# Christmas in Granite Harbor

## Candice Sue Patterson

Homefire
PUBLISHING

# Historical Romances by Candice

Saving Mrs. Roosevelt
When the Waters Came
The Keys to Gramercy Park
Lumberjacks & Ladies Romance
Collection
Beneath a Michigan Moon
Sporting For Love

# Contemporary Romances by Candice

The Farmer Takes a Wife
The Farmer and Adele
How to Charm a Beekeeper's Heart
How to Stir a Baker's Heart
Christmas in Granite Harbor
Bright Copper Kettles
Silver White Winters

# Praise for
# Candice Sue Patterson

"Patterson brings in well-researched background on the SPARs without slowing the plot. It's a fun little escape."
-- Publishers Weekly

"Deftly blending elements of history, romance and mystery, Saving Mrs. Roosevelt by talented and original novelist Candice Sue Patterson is a inherently compelling and fully entertaining read from first page to last." --James A. Cox, Midwest Book Review

"When the Waters Came by Candice Sue Patterson is a beautiful story of love and faith triumphing over the worst of circumstances. Patterson adeptly drops wonderfully believable characters into history and takes the reader on an unforgettable journey from tragedy to happily ever after." — Kathleen Y'Barbo, Publishers Weekly Bestselling Author

"Lush with historical detail, The Keys to Gramercy Park exposes the shadowed flaws in human nature, while shining hope on the glories of embracing new beginnings. This artful balance of light and dark is presented in thoughtful prose that remains with you long after you reach The End." — Rachel Scott McDaniel, award-winning author of In Spotlight and Shadow

# Maine-isms & Nautical Terms
## GLOSSARY

**Ayah**- yes or yep.
**Band**- rubberband used to secure lobster claws.
**Beans**-L.L. Bean store.
**Bugs**-lobsters.
**Counter**-overhanging section of the stern above the waterline.
**Drink**-area on a lobster boat filled with water where lobsters are kept alive.
**Flatlander**-a newcomer to the coast.
**From Away**-a person who is not a native Mainer.
**Gaff**-stick with a hook used to pull the rope attached to a lobster trap.
**Gunwhale**-upper edge of a boat's side.
**Hiya**- hi or hello
**Jimmies**-sprinkles.
**Keepers**- lobsters who measure the right size by law to keep.
**Kitchen**-first section of a lobster trap where the bait is placed.
**Pot Hauler**-electric or hydrolic device used to raise traps from the water.
**Pots**-lobster trap.
**Pound**-a place where lobsters are stored before sold to markets, restaurants, or consumers.
**Shorts**- lobsters too young to capture.

For Emily, the sister of my heart.
You will always be my dearest friend.

# Prologue

Many years ago, in the magic of childhood innocence, a six-year-old girl named Josephine stood inside a booth by the town's lobster trap Christmas tree, looking for the perfect ornament to adorn the small artificial tree in the corner of her bedroom. Her parents' tradition allowed her to choose one ornament every year so that one day when she was all grown up, she'd have plenty of ornaments and memories to fill her own Christmas tree.

This year was extra special. She was a big girl now, as her Sunday school teacher had picked her to play Mary in the nativity play. And she was learning to read. This year, it was important for her to pick the right one.

Her gaze roamed each design, stopping on a shiny clay pine tree. She lifted her hand to touch it. Bigger than her mitten. Painted yellow, red, and blue lights appeared strung with the utmost care, while tiny red hearts made up the little tree's ornaments. Josephine read the words etched on the border at the bottom. "All h-h-h."

"Hearts," her mom had said, pointing at the word.

Josephine tried again. "All hearts c-ome home for C-C-C."

She'd looked at her mom for help.

"Christmas."

"All hearts come home for Christmas." Josephine smiled.

Dad patted her back. "Good job sounding out those letters."

"I want this one," she'd said.

Her mom plucked it from the branch and laid it in Josephine's mittened hands. "Careful. Don't drop it."

"I won't." Josephine then pressed it to her chest to keep it safe.

She'd had no idea what the words meant, but she'd thought they sounded nice.

What Josephine didn't know was how much that ornament—those words—would come to mean to her many years into the future, in the harsh land of adult reality, when she'd wish for the magic of childhood innocence.

September

Why did her victim have to be so darn handsome?

Josephine Rockwell had a good feeling she was going to regret this decision. She sucked in her bottom lip, let it scrape against her teeth, and then plowed ahead.

"What I would like for the board to remember is that Mr. Mc-Clintock hasn't been part of the community for the last fourteen years." *Mr. McClintock? Good grief, Josephine, go for his jugular.* "Mind you, it was to pursue his calling, and we're all very proud of him for that. He's a very talented and intelligent man. However, his long absence has him disjointed from the needs of the commu-nity, of the fishermen. Unlike myself, who's stayed. And worked very hard to meet those needs, I might add."

The clock on the dark paneled wall ticked three minutes slow. She couldn't look at Jace. Not now. His icy blues would either communicate malice over her barb or worse—hurt. She studied the faces of the Granite Harbor Board of Selection seated be-hind the gingham tablecloth instead—the slight nod from Jack-son Goodman, the raised eyebrow from Georgina Thorogood as she scribbled notes with her perfectly sharpened pencil, Anderson Treat's poker face, and the slight frown from Henry Gratwick.

Yeah, she'd crossed a line. Josephine was humble enough to admit that. However, it was the truth, and this opportunity to become harbormaster was all she had. Jace had ancestors he could trace on a family tree, stellar good looks, and lots of money, if his shiny Lincoln swathed in tanned leather endorsed his bank account.

For crying out loud, the man had his doctorate degree! What did he want with her harbormaster position anyway? And why was he back in Granite Harbor?

He'd made his choice years ago. After graduation, he'd left for Boston. Why was he not in an emergency room somewhere, holding a scalpel, making patients feel at ease with his capable hands and lazy smile?

Her pulse pounded harder at the thought of those capable hands and lazy smile, then stabilized when she pushed it away. Come to think of it, she hadn't seen him smile since he'd returned in the spring. Four months was a long time to go without smiling. Especially since he'd been blessed with such a great one.

Raising her gaze to meet Jace's and fighting it all the way, her heart sank. His mouth pulled into a frown, eyes sagging at the corners, the irises dull with pain. Like a wounded dog.

Mr. Gratwick cleared his throat. "Anything you wish to add, Jace?"

Jace ran a hand through his artfully mussed hair, giving him that sexy Dr. McDreamy vibe. She refrained from rolling her eyes since she didn't find it that annoying. His discomfort appeared genuine and her chest ached.

Yep, she was gonna regret this one.

*Keep your eye on the prize, Josephine.*

Jace blew out a breath. "I can't argue with facts, sir. I would like to add that I worked as sternman on my father's boat from the time I could walk until I left for college. Serving others has always been a priority and that won't change just because I've been absent."

Josephine started to remind the board of Jace's abrupt change in profession but kept her mouth shut. Her interview with the town manager had been easy. Best she not kill her chances with this eclectic group. Ms. Thorogood was still scribbling and Gratwick still frowning. So much for assessing body language to predetermine their vote.

Josephine and Jace had both been recommended by the harbor committee, and they were both excellent candidates. But she was a single woman who'd worked hard and paid for her own bachelor's degree, combined with her many years' experience on the water. Throw in her intense desire to serve the town and its tourists, as well as prove herself to the natives, and she became the best option.

If she had the power to vote, she would vote for herself.

Ten grueling minutes later, the meeting ended and the scrape of metal chairs against old wood flooring filled the room. Now all she had to do was worry and fret through the next week until the harbor committee members announced their decision. Good thing she was an experienced worrier and fretter, or she'd never survive.

Jace walked away without acknowledging her, his broad shoulders slumped, sending a waft of seaweed and pine into her space. His muck boots likely accounted for the seaweed, but the alluring forest scent must be his soap or aftershave or some other manly device to attract women.

Good thing she had a strong immune system.

She thanked the board members a second time, pushed in her chair, and exited through the narrow door of the small community building. Several feet ahead, Jace walked to his fancy car, hands in his pockets. He'd always carried himself with confidence, alertness, and a pinch of arrogance. Now, he just looked. . .abused.

Her guilt meter was rising and would soon burst if she didn't make this right.

Make things right with the boy who had been a virus in her life since she'd started elementary school? The one who'd made her ride a rollercoaster of flirtation throughout high school, drove her to best him in every academic opportunity possible, made her think it was all leading up to some commitment, some declaration of his feelings only to be left emotionally bleeding when he left for Boston without a goodbye?

Make things right with that boy?

Except Jace wasn't a boy any longer and she wasn't a little girl, which made this a hundred times harder. "Jace, wait."

He stopped but didn't turn around.

This was going to be awkward.

She circled to face him but instead of looking him in the eyes like a good rival would, she stared at the loose threads on his green pull-over. "I know that we've never really been what you would call friends, but I do respect you for all your accomplishments. I—"

"Don't trouble yourself, Joey." He gazed out to sea where the sun had almost disappeared on the horizon. The breeze stirred the ends of his thick caramel hair. "You did what you had to do. I get it."

His fingers grazed her elbow in a gentle squeeze, then he side-stepped her and walked the rest of the way to his car. The engine started and purred with the sound of money a few seconds before he drove away. When his taillights disappeared around the curve, her guilt meter burst.

Josephine wrapped her arms around her middle and swallowed her emotions. He clearly wanted the job as much as she did, though she didn't understand why.

More so than him wanting it, Josephine sensed that he *needed* it.

Jace stepped through the doorway into his small one-level home at the tail of a dead-end lane. The seventies facade needed a facelift, and the worn carpet still smelled of the previous owner's terrier, but it was quiet, not in the city, and far enough away from a lawsuit he could almost pretend he hadn't been accused of malpractice.

He kicked the door closed and shuffled through the yellow-stickered mail in his hand that had been forwarded from his Boston townhouse. Bill, junk mail, a charity likely asking for a donation, bill. . .Yake and Findley, Attorneys at Law. So much for escaping reality. Not that he didn't carry the weight of the situation with him everywhere he went, even in sleep, but the large manilla envelope brought a fresh wave of grief crashing over him.

The mail pile gave a satisfying *thwack* as he dropped it onto the end table, jarring the aged shade on the ugliest lamp he'd ever seen. Like the carpet and appliances, it had been a packaged deal with the mortgage. He stalked to the kitchen and rounded the bar that interrupted the flow between the living room and kitchen. The fridge hummed when he yanked it open, and he scowled at its meager offerings. Water, ginger ale, and a quart of milk that looked more like cottage cheese.

No thanks.

Glass bottles clinked as he shut the door.

Four months and he still hadn't adapted to returning from work with every muscle sore to an empty house with no food. He'd lived alone in Boston, but at least then he'd had friends close by to watch a game or play cards, and plenty of places to grab take-out. Here, he had Dad, the open sea, and all the silence a person could tolerate.

And memories. Ones so good they felt sacrilegious to his life now. Bracing his weight on the paneled wall, he pulled off his boots and let his mind wander back to adolescence and the little girl Joey used to be. In first grade, after his mom left, he'd discovered she too had lost her mom. Car wreck when she'd been an infant. In second grade, he'd become her enemy for giving her the boyish nickname and getting the rest of the school, and eventually the town, to go along with it. In middle school, he'd teased her for having braces and boobs, though neither repulsed him. Then in high school when he'd realized his adolescent taunting was really a mad crush, he'd attempted to fix the situation by calling her Josephine. She'd hated that too. No matter what he'd called her or how much she despised him, she'd held him one hundred percent captive.

His fascination had faded with time and distance, like ripples of water from a passing boat. Until he'd seen her this spring, and she'd churned the waters again.

Except she was a strong woman now, not the timid girl he'd always known. She'd not only matured in all the right places but had grown in confidence and determination. She wanted to be harbormaster and was willing to fight for the position. And fight she had. Truthfully, she deserved the job. Even if that left him stuck on a boat he'd never wanted in the first place.

He swiped a bottled water from the shrink-wrapped case on the counter and went out to the deck to see the stars. Nothing grounded him more than remembering how small and insignificant he was in the grand scheme of things. Where was God in all this mess?

He twisted off the cap and tipped the bottle in the air in a toast, staring across the moonlit waves rolling ashore to the pinpricks of light on the other side of town. "Here's to you, Joey."

Water cleansed his throat the way he wished it'd clean his reputation.

# Two

To any other woman on the planet, the pungent smell of seaweed and briny crustaceans on a man would be a turn off. But to Josephine, that smell—on Jace McClintock anyway—was far too appealing. Partly because it meant he was home, and essentially in her life again, but mostly because since the smell wasn't clinging to her, it meant she was now officially harbormaster of Granite Harbor.

She smiled. She'd have to turn down the notch on her joy to a professional level or she might bust into a happy dance right here on the dock, the way she had in her living room a week ago when the harbor committee chairman called to tell her she'd been awarded the position. Today was her first day on the job, and she couldn't stop grinning.

"I hauled half of what I hauled last week." Nick Gentry slammed a crate of banded lobsters on the gunwale of the *Hornet's Nest*, shocking Josephine back to reality. He scowled. "Don't see nothin' to smile about."

"Hang in there, Nick." Josephine hoisted the crate from the boat to the dock. "You know the gulf. Empty traps one day, a bounty the next. These are going to the co-op, so you'll see a bonus just in time for Christmas."

He grunted, knowing as well as she that said bonus was dependent on many factors—global demand of lobsters, how many Nick was able to stock in the pound, and how much room was left. Granite Harbor was just one town of many using the co-op.

While Nick lit a cigarette, Lauren carried the heavy load to the scale. The fresh-faced woman made an excellent wharf rat, quick and efficient at weighing the crates for the local shore buyers and tracking the ones going to the co-op. She was young and pretty, a misnomer for the unflattering term.

While Lauren maneuvered the scale levers, Josephine stretched and dared a glance at Jace who stood at the helm of the *Hiley Mae II*, awaiting his turn. When their gazes connected, guilt swelled her throat, and she cut her attention to Nick, reminding herself that she'd earned the job. She had nothing to feel guilty for.

Smoke curled around Nick's face then vanished with the same breeze blowing his *Don't Tread on Me* flag. "I'm already seven hundred pounds less this month than last," he mumbled around the cigarette pinched between his lips. "I ain't hauling this winter. I'm going inland with my ex-wife and kids. A big enough bonus to see us through the winter would take a Christmas miracle, and I don't believe in that crap."

Lauren wrote the weight on a ticket and handed it to Nick. Joey turned her face to escape the cloud of smoke and animosity racing her direction and waved a hand in front of her face. "I'll count on a Christmas miracle changing your mind."

Jace coughed. Smoke inhalation or impatience?

Josephine patted Nick's arm. "The buyer from Rhett's Seafood is back today. Go get paid."

"'Bout time." Nick took a deep draw, blazing the shrinking stick a bright orange. He flicked the ashes into the water, started the engine, and chugged to his mooring.

Josephine approached the *Hiley Mae II* where it gently bumped the dock. Water lapped against the boat's hull, one of her favorite sounds. A flock of osprey chirped overhead. Jace joined Dad lifting crates onto the gunwale.

Lauren bent to retrieve a crate, angling her face close to Jace's. "How's ya haul?"

"Hit the motherload."

Lauren giggled, lifted, and walked toward the scale. Josephine moved in, cursing the irritation bubbling inside her at Lauren's flirtation. Throwing her aggravation into her work, she hefted the next crate, expecting it to be heavy, and swayed to the left. "The motherload?"

Jace pointed to a seat near the stern, suggesting Dad take a break. Then he turned to her and smirked. "I thought I'd give myself the pep talk and save my ears the speech about bonuses and Christmas miracles."

Gracious, he looked good in yellow oilskins and a once-white t-shirt. Even if his mood was as prickly as the stubble covering his cheeks.

She wagged her finger. "A lot can happen in three months, if you only believe."

"Easy for you to say, Clarence, you're living the wonderful life."

Breath escaped her like a punch to the gut. All hope of moving past their lifelong rivalry and moving into something that resembled a friendship—or more—died. Served her right for being on the dock and helping with things that weren't in her job description anymore.

Jace stared at the anchor and fidgeted with the suspenders on his oilskins. Seavey McClintock growled a warning at his son.

Josephine peered around Jace's shoulder, infusing happiness she didn't feel into her tone. "Afternoon, Father McClintock. I hope Jace isn't working you too hard. You're supposed to be retired."

The older version of Jace rubbed his lower back and winced. Was that blood smeared on the sleeve of his shirt? "I'm trying to, but until Jace finds a reliable sternman I'm retired from retirement." He shifted. "And speaking of. . .you need to retire that nickname. You make me sound like a priest, and we both know I'm far from it."

"The nickname your son stuck me with years ago makes me sound like a pre-pubescent boy." She focused her attention on Jace. "I go by Josephine, by the way. Everyone calls me that now. And I may have a tip on a potential sternman."

Lauren grabbed another crate, sending Jace a pouty smile as she did. Josephine wondered how well Lauren could swim.

Seavey coiled a rope around his palm and down to his elbow in several rotations. "You've certainly grown out of your tomboy ways, Josephine, even if Jace doesn't want to admit he's noticed."

Jace slammed the last crate and glared at Dad. "Whose side are you on?"

Seavey raised a palm. "Father McClintock thought now was as good a time for confession as any."

Deep grooves formed across Jace's forehead and around his mouth. "We're not catholic."

Josephine laughed, pleased Jace didn't deny his dad's remark. "Confession is always good for the soul, eh?"

Lauren ripped the top paper from the notepad where she'd written the total weight and held it out to Jace. He nodded his thanks, tucked it into the shirt pocket hiding behind his suspenders, and backed toward the bulkhead. "Belated congratulations on your promotion, Joey."

"Josephine."

He turned on the engine, pretending not to hear. Water bubbled around the transom then streaked the calm water as he drove away.

For a few short seconds it was as if their years apart had fallen away, and they were back to their old repartee. She loved bantering with him. Had missed it more than she'd realized until that first day last spring when she'd spotted him slogging through the mudflats in his rubber boots, carrying a shovel, digging for clams. A loneliness she hadn't known she carried melted away.

A few years ago, she'd read a book by Thomas Wolfe that said you can't go home again. Wolfe had been wrong. One could. It might be for the wrong reasons, and it might never be the same as before, but it could be done. No matter the logic, that person may have someone secretly pining for them they never would've expected.

Every time Jace started to settle into his new life, his lawyer yanked him back to reality. The cell on his dash exploded with text messages and missed call notifications as he pulled into Dad's driveway, one of the few spots on this peninsula where he picked up service with his cell carrier. With every ding and flash of the screen, Dad glanced at him, brows arched.

Jace ignored it. He'd deal with Findley after he got home and procrastinated for a few more hours. He fished his keys from his pocket and handed them to Dad. "You sure you don't mind that we swap for a while?"

"Not at all." The man admired Jace's Lincoln parked outside his window. "How fast does she go? I'm asking for a friend."

"Tell your friend she doesn't go over sixty because if she does, the car goes back to my house."

"Lighten up, son." He patted Jace's arm none too gently, releasing the briny smell of the ocean from the fibers of his shirt. "This Findley lady leave you inside out? Is she the reason you're on hiatus, so you can find yourself again? 'Cause you're definitely not yourself since you came home."

Findley, an ex-lover?

If only Findley were a woman and that was the case.

He'd let Dad think what he wanted. Jace wasn't veering from the story that he was burnt out and taking a year off to clear his head. That he wanted to return to lobstering and flip real estate as a hobby, which was why he purchased his home outright. That while he was home, he wanted to give back to the community who'd encouraged him so well by serving them as harbormaster. All points were true, but all points were just the tip of the icebergs he'd careened into when Arabella had taken her last breath.

"Sixty, not a mile over." Jace needed the car in immaculate condition in case he'd need to sell it to pay lawyer fees. In his current circumstances, it wasn't practical to drive anymore. Dad had a garage and now that he was retired—sort of—he didn't go many places. When he did, the smell of crustaceans no longer stuck in his pores. Lobster and leather didn't mix.

"Father McClintock is always available to listen to the confession of his favorite son."

"I'm your only son."

"You're still my favorite."

Jace chuckled. "Have a good night, Dad. I'll see you in the morning."

The passenger door opened, and Dad got out. "Sixty, huh? Guess Betsey will have to be satisfied with a relaxing drive along the coast then."

Jace reared back. Who was Betsey?

Dad slammed the door, grinning.

As the man rounded the front of the truck, Jace manually rolled down the window, the lever sticking a fourth of the way down. "Is Betsey a woman or your name for the car?"

"I guess that's my business, son."

Jace supposed it was but. . . "Who's Betsey?"

Waving, Dad disappeared behind his front door.

Jace blew out a breath. Was Dad dating?

His phone pinged again.

What did it matter? Dad had a right to his privacy, same as Jace. It was just weird to think of Dad dating after decades of not. At least that Jace knew of.

Grunting, he yanked his phone off the dash and returned Findley's call. He inched down the driveway while the secretary made the necessary connection. He braked for a kid crossing on his bike, then eased onto the road.

"Jace, good of you to return my call. I've only been trying for three days."

"Cell reception is spotty here. I need to change carriers. In fact, I'm driving, so I'll probably lose you soon."

"Then pull over while you have reception. This can't wait any longer."

Jace stopped by the town park, passenger wheels in the grass. He looked down at his phone. One bar. Should be enough to withstand the call. "What is it?"

Findley sighed. "We've gotta get something straight. I'm your lawyer, not your enemy. I'm trying to help you clear your name, and I can't do that unless you work with me. Willingly. That includes answering my calls and opening any mail correspondence. Are we good?"

No, they weren't good. He shouldn't even have a lawyer or a case they needed to win. Arabella should still be alive.

Jace rubbed the spot throbbing above his eye. "I'll be more proactive."

Findley's slow inhale echoed in Jace's ear. "Survivor's guilt. I've seen it before. It's why you're avoiding this whole issue. I've known you a long time, buddy, and looking over every piece of evidence I've gotten my hands on so far proves you did nothing wrong. You ran every test, did everything you could to keep that little girl alive. Time won. That's not your fault."

In all of man's intelligence, if only they could figure out how to outsmart time. To do that, they'd have to outsmart the Creator of it, and that was a feat man would never accomplish.

Jace swallowed. "I'm just trying to distract myself enough to get through each day."

"I know, but the trial has been set for December twentieth. We've got a lot of work to do before then."

December twentieth.

He was either going to have the traditional red, gold, and green Christmas, or he'd be sporting an orange jumpsuit behind bars.

# THREE

The Granite Harbor Fisherman's Association met in the back of Johnson's Grocery once a month, where the coffee pot was always on, the three chipped tables were always clean, and the mismatched chairs were always occupied. Josephine recognized every face that entered the front of the shop. Cooler weather was setting in and tourist season dwindling.

She signaled to Pete Miller, who called the meeting to order with a two-fingered whistle sharp enough to burst glass. The back of the store fell silent. Pete settled against his chair with a nod and crossed his arms. His paunch folded over his belt buckle.

Debbie, Pete's wife and sternman, slipped on her glasses. "Do I have a motion to call this meeting to order?"

Nate motioned. Seavey seconded.

Paper crinkled as Debbie held the packet closer to her face, squinting. She lifted her glasses. "Any updates on the cod restrictions?"

Clyde Hopkins, who's family had fished cod for generations, stood and reported on the latest bill in legislation to protect cod and their breeding grounds, so many fishermen, like Clyde, had hope of returning to their native occupations someday. He hated lobstering but had been forced to take it up when the state significantly lowered the legal limit of cod per fisherman several years back. The payout hadn't come close to covering the bills.

Josephine walked to the corner and poured a cup of coffee. In a rickety folding chair beside her, Jace jammed his hands in his pockets, stretched his long legs in front of him, and crossed his ankles. The discussion of "old business" played in her ears but she found it hard to concentrate when a freshly showered Jace, hair still damp and clothes smelling like fabric softener, sat mere feet away looking sexy and ticked off at the same time.

His misery was palpable. Something had sent him back to Granite Harbor with his tail between his legs, but no one knew what. Well, Seavey probably did but he wasn't saying, and no one was gutsy enough to ask. Josephine's bleeding heart wanted to help Jace find his way and ship him back to Boston. That heart had been disappointed by him many times before and didn't want to get attached again.

"Josephine?" Debbie's snap startled Josephine from her inner musings. "We're onto new business now. You requested the floor. You have it."

Heat filled Josephine's cheeks at the woman's brusque scolding. Not everyone was pleased that she'd won the harbormaster position. Josephine suspected Debbie was one of them.

Josephine leaned against the wall and took a sip of coffee, gathering her thoughts.

Hot.

She turned her face away and swallowed the coffee and the pain. Coughed. "As a representative of the Fisherman's Wives Coalition, I'm happy to announce we were able to distribute First-Aid kits to every fisherman in Azure County. We're currently raising funds in honor of Frank Swanson and hope to provide steel ladders and specialized blankets that ward off hypothermia to every fisherman by winter."

Heads bobbed and a few people voiced their approval. They all knew the lifesaving capabilities of a ladder. Once a man went overboard on a fishing boat, there was no getting back in without another person's assistance. The cold Atlantic waters would cause hypothermia long before help arrived. That's why they all tried their hardest to never fish alone, though that wasn't always doable.

"We're also working on a grant to provide scholarships to children of drowned captains. Any high schooler in the state who meets the criteria would be eligible to apply."

"Wonderful news," Debbie said. "The coalition is a blessing to us all."

Agreement filled the room. Josephine could feel the blaze of Jace's gaze on her, but she refused to glance his direction. She was curious to know if his expression was still seething or if his grouchy demeanor had softened, but she'd gawked enough at him for one meeting.

She blew into her cup and chanced another sip.

Debbie returned her glasses to the bridge of her nose and stacked her notes into a neat pile. "The floor is open for discussion. Anything else before we adjourn?

Jace raised a finger. "I'll be harvesting all winter, and I'd like to know what our current harbormaster suggests for avoiding the price decrease that hits us every year."

Josephine worked hard to not spit out the scorching liquid. That discussion had not been on tonight's agenda.

Thirty pairs of eyes fastened on her, though only nine fishermen planned to harvest during winter. She concentrated on the flickering bulb in the frozen pizza case. She'd planned to avoid this topic until she had a solid argument for what she was going to propose. Never one to back down from adversity when it came to Jace, she drank the last of her bitter coffee—which included grounds—and tossed the cup in the trashcan.

"As you know, the demand for lobster increases during the holidays. The overseas market is expected to boom after the New Year, as it'll be China's year of the lobster." She sucked in a deep breath as she could stall no more. "In a boom market, prices will skyrocket if we cut our traps by half, however, everyone will have to agree to make it work."

Before she could even declare that neighboring harbors already committed to do the same, the room erupted with voices. Several minutes passed. Sweat gathered in the dip of the small of her back. She'd be lucky to make it out unscathed.

Pete's deafening whistle quieted the room. All eyes returned to her, but this time disapproval shone in nearly every one. Josephine scratched her collarbone. "Just something to think about. The approach has been successful for several fisheries along the coast and neighboring harbormasters have told me their fishermen have agreed. I can provide data in my office to anyone interested in looking it over before I present it at the next meeting."

Debbie stood. "Can I get a motion to adjourn?"

Ron motioned. Judy seconded.

The abrupt dismissal said it all.

Josephine escaped down the cookie aisle, cut in front of the small magazine rack, and out the door, her cheeks flaming. She was going home to shower, eat, bury her head under her blankets, and not think about Jace. Good or bad.

They didn't owe each other anything—other than basic human kindness and consideration, which he hadn't graced her with tonight with his public interrogation and referring to her as "our harbormaster" in a polite tone glazed in sarcasm. Sure, he'd had the right to ask. And she had an obligation to answer. But the unspoken message that dripped through his question hurt.

She was tired of hurting over him.

"Joey!" Jace's deep timbre rumbled behind her.

Keep walking. Just keep walking.

Footsteps grew louder, closer. Her legs were already burning from the speed. She resisted the urge to run.

"Joey." He touched her elbow.

Refusing to give in, she continued walking and focused on the muted orange sun setting behind the steeple of the Granite Harbor Community Church. The dock was quiet, save for the sound of small waves splashing against the pier. The air was chilly, she was tired, and she wasn't in the mood for this Boston doctor turned handsome lobsterman of her dreams and his egotistical attitude.

Just keep walking. *You're almost there.*

The empowering escape she'd envisioned crumbled when her office door stuck upon entry. Her right kneecap slammed into the metal, and she swallowed a yelp. That would be the first thing she'd replace in her office.

Her second attempt at a grand exit shattered once she got the door open and Jace deflected its slam and followed her inside. Tonight was not her night.

"Joey."

She turned on him. "Josephine."

Her breaths were coming hard and fast. She needed to calm down before the tears that always sprang when she got angry joined this crazy train and gave him even more pleasure. Flexing her fingers, she went around her desk and dropped onto the plush chair. She planted her elbows on the desk calendar that swallowed her workspace and rubbed her forehead. "Was your attack premeditated, or did you improvise?"

"It was a legit question."

She looked up at him. "A legit question you purposely threw out to stir conflict. You knew how they'd react. Before I had a chance to broach the subject at the next meeting with statistics and facts, you threw me to the wolves!"

"We're wolves now?"

His hair stood in spikes, as if he'd raked his fingers through it.

She huffed. "You know what I mean."

Here came the tears.

Quiet descended over the room like a weighted blanket. Jace kneaded the skin between his eyes. She rubbed her hands along the thighs of her jeans, blinking to dry her eye sockets. The clock on the wall ticked a steady and annoying rhythm.

Jace dropped his hand, huffing a breath. "Remember the day with the board of selection when you threw me under the bus?"

"This is revenge?"

"You know me better than that." When she raised her eyebrows, he said, "No, I guess you don't. Look, truth is I can't afford to take a hit this winter. I need the money."

That certainly hadn't been the response she'd expected. He'd been a doctor in one of the most prestigious hospitals on the east coast, raking in thousands of dollars a day and now he needed money? The weariness sagging the skin around his eyes and pure misery radiating from their depths hit her heart's center.

She clasped her hands, leaned forward, and gentled her tone. "What happened in Boston? I know we've never been close enough to share personal information, and you certainly don't owe me any explanations, but misery radiates off you like the Texas sun on blacktop."

*Trust me, Jace. Confide in me.*

He fixated on the wall behind her. Swallowed. "Have a good rest of your night."

His words were a decibel above a whisper.

Cue her disappointment. She was sure it played on her face because he started to fidget as he backed away.

Now she was deflecting a slamming door. A door to a room full of secrets that made Jace. . .Jace. A door she'd always wanted to walk through but was only allowed to pass and stare at. Never enter.

She was dying to know what lay behind that door.

To feign indifference, she poised her fingers over the adding machine where she checked imaginary sums. Twice. She grabbed a pen, opened the ledger, and wrote numbers in a column she'd erase as soon as he left.

Why was he still here?

Her stupid self glanced at him.

Jaw flexed. Blue eyes fierce. "I'm sorry, Joey."

He turned to walk out.

"We're not twelve anymore. It's Josephine."

One foot in her office, one foot on the sidewalk, he faced her, brows pinched, mouth tight. "Sorry, again. I guess you'll always be Joey to me."

He tapped on the doorframe, as if wanting to say more, then closed the door behind him and vanished into the darkening evening.

What did that mean? He couldn't speak those words with softness and conviction and then just walk away.

Josephine rubbed the skin between her eyebrows where tension pulsed. She wanted to run after him and ask for more details but wouldn't abase herself. This tug-of-war between them had gone on for years and every time she'd try to leave the game he'd say or do something to reel her back in, drop a morsel that kept her following. Something to give her false hope.

This had to stop. She was thirty-one now, strong and independent. And she was done playing games with Jace McClintock.

# Four

Jace throttled down the motor and slowed the boat to a crawl. Sunlight sparkled on the rippling waves formed by their wake. The only thing that stood between solid ground and his boat was the most vivid blue water he'd ever seen outside of a filtered photograph. The air was so tangy, so salty, he could taste it.

He'd never minded acting as Dad's sternman growing up. Perhaps because he knew the profession wasn't his future, and when they returned home—and after a good meal and a thorough shower—he could hit the books. The twenty-percent pay covered his minimal teenage needs and gave him enough for savings. His future had lain before him like an endless yellow brick road. He'd worked hard, seized the day, saved lives.

Then the road had dead-ended and all the things in his life he'd thought had substance turned out to be as flat as the cardboard props on a movie set. Career, suspended. Girlfriend, gone without notice. People he considered friends, silent.

Life had done a one-eighty and now he was as trapped as the banded lobsters piled in the drink.

"Right here." Dad yelled, tossing up a hand.

Jace let the boat idle and walked to the pot hauler. He grabbed the hook and secured the gaff, dragging closer the plum-colored buoy with two yellow stripes. It was tricky maneuvering the boat through areas saturated with multi-colored buoys. A line in the propeller was never a good thing, for the boat or the fisherman who owned the lines.

"Beautiful day." Dad rested a hip along the counter.

"Ayah." Jace grasped the line in his left hand and handed the hook to Dad, who laid it along the gunwale.

"Fall's soon to settling in. Won't be many more days like this."

"It's only the end of September. We've still got nice days ahead." Jace ran the line through the hauling block and between the plates of the hydraulic hauler.

"That's the first positive thing you've said since you've been home."

Ignoring the comment, Jace twisted the brass handle toward himself. The plates spun counter-clockwise and pulled the line out of the water, coiling it onto the deck. After a few minutes, he slowed the hauler and waited for the trap to break surface.

Four lobsters waited inside the kitchen attempting to snack on the herring inside the mesh bag. He slid the trap down the counter and continued hauling line while Dad measured each lobster, throwing back the shorts and banding the keepers. They were a well-oiled machine, even if Dad worked slower nowadays.

After the mesh bags were filled with fresh herring chunks and the traps reset along the craggy ocean floor, they hosed down the deck, the counter, the gunwale, and themselves, then washed up for lunch.

The meal consisted of deli turkey and Havarti cheese on white bread, a bag of plain Lays, a pack of Oreos, and a Mountain Dew. The same lunch they'd eaten almost every day since the season began. What he wouldn't give for a plate of chicken cacciatore and a loaf of garlic bread from Mario's, his favorite Italian restaurant back home. Except Boston wasn't home anymore.

Heck, he'd even go for Bos Med's cafeteria food over another turkey sandwich.

Dad tossed his last crust of bread in the water beside a gull. The bird scooped up the morsel then flew away.

"Hand me the ibuprofen?" Dad stretched out his left leg, eyes closed, lips tight.

Jace retrieved the bottle and shook two pills into Dad's open palm. Dad popped them into his mouth and chased them down with the caffeinated liquid.

"You can't keep going like this. You'll ruin your liver." Jace tossed the bottle into a duffle in the cabin. "I'll get with Joey—*Josephine*—this week about that sternman."

Boy, did he dread that conversation. Not only because he hated the thought of losing Dad but because his relationship with Joey, like every other aspect of his life, had lost its footing. They'd always competed, always riled one another. Except now it didn't hold the undercurrent of flirtation or the innocence of childhood.

Dad tossed his empty can into the cooler. "I know you're bitter about the town electing her for harbormaster, but she earned it. Go easy on her."

"I'm not bitter." Not entirely. She *had* earned it. And it was best she was awarded the job. Usually, trials like his take much longer to receive a court date. He'd thought he had time to establish himself here before he faced a judge. If he'd have gotten the position only for a jury to find him guilty a few months later, the town would feel betrayed.

Jace sighed and plopped down on an upturned bucket. "I don't want to be on the water for the rest of my life. I thought I'd come home, start over, manage the harbor. . ."

Try and forget.

Dad barked a wry chuckle. "Be as reclusive as you could get away with and ignore years of hard work and thousands of dollars' worth of education?"

Jace threw his head back and groaned at the sky.

"Do something else, then."

"Like what?" Jace worked the kinks from his neck.

"Doc Greenwell paid me a visit not long before you moved back. He wondered if you'd ever consider leaving the hospital, moving back, and taking over his practice when he retires next year."

"You never told me that."

"Never had a chance to. 'Fore I knew it, you'd resigned, subleased your apartment, bought the house on Tanabe Road, and told me not to ask any questions."

"You haven't, and I thank you for that."

Dad nodded. "I figure you'll tell me when you're ready."

He'd never be ready to confess that because of him three lives would be changed forever. He could barely live with himself as it was, but once the information leaked, the entire town would know what he'd done by days end. He couldn't live with their knowing eyes assessing him, judging him. For the few relationships that remained to change, for the connection to his community to break.

For Joey to think him a murderer.

That's why he'd wanted to be harbormaster. If his secrets came out, he'd be in a position to serve and prove he was the same Jace they'd always known, not just a citizen with a dark past.

But Joey'd earned it, so he'd continue hauling pots with little hope of getting ahead, of finishing payment on his student debt and lawyer fees, of ever having the life he'd planned for.

Josephine's office door squeaked open. She peered around her desktop monitor at Seavey lumbering toward her in dirt-caked boots, a hand pressed to his back. She was giving up on keeping a clean floor. Every captain or mate that graced the doors left something behind.

She stood and smiled. "What can I do for you, Father McClintock?"

He smirked and handed her the weigh ticket. "Jace heard that Maine Lobster Today was inquiring about fisherman. Asked me to check into it for him."

Her stomach turned sour. After their confrontation the other night, he obviously didn't want to be around her. In fact, most of the fisherman had either avoided her the last two days or, if they'd had to converse, made it brief.

"Of course." She opened her email, reached for a sticky note, and copied down the number. "They're a hot new overnight seafood delivery company. Impressive numbers for their first fiscal year. I understand they plan to purchase from the co-op through winter but would like to buy straight off the dock next summer if enough area fisherman partner."

Seavey took the note.

"Is Jace okay?"

"He is. He's getting some things from the boatyard to make a repair, so he asked me to see you."

"No, I mean, is he okay. Like. . .with life?" Her fingertips skimmed the edge of her desk. "He just hasn't seemed himself. The Jace I remember, anyway. He seems. . .well, time passes and people change, so I. . ."

She ceased her rambling, stomach tightening in a hard knot.

Seavey tucked away the note. "Girlie, your guess is as good as mine. I've no idea what happened in Boston. I do know he could use a friend, though. Even if he thinks he doesn't need one."

Friends? That word didn't accurately describe their dynamic. Enemies? Rivals? That was more like it. Had it not been for her determination to best him in every school subject growing up, she might not have had the motivation to get good grades at all. Sometimes she'd come out on top, sometimes she hadn't. Winning the harbormaster election over him had been the ultimate victory.

Except victory hadn't tasted as sweet as she'd anticipated. Not when the hard lines of disappointment on his face poked her conscious every time she saw him.

"I'll see what I can do." She reached for her mug of tepid coffee and stared into its rich roasted color.

"He's back." Seavey pointed out the window that was in desperate need of cleaning. Through the grime she could see his unmistakable form carrying some unidentifiable object toward his truck.

"In case you're in need of confession." He backed away, a grin splitting his face.

"What exactly would I be in need of confessing?"

Seavey shrugged. "That's between you and God."

He winked and left the way he'd come. Dirt clods marred the floor. Confession her great auntie—whoever she was. The branches on her family tree were shaped like question marks.

Josephine sat and glanced at the pile of papers in front of her. Then to her computer screen. She lifted the mug to her lips and cringed at the bitter liquid. The dull roar of a boat engine sounded outside. Deep laughter from jesting fisherman. She shuffled papers.

Okay, she'd go talk to Jace. Good grief.

She stood, rolling her chair into the wall behind her. Skirting the dirt clods, she twisted the doorknob, abandoned her mug on the window ledge, and stepped into the afternoon sun.

Jace shuffled items in the toolbox attached to the truck bed. His strong back rippled beneath the suspenders of his oilskins. Sweat glistened on the back of his neck and dampened the neckline of his t-shirt. He reeked of herring and briny water and yet she fantasized wrapping her arms around his middle and pressing a kiss to his stubbly cheek.

Stupid woman.

"Jace."

Seavey got into Rand's truck, and they pulled out onto the road.

He was abandoning her. Didn't he know confession included a priest?

Jace continued fumbling around, metal crashing against metal. A few seconds passed, and he pulled out a wrench and slammed the toolbox lid.

"Jace."

He whipped around, and she jumped.

"Sorry." She pressed a hand to her chest.

"Don't ever sneak up on a man with a tool in his hand."

"Good advice. But I didn't sneak. I called your name, twice. You just didn't hear me."

He inhaled his frustration. "What can I do for you, Josephine?"

While she liked the sound of her given name rolling off his tongue, she missed the personalization of the nickname he'd branded her with. Odd since she'd always hated it. But after he'd declared she'd always be Joey to him in that mopey, breathy way that had kept her awake most of that night, as if it were a secret between just the two of them.

His eyebrows arched, waiting.

She'd answer him if she could curb this attraction that had returned to engulf her like a tsunami. She hadn't sought it out, didn't welcome it, but, oh, she wanted to give into it.

"I came to apologize." See? That wasn't so hard.

Wait. What?

He leaned against the truck and crossed his arms. "Apologize. You?"

How she wished she'd brought that disgusting coffee along, so she'd have something to occupy her hands. "I'm not above admitting when I'm wrong."

Except she wasn't quite sure what she'd done wrong that would warrant this apology.

Jace tipped his head back and squinted at the sky. The defined lump of his Adam's apple was driving her crazy, so she gawked at the sky too. "What are we looking for?"

He returned his attention to her. "I was checking to see if the sky was falling."

"Ah, hilarious. And here I was trying to offer a genuine apology."

"For what?"

His guess was as good as hers.

Jace took a step closer. "For suggesting that I risk my livelihood on a whim by cutting my traps by half, hoping it might raise the price?" Another step. "Or for the little victory dance you performed on the dock after the election? Yeah, I saw."

That spark of defiance he was perfect at igniting flamed. She closed the remaining distance, her finger pointed his direction. "You're the one who taught me that victory dance, if you remember, and to be fair—the winner has always gloated after a battle."

"We're not kids anymore, as you've so eagerly reminded me, *Josephine*." He rested his elbow on the tailgate, bringing them even closer. The pungent scent of crustaceans and hard work filled the remaining space. The hard blue of his eyes softened, as did the sharp angles of his face.

Oh, she was aware. In the boldest move she'd ever made toward him, she gripped his forearm. His muscles flexed beneath her fingertips.

She swallowed her pride. "I'm sorry for getting angry at you at the meeting for asking a fair question. I'm sorry for my gloating, for reminding the board you've been absent the last fourteen years, and for not welcoming you home the way I should have."

Yikes, that last part had come out flirtier than she'd intended.

"I'm also sorry for whatever happened that brought you home. I mean, I'm not sorry you're home, but something devastating happened—obviously—to make you give up your life in Boston and—"

He turned, ripping his arm from her fingers, opened the truck door, and climbed inside.

Idiot! Why hadn't she stopped at flirty? Flirty wasn't so bad. Flirty was better than furious.

The engine started and the truck rolled forward. She couldn't let him drive away. How could she fix this? "Wait, I. . ."

Jace braked. He rolled his window down and stared at her in his sideview mirror. "Don't concern yourself with the latter." He sighed. "Thanks for the rest, though."

Slowly, he drove out of the harbor, leaving her feeling as unsteady as a rubber ducky in high tide.

# Five



*Sixteen years earlier*

The moment of truth.

Josephine's stomach twisted harder with each paper Mr. Hedlund rummaged through on his messy desk. She filled her lungs with what was supposed to be a cleansing breath, only to fill her nostrils with the enticing scent of Jace's cologne. A scent that would calm her if she had the privilege of snuggling close and enjoying it. Instead, it spiked her anxiety as she waited for Mr. Hedlund to announce who'd won UMaine's Maritime Conservation internship for the summer.

Jace swiveled from the desk in front of her, extended his long legs into the aisle, and crossed his ankles. He propped his elbow on her books in that casual, annoyingly confident way he did every time they competed. He loved reminding her how unshaken he was by such things. Still facing the teacher, his neck strained from the angled position. Enough so that his pulse visibly thumped through the skin where he'd placed the devilish potion that smelled so wonderful.

She wasn't sure which of her desires pulled stronger—wanting to touch the spot where his pulse beat or wanting to wrap her fingers around his neck and squeeze. As if sensing her warring thoughts, Jace looked at her and winked. Strangulation weighed heavier on her desire scale.

Before she could analyze the tingly warmth that spread through her from that wink, Mr. Hedlund unearthed a certificate and held it in the air. He planted his feet in front of the chalkboard and cleared his throat. "Two of our juniors tied in academics this year, making it difficult for the conservation board to choose a recipient. Based on the submitted essays and interviews with the provided references, this year's maritime conservation internship goes to Jace McClintock. Congratulations."

Josephine's body continued tingling, only it had morphed into tingles of disappointed shock. Her hands languidly clapped with the others in the room, but her breaths came fast and her eyes watered. She'd worked harder to win that internship than she'd ever worked before. It had all come down to Jace being the more likable person.

She shouldn't be so surprised.

Jace stood to receive his certificate, jarring her desk into her ribcage. She grimaced. How unfair. He didn't even want the internship. He didn't plan to have a career in marine studies. His dream was to apply for medical school and save lives in a hospital so large it took up three city blocks. Granite Harbor was just his steppingstone. It was Josephine's haven. She couldn't imagine a better place to grow up and work and raise a family. That scholarship was the first step in accomplishing that life.

As Jace performed a victory dance back to his seat, their gazes locked, and she made a weak attempt to smile. She'd never been good at keeping her thoughts from playing on her face. She did such a poor job at acting happy for him that he frowned, as if he read every single thought running through her brain right now—like what an awful dancer he was. His steps faltered.

"Congratulations," Josephine murmured as he sat. Now the waft of cologne made her stomach churn.

"Thanks, Joey. I know how much you wanted this."

Understatement of the century.

The rest of the afternoon passed in a slow torture. Her lunch tasted like cardboard, and numbers, which normally made sense to her, were a jumble of insignificant code during calculus. When the last bell rang at three o'clock, she snatched up her backpack and raced down the hall to the exit, not caring that some of her fellow students were staring.

Outside, sunlight whispered across her skin. The air held a nip, but spring was expanding its wings along the coast. Branches with tiny buds rustled in the breeze and a buoy bell clanged in the distance. She couldn't wait to get home, bury her face in her pillow, and scream her frustration into the downy feathers. After a good cry, she'd eat an early dinner where she'd pretend everything was fine, then clock in for her shift at Johnson's Grocery. Where she'd work nearly every day. All. Summer.

"Joey, wait." Gentle pressure on her elbow spun her around.

She yanked away from Jace and moved forward. Gloating was not on her watch-list today.

"Josephine Elaine Rockwell."

She froze. He did not just use her full name the way her father did when she was in trouble.

She turned on him. "I'm sure you think winning that internship has now given you some kind of authority over me, but I assure you it hasn't."

"I never claimed it to."

"Then why are you scolding me like a small child, using my given name you've refused to call me by since the second grade?"

"I wanted your attention." He shoved his hands in his coat pockets.

She thrust out a hand toward the school. "Was everyone else's attention today not enough?"

His eyes searched her face the way they did when he was engrossed in a book. "No. I wanted yours."

"In that case, let me give you my undivided attention." Her backpack slid off her shoulder and plopped into the grass. She bent at the waist as if meeting a king. "I am humbled merely to stand in your presence. I offer you my most heartfelt congratulations on the internship and wish you nothing but happiness now and forevermore."

Jace rolled his eyes.

She snatched up her bag, hoisted it back onto her shoulder, and continued toward home.

"That's not the kind of attention I want from you." He caught up to her. "Stop acting like a petulant child. It's not attractive."

Well, she felt like a petulant child right now, so why not act like one?

"Since when has attraction mattered? You've been nothing but repulsed by me since the day we met."

His eyes turned stormy. The kind of raging storm that warns a person to run for cover, but they stupidly stand in fascination of the atmospheric disturbance. Jace stepped closer. "Is that what you think?"

The softer tone of his voice sucked the anger right out of her. Was Jace admitting feelings for her? Her teeth clamped down on her bottom lip. Had she left school and fallen into some kind of portal that sent her to an alternate universe? Because if Jace was admitting he was attracted to her, that was the only logical explanation.

He stepped even closer, and she felt her eyes widen. "What do you think all this madness between us over the years has been, if not chemistry?"

Yowzers. If that was true, good thing they'd not been partnered together in chemistry class, or they might've blown up the school. She'd been well aware of her own attraction for the last couple of years, but his? She'd no idea it existed.

An arrogant grin lifted one side of his mouth. "I've rendered you speechless. That's a first. Hopefully, it won't be the last."

"If this is how you flirt, you really stink at it."

Jace threw back his head and laughed, gaining the attention of the other students walking home. "Don't hate me for too long, Jo. You'll break my heart."

He caressed her arm, sending another wave of tingles through her limbs, then strode away as if he hadn't shaken her world for the second time today.

# Six

Josephine opened the front door of her parents' home and stepped back into childhood. Not much had changed, like the hunter green couch in the living room, worn in the right places, where Moby, their nearly deaf terrier, lay snoring. The knickknacks and wall décor were still the same, and so were the scents of pepper, warm cream, and veggies. Mom was cooking.

"Smells great," she called on her way into the kitchen, not wanting to startle anyone.

"It is." Mom turned from the stove. "First chowder of the season."

"Clam?"

"Ayuh. I'm determined to beat Cinda Willard at the festival this year if it kills me. What do you think?"

Mom retrieved a spoon from the drawer, dipped it in the pot, and carried it across the kitchen above her cradled palm. "Be honest."

Josephine opened her mouth.

Hot liquid spilled over her tongue and coated the back of her throat. "Ah!" Josephine ran to the sink, turned on the tap, and drank straight from the stream of water.

Mom patted her back. "Sorry. I didn't realize it was that hot. Better not do that to the judges, eh?"

Josephine shut off the tap and patted her mouth with her sleeve. Words scraped against the back of her throat. "No. Best not."

Tongue flaming, Josephine plopped on a barstool and hooked her ankles behind the foot rung while Mom poured her a glass of milk. She stared at the beautiful hardwood floor her parents had installed last year. It was durable, functional, and attractive. Yet, she couldn't help but miss the old familiar floor too, chips, dings, and all.

"Are you okay?" Mom set the glass in front of Josephine, pulled out a stool, and tossed the dish towel she wore on her shoulder onto the island.

Josephine brought the glass to her lips and drank half of the milk.

"I'm sorry about the soup."

The glass met the island with a clink. "I'm fine."

Mom probed with her all-knowing eyes.

"It's my job." Josephine dropped her chin into her hand. "At least three-quarters of the town bucks at the mention of change. The other quarter either heads south for the winter or is too old to care."

"You knew all this going into it."

"I guess I figured if they trusted me enough to elect me, they'd trust me enough to lead. Really, all they want is someone to be in charge of keeping things the same."

"We are creatures of habit."

"I understand tradition—traditions are wonderful—but change is not always a bad thing, and new traditions can be started. The traditions we have today were once new, for crying out loud."

Mom tilted her head, and her expression eased into patient understanding. "True, but traditions can't be forced, or they lose their value. Could it be that your approach to these new ideas are more offensive than the actual idea?"

Josephine thought back to the night of the meeting. She hadn't planned to broach the subject of limiting traps that night. She'd purposefully tried not to be forceful, as she'd known they wouldn't immediately embrace the idea. They needed data and comparisons and faith. Lots of faith.

"No." Josephine drank the last of her milk. "I know I can be overwhelming sometimes, but I wasn't about this. I wanted to wait to suggest cutting the number of traps we place in the water by half to control the market. To present it when I had time to draw up reports and prove an alliance with other harbors. Jace ruined it."

Mom took the empty glass and rinsed it. "You two have never been able to get along. I've always suspected there's something deeper going on than friendship."

Josephine barked a laugh. "For there to be something more than friendship, we'd have had to start as friends. We've never been that."

She'd almost given in a time or two, on a bad day when she had her guard down. That would be the time he'd embarrass her or throw down a new challenge. She suspected there'd been a time or two when he'd come close to giving in as well, but truth was, they were oil and water. While he'd dreamed of leaving Granite Harbor, she'd dreamed of never leaving.

Mom swept a section of Josephine's hair off her shoulder and finger-combed it down her back. "You've always known your own mind. Courageous and headstrong. Laser-focused on what you want in life. Just like your mother." She smiled. "Looking at you is looking at her."

Josephine stared at her calloused hands. Would her birth mother be proud of who she'd become? She was grateful for how her adopted parents had kept her mom alive over the years with stories and photographs and memorabilia. Even so, there were many unanswered questions, empty spaces, and insecurities. Especially where her birth father was concerned. Whoever he was. Was he still alive? She'd never understand why he hadn't wanted her.

Mom's hand cupped Josephine's cheek, and her brown eyes pooled with unshed tears. "Anne was my very best friend. And now, you are."

Warm lips touched Josephine's temple. "Thanks for always being here for me."

Mom waved a hand in front of her face to dry her watery eyes. "Now, for my invaluable motherly advice." She winked. "Sometimes the most powerful statements are spoken with a gentle voice. Like when Jesus went down to the docks to find disciples. He simply said, 'Follow me.' He didn't shout it. Or provide a PowerPoint presentation."

Mom smiled to soften the blow. "Take baby steps, sweetheart, and have patience. With the fishermen, and with Jace."

"What does Jace have to do with anything?"

"Because I know my girl. You care for him, despite trying to convince everyone—and yourself—you don't." Mom leaned close. "I love you," she whispered.

"I love you, too."

"Send you home with some chowder?"

"Sure."

Mom dished the food into a glass container, while Josephine told her about her fundraising efforts to improve repairs on the Granite Harbor lighthouse. She handed Josephine the container and gave her a hug. "You care about and love this community. You can't get a better harbormaster than that. I'm about to start a batch of blueberry muffins if you want to stay until they're done."

"Thanks, but I should go."

The warmth of the glass seeped into her middle as Josephine pressed it against her side. Moby was still tucked in his mound of blankets in the corner of the couch, snoring. Not wanting to startle him, she settled for a light kiss to his head, which didn't stir him in the least, and headed for the door.

The cotton candy colors of sunset in the painting on the wall caught her attention. The artist, D.C. Jones, did a fantastic job of capturing the sky's calming hues in the background of the harbor. Mild, rippling water disturbed by a lobster boat in the distance, bright orange buoys dangling from its side. The boulders on shore dusted in snow. Painted with such detail and clarity, Josephine had always loved this picture for its ability to suck her in, even as a young child.

This landscape, these people—this was her home, even if she wasn't a true native. Though everyone had come to accept her in the flesh, she wanted to be a part of them in heart. Prove she belonged amongst them.

Mom's words echoed across her heart. *Sometimes the most powerful statements are spoken in a gentle voice.*

Maybe it was time Josephine learned how to whisper.

If Jace didn't eat soon, his gut would be howling like that cougar making an awful racket behind the boatyard. He halted outside of the gate and listened, his grip tightening on the old propeller. Except there weren't any cougars along the coast and the noise was coming from. . .inside the boathouse?

He approached the shingled building in need of a new roof. He'd never seen anyone use the place, even when he was a kid. Owned by the town, the harbormaster was the only person allowed access, and from what he'd heard it had been little more than a storage shed for decades.

The feral animal screamed again. A cat, for sure. How large was hard to judge with the sound echoing off the rafters. A cry for help or warning?

He tugged on the door handle. Locked. The yowling ceased. He tried again. Something crashed to the floor. All went silent except the water splashing against the concrete supports. He needed to report this to Joey but didn't much feel like seeing her after their last encounter. Those eyes, that touch. It may have only been a squeeze on this arm, but he'd nearly come unglued.

He'd waited years for her to touch him. To warm to him in even the slightest of ways. To treat him as anything other than competition. The gesture had been comforting after every relationship he'd built the last ten years had turned their backs on him. Joey probably would too if she knew his secret.

Grief sprung in his chest. He'd almost taken her in his arms to make up for all the time they'd wasted arguing, but pursuing a relationship for solace wouldn't be fair to either of them.

Another scurry sounded from inside the boathouse. A cat chasing a rat most likely, but he'd better mention it, so no one got hurt. If he saw Lauren first, he'd tell her and let her pass the word to Joey.

His footfalls rustled the grass along the shore. The propeller was cumbersome, but it would work great for the table lamp he was working on. The discarded items in the boatyard were meant for the community's use in the industry, but he didn't think anyone would mind him using it, as one of the blades had broken off. His former colleagues always teased him about his hobby, but his online sales were helping pay the bills. The student loans were accruing interest, and his lawyer fees were mounting. It didn't feel as if he'd ever escape from the weight of it all.

The sweet smile and rosy cheeks of a fair-haired toddler flashed in his brain. The propeller hit the truck bed with more force than he intended. Then again, he hadn't intended to conjure up thoughts of Arabella either.

Jace searched the dock but to his rotten luck, Lauren wasn't there. No one was. His stomach growled. It was lunchtime. If Joey wasn't in, he'd leave a note on her desk and call his duty fulfilled.

It took a moment for his eyes to adjust to the dim light of her office. The open windows stirred the gauzy curtains. An empty computer chair meant Joey was out to lunch, which meant he could evade her for another day.

A notepad and pencil lay beside her mouse pad. He reached for it as a door in the back corner opened. Joey entered, wiping her hands on a paper towel. "Sorry, I didn't hear you come in."

Jace straightened and pointed to the notepad. "I didn't think you were here. I was leaving you a note to tell you that there's an animal in the old boathouse. Cat, I believe. Sounds like it's making a mess of things in there."

She tossed the wadded paper towel into the trash. "Thanks for letting me know. I'll check into it."

He nodded. Turned to leave even though a part of him wanted to stay.

"It could be the ghost of a Civil War captain with a peg leg."

He recalled the summer they'd turned ten. A memory long forgotten. He laughed, turning around. "Horrible noises were coming from in there. If it's him, he's removed his leg and is using it as a weapon."

She opened her mini-fridge and pulled out a Moxie. "I would too if I'd been locked in a boathouse for a hundred and sixty-three years. A boathouse I now realize hasn't been around for half that long." The can hissed. "Imagine explaining to my dad why I was soaking wet and how my arm got sliced open."

"You didn't have to accept the dare."

"And lose to you? No way!"

"You did lose."

"But—" she raised the can toward him—"I kept my dignity."

Her slender throat worked as she drank. Curse his male senses for noticing.

"What ever happened to that girl? The one that was with us that day. What was her name? Melanie?"

His brain had trouble switching subjects.

"The one you dated a few times after you realized girls didn't really have cooties."

"I have no idea. She was from Chicago and only summered here. Haven't seen her since eleventh grade."

She relaxed in her chair. "Soda?"

His stomach rumbled. "Sure."

She reached in the fridge and tossed him one.

He tapped the lid to avoid an explosion. "What about you and that guy with the glasses? The one with the spiked hair and frosted tips who looked like a generic boyband member."

She giggled. "David? He's well. Lives in Bangor. We talk every Saturday night. Meet up once in a while."

Every Saturday night? He refused to examine why that thought made him want to Hulk-smash the aluminum can. "And the hair?"

"Nonexistent. Apparently, male-pattern baldness runs in his family."

That shouldn't give Jace satisfaction.

"That's the first smile I've seen on you in a long time. It's a nice change."

That hit him in a tender spot. "Later, Jo—Sephine." He backed toward the door. "Thanks for the drink."

"Anytime."

He let that end their exchange. They'd already talked longer than he'd intended.

The sun warmed his shoulders. Summer lasted such a short time here, while winter seemed to go on forever. He dreaded this winter, hauling in the harsh conditions. Going home to an empty house.

Though he'd take that option any day over spending it in a jail cell.

He climbed into Dad's truck. The engine turned over three times before it fired. He smacked the steering wheel. Not another expense. He may know a little about electricity, but he knew nothing about auto repair.

The truck rolled backwards, then he switched gears. As he left the dock, he swept his gaze over the harbor. A middle-aged man sitting on a park bench stared at Joey's office. Or the part of the harbor that lie beyond it.

Concern flared in his chest. Then he reminded himself this wasn't the city. It was a popular spot, as the bench rested on a knoll and offered a great view of the water. He needn't worry. Joey was a grown woman, and smart. The guy was probably a seasonal tourist who'd yet to leave.

He stopped at a four-way heading outside of town. He motioned for the older man on the sidewalk to cross the street. The man waved his thanks, but instead of heading to the other side, he advanced toward Jace's door. Doc Greenwell. Jace swallowed a groan and rolled down his window.

"Afternoon, Jace."

"Doc."

"I've been wanting to speak with you. You're a hard man to track down."

"Is everything okay?"

"Sure. Sure." Sunlight glinted off the gold frame of the man's glasses, making Jace squint. "The crux is I plan to retire within a year, and I'd like you to consider partnering with me and then taking over."

Air escaped Jace's lungs. An opportunity he'd have snatched had it come six months ago. Was this some kind of sick joke? Of course not, Doc had no idea what happened in Boston. No one here did. And Jace wanted to keep it that way.

Words scraped the back of his throat. "I can't. I'm sorry."

Doc Greenwell frowned. "But. . ."

A car pulled up behind Jace. "Thanks for the offer, but I'm not your guy. Take care, Doc. Good to see you."

The ascending window sent the doctor on his way. Jace hated being rude, though the man seemed more confused than offended. Jace couldn't entertain the idea. Couldn't let himself hope a return to medicine was possible. His spirit couldn't take anymore disappointment.

Doc Greenwell wasn't stupid. With his resources, he'd eventually figure out why Jace had left Boston. Jace hoped that when he did, he kept it confidential.

Until then, all Jace could do was push it out of his mind and ignore how appealing the doctor's offer sounded.

# Seven

The town hall was located in one of the oldest homes in Granite Harbor, the closest thing they had to a courthouse. Historic authenticity intact, offices had been placed on the main floor in the 1940s, the only changes made being the technology used and the new decor every twenty or so years. Though the home was large, the entire building housed local government offices, the water company, sanitation department, police station, and license branch. The harbormaster's office probably would've been crammed in too, but it was more convenient for the fisherman at the dock.

The entryway smelled of the spearmint and eucalyptus candles Vicki Von Trapp sold in her home goods store. Derek Hopkins, one of two town officers, stood from his perch on a sturdy wooden chair when Josephine entered.

"Good morning, Derek."

"Josephine. Please empty your pockets and place everything in the plastic tray."

Derek, always the professional.

Even off duty.

Josephine knew the drill by now. She visited at least once a week. Her pockets turned up a five-dollar bill, a waded-up receipt, a stick of gum, a keychain flashlight, and her office key that she dumped into the tray. He waved a metal detecting wand around her, then inspected the tray's contents.

"I learned my lesson and left my lightsaber at home this time."

He pursed his lips and handed her the tray. One of these days, she was going to rouse a smile out of him. She tucked her cash, gum, and keys back into her pocket and tossed the receipt in the trash on her way to the clerk's office.

Where Derek's facial muscles were in a constant state of paralysis, Meghan Dower's worked overtime. "Hey, what can I do for you, Joey?"

The woman's midwestern accent crooned throughout the room.

"I'm here to get the key for the boathouse."

"Oh, did we not get that to you yet? I'm sorry." Meghan pushed up on the desk and stood. Her necklace swayed along the neckline of her trendy blouse. The woman always looked impeccable, making Josephine wish she dressed more feminine. But polyester and fish guts didn't pair well.

"I haven't had need for it yet. After my last experience there, I'd planned to never enter it again." She looked at Derek over her shoulder, standing tall, hands clasped across his front. "Remember that day, Derek?"

Nothing. She swore the man was part statue.

Meghan raised a curious brow, but Josephine waved the comment away.

"Jace said he heard a wild animal crashing around inside. Guess I'll check it out. Hopefully it isn't a ghost."

Derek remained deadpan.

Keys rattled from the wall-mounted lock box. Meghan returned to her desk, hand outstretched. "Here you go."

"Appreciate it."

The woman made a notation in a small notebook. "The clam bake is next week. Don't forget, it's your job to choose and announce who's going to display this year's lobster trap Christmas tree on the dock."

Josephine tucked the key into her other pocket. "How could I forget? It's harbormaster tradition."

Except she had forgotten. Meghan's intuitive gaze said she knew it too.

"It's a great honor to be chosen." Meghan's eyebrows wiggled up and down. "Choose wisely."

Josephine leaned over the desk and stage whispered, "Maybe I'll pick Derek."

He glared at them.

Meghan giggled. Josephine tapped the desk and moved to the exit, halting directly in front of the stern officer. She craned her neck to look up at him. Wow, he was tall.

"Have you ever thought about moving to the UK and joining the Queen's Guard? You'd be phenomenal. Wait, did I just see a corner of your mouth twitch? Hmm. . . No. Just wishful thinking."

Maybe she would choose Derek for the Christmas festivities. Surely some holiday spirit could elicit a reaction from the man.

She patted his arm. "Well, don't have too much fun. You're on the clock after all."

The boathouse was a good mile from the town hall, but a cloudless sky made the walk enjoyable. A part of her missed being on the water. Unbeatable atmosphere, quiet environment, accountable to no one. She also liked a reliable, steady income and going home at night without an aching back.

That's what she needed to express to the fisherman at the next meeting. She'd been in their position. Had the same troubles. The same fears. Her decisions would be made with their livelihood in mind.

She took the forked path that led away from the main drag to the boathouse. Few homes laid this direction. She waved to the Thomases, who were harvesting the last vegetables from their raised beds. Save for the pumpkins. In another month, every kid in town would flock to the Thomas home for a fat quality squash.

Murphy, the world's sweetest mutt, left the garden and trotted up to her for a scratch behind the ears. He groaned, moving his head from side to side before collapsing to the ground and sticking his paws in the air. She grinned at his expectant expression, tongue lolling out of his mouth. She obliged, rubbed the velvety fur on his nose, then sent him back to his owners.

Maybe she should get a dog. She missed Moby, and her house, at times, was a little too quiet. A little too lonely.

A muffled crash sounded from inside the boathouse. Josephine jogged to the main entrance and yanked on the door. Locked. That meant that whatever was trapped inside was less likely to be human and more feline like Jace suspected.

She glanced around for backup. *Lady and the Trap* cut through the water near Otter Point, too far away should she require assistance. If worst case scenario lie behind the door, like a bear or a puma—or an angry Civil War ghost—she'd have to scream like a banshee and hope the Thomases heard her.

The lock resisted the key. Rust to be sure. She jiggled the key as she pushed until it fell into place and turned. Easing open the door, she peeked inside. Smells of every nature hit her nose--varnish, gasoline, damp wood, seaweed. Plank flooring covered most of the bottom, leaving limited space at the back doors for a skiff to dock. At one time, the floor would've been mostly open to allow for larger boats. For decades now, the boathouse was used for little more than storage.

She threw open the doors and tiptoed inside. Old life jackets hung on pegs. Faded buoys lined the walls. Metal gas cans, oars, rope, reels, traps—a nautical pickers paradise. Something alive was amidst this junk, but how was she ever going to find it without cleaning?

Her pocket-sized flashlight was little but mighty. She swept the LED beam along the floor that was rotting in spots, the back doors, the walls. The place was eerily still. "Kitty? Masked bandit? Whatever you are, it's time to come out."

She crept forward, her steps causing some of the floorboards to creak. With every second that passed, anxiety raced with a Jack-In-The-Box quality that made her want to run back out.

"Hello?" She kicked a coil of metal chain and braced herself. Was that a purr or a growl? Forcing bravery, she swept the beam around the room.

"I'm not going to hurt you. I just wanna see what you are. Well, maybe. As long as your teeth won't do lasting damage."

She rattled a stack of wooden lobster traps. A feral scream split the air. Josephine jumped back. A dark figure dashed from behind the traps and up the wall of life jackets. Clutching her chest,

Josephine spilled light into the rafters where it reflected two glowing eyes staring back at her.

She examined the creature. Pointed ears with tufts on the ends, bushy tail whipping in a dare, large paws, thick coat. A Maine Coon. A big one. Josephine released a breath. This she could handle. Some food, a live trap, patience.

The stack behind her swayed and she reached out to stop it from toppling. Upon further inspection, she noticed how ancient the traps were. Fisherman around these parts hadn't used wooden traps since the mid-80s, but these were much older than that, the design and material different.

Why so many? And why keep them? Why keep any of this stuff?

Deciding to inquire more about the contents later, she craned her neck to the ceiling. "Are you hungry, boy? I'll be back with food and tools to fix the spot you're coming in from. This old boathouse is no place for a handsome kitty like you."

It growled a response from its lofty perch.

She exited, turned off her flashlight, tucked it into her pocket, and locked the doors. The cat would be fine overnight. It was plump and healthy, so it obviously had a means of leaving if it needed to. For now, she'd gather the supplies and return in the morning.

The Thomases weren't in their yard on her way back through. Josephine's stomach growled. They were probably eating lunch. She glanced at her watch. Or preparing for dinner, more like. No wonder she was hungry. She'd skipped lunch and hadn't even realized it.

A boat horn tooted in the distance, two quick blasts in greeting. The fisherman communicated that way, much like Morse Code.

She'd memorized every single sound over the years, learning the short and long pulses, the meaning behind the duration of the sounds. They communicated plenty through radio, but like many things in Granite Harbor's history, this tradition was still going strong.

Which made her choice for the town citizen to build the lobster trap Christmas tree vital. She had to prove her number one goal was to bring the community together mixing traditional and innovative ways. She needed to choose someone who was on her side, as well as someone who was highly respected. And the unspoken rule was to choose someone who'd never been chosen before, so she had a lot to consider.

The harbor was filled with its usual sounds—engines running, crates sliding along the dock, the low hum of voices with an occasional bellow, water slapping the pier. Sounds and smells she wished she could bottle and share with the rest of the world.

Except the rest of the world had already caught on to coastal life. For years, towns around them had slowly suffocated with the influx of flatlanders buying up property for their vacation homes, raising taxes so high the average Mainer couldn't afford to live. Many a fisherman were forced to move as far away as an hour from the coast and drive to their boats every morning. Granite Harbor hadn't felt the squeeze yet, but the grip was there.

She angled off the path into the parking lot and toward her office. Jace stalked around the side of the building, carrying a tangle of rope and the intimidating scowl of a WWE wrestler right before they body slam their victim. Maybe she should have stayed hidden in the tree line until he'd left.

Seavey followed his son, steps swaying, pain evident on his face. Jace threw the rope into his truck bed at the same time he saw her. Too late to hide now.

"Someone cut my rope." Jace's nostrils flared.

Her stomach knotted. "That's a tall accusation. Are you sure?"

He leaned over and grabbed the rope, holding up the neatly spliced ends. "If it had been a propeller or a seal, it wouldn't be this clean."

Josephine knew this, but she didn't want to believe someone would be so cruel. She looked at Seavey.

The man shrugged. "The other lines were fine. Could've been an accident."

She gazed across the water. "Or a warning."

Might as well say it. She didn't want them thinking she was naive to the possibility of a trap war. Though she had hoped the scenario would never play out while she was in office. She'd read accounts where men had lost their lives over space along the ocean floor. As if anyone but God owned it. However, there were jurisdictions in place to protect fishermen and their areas, and she would see that those jurisdictions were obeyed.

She met Jace's furious stare. "I'll check into it."

He released the rope. "See that you do."

Seavey cleared his throat.

Jace ran a hand down his face. "Please."

"I'll let you know what I find out." She took two steps, then paused. "By the way, I just left the boathouse. It's a feral Maine Coon."

She'd hoped by changing the subject it would coax softness into his demeanor, but to no avail. "I hope your evening gets better."

Jace opened his truck door and shook his head. "Thanks."

Seavey patted her arm as she passed. "Hang in there, girl."

She spoke into his ear. "I don't think that block of ice is ever going to warm up."

He placed a hand to his back and whispered a groan. "He will. What he needs is a good and patient woman to soften him up."

Heat swirled in her veins at the idea of that woman being her. Holding him, uplifting him. Being the reason he smiled again. "I don't think even Joan of Arc had that much talent. But if I find a woman that fits that description, I'll send her his way. Take care, Father."

"I'd say what he needs is right in front of his face."

She started walking. "I'm going to ignore that comment."

"You two can't run forever."

A door shut behind her, followed by the start of an engine. They were both good at running, especially when it was away from each other. But something needed to uplift him. He needed a good dose of—

She whipped around in time to see Jace's taillights disappear. Goosebumps covered her arms, and she rubbed the sensation away. What Jace McClintock needed was a dose of Christmas spirit. He was respected, understood her position as well as the position of his fellow fishermen, and had once taken an oath to help and heal humanity. He just needed to find his way again.

She'd never imagined herself playing Santa, but for Jace she would.

# Eight



Jace hadn't attended a clam bake since he'd been accepted to med school. The sights, the smells, were almost enough to put him in a good mood. Take him back a decade when life didn't weigh so hard on his shoulders.

Steam lifted from the seaweed covered pit. A mingle of appetizing scents filled the air, reminding him of childhood, comfort, and the importance of breaking bread with family and friends. The fishermen had adjusted their hauls to accommodate for a Saturday off. Instead of heading out to sea at dawn, they'd gathered at Otter Point, collected enough seaweed at low tide to last the day, prepared the fire pit, and helped with anything else needed.

The water was flat calm, *Home on the Grange* the only disturbance as it transported passengers for the affair. Most tourists and summer dwellers had returned to their lives elsewhere, making the clam bake an unspoken celebration for locals that the area was theirs again. It was hard serving two masters—the seafood industry and tourism.

Pete ripped a square of aluminum foil off the roll and grabbed a potato from the wooden crate. "And then, with her nose stuck up in the air, she asked me where the spa was located. Can you believe that? I told her it was right there." He pointed to the ocean. "Told her the fresh air and cold water had the same healing powers as those stinky ones her ancestors use to soak in."

Jace chuckled. Nick tossed onions and clams in the net bags. "What'd she say?"

"She flipped me off and teetered away on her red heels." Pete added the foil wrapped potato to another crate.

Nick shook his head. "Maybe you're onto something. Why don't you take all those millions you make from fishing and build a spa, so the tourists feel more at home when they visit?"

Jace ignored the jesting curse that followed. Living in Boston had changed him. He saw both sides, the need to escape the chaos of everyday city life and enjoy some luxuries, and the need to live small-town life without the scrutiny of outsiders. Catch-22 Dad called it. The money tourists circulated kept the locals going during winter, but with the tourists came higher prices and crowds that made everyday living difficult. And plenty of demands for the locals to change their way of life to better suit their comforts.

Pete lifted the wet canvas. Jace and Nick used industrial tongs to lift the cauldron of cooked lobster, clams, and veggies. Jace's stomach roared. Thirty more minutes and he could swap places with Ron and eat.

"Back again." Lauren waved her fingers encased in welding gloves. Whoever they belonged to must have long arms because the gloves went up to her armpits.

"Still comin'?" Nick looked up the embankment where the food was being served.

"They're lined clear out to Johnson's Grocery." With awkward coordination in gloves so large, she gripped handfuls of seaweed and tossed them aside while Jace put on the food safe, heat-resistant gloves Pete's wife had loaned him.

He pulled dozens of red, steaming lobsters from the top of the pile and lined them on a tray. Next, he worked the bags of clams, potatoes, onions, and corn still wrapped in husks. Lauren and Nick carried filled trays to the serving line and returned with empty ones.

Jace dripped with sweat from the heat escaping the huge metal pot. He'd forgotten how much work went into the annual celebration. Games and contests for children were set up along Ore Street. Merchants held extended hours. The pie contest would begin at two. If a person was feeling really crazy, they could enter the Logger Games, an American Ninja Warrior-like course in the harbor. Though most contestants only entered that after a few beers from the local brewery.

Together, they refilled the cauldron, lowered it into the pit, and covered it with fresh seaweed and the wet canvas. Tonight, they'd pile all the natural materials they'd used at the edge of the cove and high tide would wash them away as if they'd never been there.

Jace checked the time on his phone.

"Got somewhere to be?" Lauren pulled off her gloves and tossed them on the picnic table.

"In line for the food. I'm starving."

She smiled. "Me too. How much longer you got?"

"Ten minutes." He lifted the hem of his shirt to wipe sweat off his forehead.

When he dropped the fabric, he realized his mistake.

Lauren's heated gaze roamed over him. One side of her mouth quirked. He was flattered. She was a pretty woman with a mass of blonde hair, delicate features, and tan skin. Excellent at weighing crates and mediating with the local shore buyers. But she was young. Too young for him, and too easily persuaded. He wasn't looking for a relationship but if he were, he wanted a challenge. He enjoyed the pursuit.

She tucked her hands in her back pockets. "We could eat together. Take in the festivities."

Seconds ticked by as he scrambled for an excuse. Nick flicked him in the back, prodding Jace's tongue to unhinge. "Uh, sure."

What was he saying?

"I'd like to go home and change first." Which made him sound even more interested, which he was not.

Lauren backed away. "Meet you in line in twenty?"

Jace nodded.

After another lingering look, she started up the hill.

Nick snickered. "Man, you really know how to wax poetic with the ladies. Is that how they do things in Boston? 'Uh, sure.'"

Jace shrugged at the dopey impersonation. "Like you're any better? You're single too."

"Divorced." Nick punctuated the word with his finger. "There's a difference."

"Then you go out with Lauren."

Nick made a face. "She's young enough to be my daughter."

"She's too young for me, too."

"By like what? Six or seven years?"

"Exactly. Too young."

Nick touched his chin with a thumb and forefinger, squinting into the distance. "Me thinketh thou dost protesteth too much."

Jace rolled his eyes at Nick's sorry attempt to sound literary. "Very eloquent. It must be hard for you to go out in public being so smooth."

Nick made a gun with his thumb and forefinger and winked while clicking his tongue. "You know it."

Dismissing Nick with a swat of his hand, Jace walked the short distance to his house and changed clothes. One meal with Lauren couldn't hurt, could it? It might not be so bad to spend some time in female company. It had been a while. But if he could find a way to let Lauren know he was only interested in friendship, transferring his haul at the dock would be a lot less awkward when this lunch was over.

He approached a group of picnic tables covered in red-and-white checkered tablecloths. Mrs. Green, his high school choir teacher, waved at him across the crowd. He returned the gesture, half-scanning the faces for Lauren.

Someone tapped his shoulder. He turned.

"You clean up well." Lauren rocked from heels to toes. She, too, looked different, but he couldn't decide how.

"Thanks." Jace glanced at his plain gray tee, not seeing anything special. She waited for a return compliment, but he didn't want to encourage her. "You ready to eat?"

Her smile dimmed. "Yep."

He led the way but allowed her to go first in line. Volunteers served the food in a buffet-style manner. Lauren conversed with everyone around her as the food filled her plate. Her smile, her bubbly personality was infectious, though he wasn't drawn to it in a romantic way. He could see, however, why Ross, groundskeeper for the area lighthouses who sat ten feet away, couldn't take his eyes off her.

Jace lifted his chin at Ross in a friendly I'm-not-stealing-your-girl gesture. Ross's stone jaw softened a bit, and he went back to eating his food. Jace sensed a backstory a mile long, but since he wasn't a psychologist and he wasn't looking to start a relationship with Lauren, he'd let Ross work it out on his own.

Vacant seats were hard to find. After walking around, they managed to find two next to the makeshift stage used for live music and announcing the various contest winners.

Lauren tore meat from her lobster shell and dipped it in a cup of melted butter. "Mmm. I love lobster."

Jace did too, though he rarely ate it. Every lobster kept meant less profit and he'd rather have money in the bank than a freezer full of meat. He popped a french fry into his mouth.

"We vacationed in Camden the summer I turned ten." Lauren took a sip of Coke. "I ate so much seafood I had to be hospitalized."

Jace wiped his fingers on his napkin. "Mercury overload or shellfish poisoning?"

Lines formed between her brows. "I don't remember. I just know I couldn't stomach the thought of seafood until I was twenty."

"Most likely shellfish poisoning. It's caused from eating seafood contaminated with bacteria or a virus produced by toxic algae." How easily he'd slipped his doctor coat on. He scrambled for a way to keep the conversation flowing but distract her from asking questions about his previous life. "That's why it became illegal to serve it to orphans and inmates more than three times a week."

Lauren leaned closer. "What? No way."

"You didn't learn that in school? What are they teaching nowadays?"

She raised a brow.

"Sorry, I didn't mean that as an insult. I'm shocked. We were taught that in fourth grade, and I never forgot it."

"I grew up a few hours inland in the small town of Garland. Attended U of M and worked summers in Acadia. Loved it so much on the coast I decided to stay."

Made sense. The coast was a hard place to get out of your soul once you'd experienced it. "Well, in the nineteenth century lobsters were so prevalent that when high tide washed out to sea, they covered the beaches and boulders like a blanket. They used pitchforks to scoop them up and toss them back into the water."

He paused for a bite.

"Like anything overindulged, eating it got old quickly." He wiped his mouth with a napkin. "They began serving it to inmates, widows, orphans, servants, and livestock nearly every day. Lobster soon became synonymous with the lower-class, while the upper-class switched to valuable cod, mackerel, or grain."

Lauren placed her elbow on the table and leaned her face on her fist. A sideways grin lifted one side of her face.

"My nerd side is showing. I apologize."

"No, please, continue. I'm fascinated."

Hopefully more so with the history lesson than him. "Some indentured servants from Massachusetts, I think, took their owners to court, and won a judgment that they couldn't be fed lobster more than three times a week. The rule eventually trickled through the entire lower class."

"Amazing. They don't teach that to fourth graders in Garland."

"Tell me something you did learn then." Anything to shift the focus away from him.

"I learned how to milk cows, behead chickens, and ride horses."

"You've beheaded chickens?"

"Does that appall you?"

"I'm just imagining all the feathers and blood."

Her eyes narrowed in playful consternation. "Surely, Doctor McClintock isn't afraid of blood."

His mood took a dark turn at the use of his title. "No, blood doesn't bother me."

She blinked. He hadn't meant to be gruff, but the mention of his doctorate was like pouring whiskey on a raw, open wound.

He scanned the crowd as he thought of some way to backpedal or change the subject and landed on Joey's profile. She stood by the stage talking to the clerk from town hall, hands tucked into the back pockets of her fitted jeans. Her thick copper hair hung in wavy layers down her back instead of pulled up in her customary ponytail.

She noticed him seconds later and smiled. Was she wearing makeup? This seasoned, very womanly Joey spilled sunshine on the moment. He didn't want to stare but her green shirt drew attention to her curves in a way her oversized tees and hip waders did not.

"You know what else I learned on the farm?" Lauren's voice yanked him from his gaping. She crossed her arms on the table and leaned toward him. "How attraction to the opposite sex operates."

His neck flushed hot. "What do you mean?"

She wasn't about to come onto him was she?

Lines of disappointment bracketed her mouth. "I mean it's obvious you have a thing for Josephine."

Oh. He shook his head.

Okay, he had a thing for her. A thing that had been festering for years. Even more since his return, though he tried to ignore it. Would it hurt to finally admit it?

Joey's laughter hit him from here. He wanted to curl up in it, draw her close, and be the reason for it.

She grasped the town clerk's elbow then started up the stage steps.

Yes, it would hurt to admit it. They'd only ever been rivals. Friends in the rare occasion it was called for. The transition to something deeper would have to be executed precisely to be successful, and he didn't have the stamina right now.

Before he could respond properly to Lauren, a high-pitched screech blasted through the speakers, followed by a thumping finger on the microphone. "Sorry. May I have your attention, please?"

Joey waited for the crowd to quiet. "First, I'd like to announce that Berkley Perry is the winner of this year's coloring contest." Everyone applauded. "Berkley won a twenty-five-dollar gift card to The Treasure Chest Toy Store."

A cute toddler in striped leggings and one of those fluffy ballerina skirts walked shyly to the stage. Joey bent and handed the girl an envelope. The tot ran back to her mom holding out her prize, blonde hair flying behind her.

"Next, the winner of the Nautical Knots race is Liam Myers. Congratulations, Liam, you've won a fifty-dollar gift card to Pelican Sporting Goods."

A teenage boy tall enough to play in the NBA accepted his gift, then shook hands with the owner of the store.

"And lastly—" Joey wiped her palms on the thighs of her jeans—"I would like to announce who I've chosen to build and present this year's lobster trap Christmas tree. As you know, the citizen is always chosen with special care, and the position is a great honor to the one it's bestowed upon."

He'd forgotten all about the tradition of the harbormaster announcing it at the clam bake. He didn't know who he would've chosen had he won the election. Not that it mattered. He'd always loved walking along the dock in December as a kid, though, seeing the stacked traps rimmed in white lights, ornaments and buoys hanging from the cages. Especially after a light snow. Once when he and Dad—

His name boomed through the speakers.

Lauren turned and beamed at him. "Congratulations!"

Ron walked up and slapped his back, offering his sentiments as well.

Jace went numb.

Joey stared at him from the stage, biting her lower lip. "Jace?"

He pointed a finger at himself as the crowd continued to clap. She nodded.

Anger rolled through him, swift and deep. Inhaling a breath, he stood, untangled himself from the picnic table, and went to the stage. He wore the appropriate mask, though he was seething on the inside. This was payback for putting her on the spot at the last fishermen's meeting. Like in their childhood years, he'd unknowingly thrown a challenge, and she was running him through the gauntlet.

She knew he was hauling traps all winter and didn't have the time to mess with Christmas trees. And where was he supposed to find traps? All his would be in use.

Joey handed him the customary ornament, his name and the year etched on the back. She must have read his anger because as their fingers brushed, her guilty eyes widened, and she swallowed.

"Congratulations, Jace." Her voice was timid. "We look forward to the coming season and our honorary citizen leading the festivities."

More clapping ensued. A few whistles.

Who was he kidding? Precisely executed or not, they could never supersede their opposing relationship now.

# Nine



Josephine walked the shoreline of Puffin Point, pebbles crunching beneath her shoes. Dusk rushed in with an artistic blend of pinks, purples, and blues. Wind rustled the autumn trees and the thinning pink blossoms of mayflowers beneath. Soon they'd be gone, and a heavy frost left in their place.

She zipped her fleece jacket and stood facing the choppy water. A couple holding hands were combing the beach to her left and a family of four played catch to her right. Happy little girl squeals carried through the air.

The clam bake had been successful and had kept her so busy she'd barely had time to eat. Now would be a good time to walk home and indulge in the blueberry pie and homemade whipped cream she'd stashed away earlier. If only she had someone to indulge with.

Josephine had always been independent and comfortable in her own skin. But occasionally, like tonight, insecurity and loneliness crept in and reminded her she wasn't getting younger. Reminded her that despite a wonderful childhood with her adopted parents, she hadn't a clue where she really belonged.

A certain ex-doctor lobsterman came to mind, but she shook the thought away after recalling the murderous look in his eyes when he'd joined her on the stage. Okay, murderous was a bit melodramatic, but definitely unhappy. Very unhappy.

She turned for home and jerked to a stop at the sight of Jace standing not six feet away. Pain and confusion radiated from his gaze, cutting her in two. "Why me?" he asked.

One, he was intelligent.

Two, he was gorgeous.

Three—in his annoying way—he'd always pushed her to be her best. Now, she was going to push him to be his.

Four, the whole broody thing he had going on since he'd moved home had awakened her feminine instincts.

But he wasn't asking for her list of why he'd make a good pie partner. He was asking why she'd chosen him to build the lobster trap Christmas tree. "Why not you?"

Jace's mouth opened, and some caveman-like grunt escaped before he closed it again. It wasn't often the man was speechless.

"I have many reasons." The wind at her back blew her hair into her face. She tucked large sections behind her ears and chose the humor tactic. "The main one—you're grumpy and reclusive, and before you completely turn into the Grinch, monologuing and eating onions for dinner on a secluded cliff, I decided to save you." She scrunched her nose with a grin. "I'm your Cindy Lou Who."

He blinked.

She tilted her head to the side and studied him. "Come to think of it, you might be more of a Shrek."

Jace rubbed the back of his neck. "I don't mean to be grumpy and reclusive. Or an ogre."

She grinned at his terrible attempt at a Scottish accent.

"I need time to settle back into life here before people start needing things from me." He ran his fingers through his hair. "I'm not ready to be the town's Holiday Cheermeister."

She smothered her grin at his mention of Grinch pop-culture and swallowed the questions about his Boston life building in her esophagus. "You ran for harbormaster. To me, that meant you wanted to dive back into the community headfirst."

"There's more to it than that, oh chosen one."

Shrek had a sense of humor after all.

Jace flipped up the hood of his sweatshirt to cover his ears. With the sun nearly set, their position by the water was turning cold. He cracked the bones in his neck and loosened his shoulders. Josephine took small steps toward home, pleased when he stayed beside her. "You are every bit as capable of doing this job as me. Everyone knows that. Everyone also knows that your passion isn't in fishing and water patrol. It's in healing."

He stopped walking. So did she.

His hands were hidden in the pocket of his hoodie, but she instinctively knew they were clenched. The intensity of his gaze made goosebumps fan across her skin.

"You think you know me so well." He inched closer until their toes touched. "Truth is, you've never let me get close enough for us to know each other."

"I know you better than you think I do."

Why were her knees wobbly?

His lips curled in a satisfied smirk. Those lips caused lava to pool low in her belly and he knew it. "Why have we never moved past this?"

"Past what?" Darn that lump in her throat.

"This childish opposition."

It had been a rather forcible game of tug-of-war, and she was exhausted.

He shrugged one shoulder. "You think we can finally lay down our weapons?"

Their rivalry had always given her motivation to try harder, be better, dream bigger. Friends or more, she wasn't sure how to bury old habits and act around him.

"Sure."

Brilliant response.

"Good." He resumed walking. So did she.

Waves rolled in faster than when she'd first arrived. It was hard to imagine that in a few hours, the spot they were standing in would be submerged. A good example of the nature of things, constantly changing.

Jace bumped her elbow with his. "For future reference, friends don't foist unwanted time-consuming holiday traditions on each other unexpectedly."

She smiled. "Duly noted."

Streetlights blazed to life as they reached the empty sidewalks. Closed signs hung in shop windows. The decorations and displays packed away until next year. It had been a busy but good summer.

To break the strained silence, she told him about the cat in the boathouse and how it was smart enough not to fall for her trickery. He offered a couple of suggestions, and they reminisced about childhood pets until they reached her front porch.

Jace removed his hood. "Thanks, by the way. For the lead on a sternman. I think he's going to work out great."

"Happy to help." She meant it.

Her neighbor's living room light radiated through the curtains. Duke, their adorable golden retriever puppy, shoved the fabric aside with its nose and pressed against the glass, tail swaying like a metronome. Maybe she should get a dog too, so someone would be happy to see her come home.

It was easier for Josephine to concentrate on the dog than on how she'd like Jace to conclude their walk. "Thanks for seeing me home."

He glanced around the porch as if only now aware of his gesture. "Ayuh. Goodnight."

He headed toward the street.

"For future reference. . ."

He turned. The glow of her porch light cast shadows on the planes of his face.

"Remember that some people are meant to go out into the world and do great things. Others are meant to stay where they were planted."

The grooves in his forehead grew deeper as he thought about what she'd said. He gave a slight nod. "Understood, Fiona."

She giggled as she unlocked the door and stepped into a dark house. Her mood sank. She should've invited her new friend in for pie.

Joey's statement hit Jace between the eyes. He'd tried to go out into the world, leave his mark. Make a positive difference.

He'd failed.

Darkness engulfed the town. Streetlights grew thinner the farther he walked. A half-moon offered enough light to see his way. He had a couple miles left to go before reaching his home at the cusp of his dead-end road, but he didn't mind. He often took night walks when he couldn't sleep, when grief and guilt consumed and the air in his house felt suffocating.

Many of those nights, the galaxy glittered in a way only God could design. The view had a way of calming his racing heart, of humbling him, of putting things into perspective, though he'd never understand why God was putting him through this.

Joey had been the better person for harbormaster. Dirk Schlagel, the town's oldest bachelor before he passed away, had taught her the trade as well as any apprentice. He'd left his boat to Joey, and she'd inherited his license and buoy colors through hard, honest work. Jace needed to give credit where it was due and stop pouting like a child. Being one-track-minded when he decided to go after something had always been his double-edged sword.

He had to admit, a part of him had latched onto the competition with Joey like Linus with his security blanket. It was familiar. Comforting even. It had given him a distraction from lawyers, court documents, and death.

Joey, herself, was a distraction.

From the moment he'd spotted her on the docks during April mud season, wearing a stained pair of jeans with a rip in the knee, a flannel, and a ratty ballcap, her hair spilling out the hole in the back, he'd been distracted.

His old adversary had lost her girlish freckles and grown a few inches taller, slimming in areas that created beautiful curves in others. He'd remembered how pretty she'd looked at their high school graduation, all fifteen graduates in folding chairs on the front row. During his valedictorian speech, his gaze kept returning to her, part gloating, part to keep himself steady. The teenage Joey and the grown woman Joey were two very different beings.

Adoption may have planted her here, but she was as synonymous with Granite Harbor as any native. That woman had done great things without ever having to leave home.

Lucky her.

# Ten



*Sixteen years earlier*

Jace leaned against the hood of his car and watched Joey sitting on the shoreline below. Her knees were pulled up to her chin, and she wrapped her arms around her legs, staring out to sea. The breeze played with her hair in a way he'd like to. But since she despised him, he'd have to be satisfied watching nature do the job.

Maybe after listening to what he'd come to say, she wouldn't despise him anymore.

The beach was secluded this afternoon, save for the gulls and a few puffy clouds overhead. He pushed away from his car and moved toward her, wishing his shoes didn't crunch the pebbles so loudly. He'd planned on a sneak-attack. That way, she wouldn't have time to react to his approach and build her wall.

She tossed her head to the side, sending hair away from her face, and met his gaze. Her eyes were rimmed in red. Had she been crying? His palms sweat. If now wasn't a good time for his announcement, what would he use as his excuse for seeking her out?

"Hey." He lowered his body next to hers.

Man, this was uncomfortable. He wiggled to flatten the rocks away from his tailbone.

She sighed and wiped her cheeks with her sleeve. "Shouldn't you be packing for your summer stay at the marine institution?"

"Is that why you're crying? You gonna miss me?" He kept his tone light to show he was teasing.

Her glare shot daggers at his vital organs.

"Apparently not." He knocked her shoulder with his. "What's wrong then?"

Tomorrow was the last day of school. Surely it wasn't that.

Joey pressed her lips together and tucked her hair behind her ears. Up went the wall. Man, she was a fast builder.

He picked up a pebble and rubbed his thumb over the smooth shape. "I'm sorry if this is bad timing, but I came to tell you I'm not taking the internship this summer."

She made a face. "Why not?"

"Doc Greenwell heard that I plan to apply for medical school in a few years and offered to mentor me. I figure that's a better use of my time."

*And because I saw how crushed you were by not earning it yourself and decided I couldn't do that to you no matter how much I like to win. So, I gave it up the internship to make you happy.*

He'd keep those remarks locked in his own head, however.

A knot formed between her brows, and he resisted the urge to smooth it away with his lips. "You're just giving it up?"

"Actually, I'm gifting it to someone."

Hope lit in her mesmerizing eyes.

He grinned. "Stop sitting here and moping and go home to pack your suitcase."

She touched his arm. Her fingertips curled around his bicep in anticipation. Wow, that felt good. "What do you mean?"

"The internship is yours, Jo. The grant committee agreed to let me give it to you, since you were the runner up, and I've already discussed it with your parents. They agree it's a once in a lifetime opportunity. Now go. Discover a new species or solve the ocean's problems or something."

Anything but look at him like he was her hero. *That* might make him do something stupid like lean closer and see if the salt in the air also clung to her mouth.

"But why? How?" She shook her head, as if it would clear her jumbled thoughts. "Are you certain?"

"Yes. This isn't a dream, but I can pinch you if you want me to." He winked.

She laughed. Her face glowed with a happiness he rarely got to witness. And this time, he was the cause. He'd finally scaled the wall.

He resisted the urge to throw his hands up in victory.

Her arms flew around his neck and clamped hard, pressing the soft curves of her body against his side. Before he could react and press her closer, she moved away as if he'd scalded her.

"Sorry." Her eyes were huge. "Gut reaction."

Rosy cheeks looked great on her, and he wished she'd stayed against him a little longer.

When he didn't respond because he couldn't, she winced. "That was awkward."

Awkwardness wasn't what was keeping him silent. The lingering feeling of her against him was. He cleared his throat. "Totally. Don't ever do that again."

He smiled.

She did, too.

"I can't believe you'd rather be around sick people and medicine than the ocean. Just look at it. It's so vast it would take all of eternity to learn its secrets."

"The human body is just as complex." He adjusted his position on the rocks to relieve his tailbone, which put him a few inches closer to her. "We all have different dreams, Jo."

"That we do." She shifted closer as well. "Thank you. So much."

Their arms brushed, sending a jolt of heat through his body. This moment with her, this connection they shared for the first time, was worth spending the summer on Dad's boat and working with Doc Greenwell on Saturdays just to see her happy.

"Don't think this means I like you now." She stretched her legs in front of her.

The wind picked up the ends of her hair and tickled his face. "Of course not. That would make things even more awkward."

She bumped his shoulder with hers.

For the first time in their history together, they sat in comfortable silence, bodies touching, and watched the waves roll ashore. If only their lives weren't drifting in opposite directions.

# Eleven

Talk about a manic Monday. Josephine's office had seen enough foot traffic to wear grooves into the floorboards. The rank smells of fish bait and body odor lingered in the small space, despite her diffuser pumping orange and clove essential oils into the air.

A middle-aged man with tan weathered skin and salt-and-pepper strands in his hair and beard walked in as Caleb Morris was leaving. One of Caleb's ropes had been cut too, meaning she was going to have to open an investigation. The idea made her stomach churn. Cut ropes was a harbormaster's worst nightmare.

"May I help you?" she asked without her usual enthusiasm.

"I need to renew my mooring permit, please."

The request surprised her. Josephine had seen him around the last few months, though he kept mostly to himself. Fit for his age, there was something about him that was familiar in an eerie we-knew-each-other-in-another-life sort of way. Not that she believed in that mystical stuff. Still, the guy's presence set her on edge.

She nudged her mouse to wake up the sleeping computer. "Name?"

"Colin Warner."

She didn't recognize the name. Was he a new sternman or a transplant from away?

"That'll be eighty-five dollars, please." She opened a file cabinet and retrieved an application. "Fill this out while I update your record."

She held out a pen and clipboard.

Mr. Warner walked to the chair in the corner and filled out the paperwork, the sleeves of his shirt straining against his biceps. He had a military air about him, direct, professional, his gaze absorbing pertinent details within seconds. Much like her uncle Trey, a retired Army colonel.

She plopped into her desk chair and clicked the icon to pull up the mooring records in alphabetical order. There he was. His record dated back to 1989. He hadn't always held the same spot, but he renewed his license at least every few years. His last mooring was on the backside of town where the seasonal boats moored, but his spot had sat empty for the last few years. Lucky for him it was still available.

She made the appropriate notations and waited.

His chair creaked when he stood. Mr. Warner handed her the clipboard and fumbled for his wallet. "Have you been harbormaster long? Last time I was here, it was a short man with black hair."

"Regis." The town celebrity, even if only because his fashion sense resembled Elvis in his later years. Bad attempt at a comb-over and all. But the Elvis lookalike knew the industry well and had done a wonderful job before his retirement.

"I was elected last month. Regis is wintering in Florida now." She envisioned the man lying on the beach singing "Burning Love" and swallowed a laugh.

She scanned the application and made an additional copy.

The certifying stamp thwaked against the papers, leaving its mark inside each black square. She passed him his copy, stood, and held out her hand. "I'm Josephine Rockwell. Nice to meet you."

He stared at her hand and blinked as if unsure he should make contact. Germaphobe? Or did he think the funky smell in here was her?

She retracted her hand and rubbed it down the leg of her jeans. "It looks as if you've been mooring with us for many years. I don't see you around often. Do you—"

Jace stormed in. "Sorry to interrupt, but Hemingway is causing a scene, cursing and spitting because he thinks my boat's in his spot."

"Spitting?"

Gross.

Jace closed his eyes, the way a mother does to a child with whom she's quickly losing patience. "Hurry, Jo. It's bad."

She acknowledged Colin. "Duty calls. It was nice meeting you."

Josephine rounded the desk and rushed after Jace, around the backside of the office to the opposite side of the dock. Sure enough, Hemingway was perched on an upended barrel, red-faced, ranting, and creating a small pond of saliva by his feet.

His eloquent storytelling had earned him the nickname decades ago, coupled with the fact he could be spotted on his boat with an open book on many an afternoon. Since dementia had taken over, his storytelling had mostly turned into sailor dialog and his old addiction to smokeless tobacco was stronger than ever, minus the tobacco.

She approached with caution. "Hey, Hem. Remember me? I'm Josephine Rockwell, the new harbormaster."

The old man scowled at her, spittle dripping from the gray whiskers on his chin.

She pressed a palm to his back and rubbed circles the way she'd seen her best friend Ciara do to calm her autistic son. "What's got you maddah than a wet crittah at suppertime?"

Hemingway harrumphed at her exaggerated dialect but softened under her ministration. "This juvenile here has his boat tied in my mooring." He pointed a crooked finger at Jace. His thick, yellow fingernails were long and starting to curl. "I've owned the same mooring since 1961."

She didn't doubt that. In fact, she would have guessed longer.

Hemingway thrust a few insulting barbs at Jace while she thought about the best way to deactivate his anger bomb.

Josephine stopped rubbing circles and slipped an arm around his bony shoulders. "Mr. Hemingway"—what was his actual name?—"you've worked hard for many years, haven't you?"

"Ayuh."

"It's said that you're an expert fisherman. A legend in these parts, if you will."

Hemingway perked. "I know these waters like the back of my eyelids."

She refrained from smiling at the misnomer. "You've seen this town through the greatest of times and through the worst of times. What right does this juvenile have to park in your mooring?"

She hitched a thumb at Jace.

Jace threw his palms out and mouthed *what are you doing?*

Hemingway spit again, this time dangerously close to her shoe. "Yeah, you babyface—"

Josephine grimaced at the rest of the sentence.

Hands on his hips, face to the sky, Jace let the slander ricochet.

She squeezed Hemingway's shoulder. "But you see, you worked so hard and helped this town so much that five years ago you decided it was time to retire."

"What?" Hemingway scowled.

"Yessir. You sold the *Trapper John* to a newbie in Stonington and have been living the good life ever since."

His ruddy cheeks calmed from purple to red. "You joshin' me?"

"I wouldn't do that to a rock star. To prove it, there's a framed picture of you at your retirement party hanging in the harbormaster's office in honor of all your years of service. I can show it to you if you want. While we're there, I can also prove to you that Babyface has a legal permit to be moored in your old spot."

Jace turned to the side to hide his amusement, but she caught it anyway.

"Well. . .I wouldn't mind seeing my picture in the hall of fame."

More like wall.

She helped Hemingway stand and linked her arm through his. Other than a small tear in the sleeve, and the fact it was wet, his coat looked brand new. She would not allow her brain to wonder why the fabric was damp.

Jace held out his hand to Hemingway to show they were good, but Hemingway waved him off. "Sorry, junior, I don't do autographs."

Josephine held in a snicker the entire painfully slow walk back to the office. As she helped Hemingway over the threshold, she remembered that she'd failed to collect Colin's permit fee.

What a rookie mistake. Now she'd have to track him down.

"Here's your picture, Mr. Hemingway." She led him to the wall opposite her desk and offered him a bottle of water that he refused.

Leaving him to stare at his picture, she went to her desk to look at the address on Colin's permit. Four twenty-dollar bills and five ones peeked out from beneath her wireless keyboard, her copy of his permit folded around it. Thank God for honest citizens.

For the second time in the last half hour, she went to the filing cabinet and, this time, searched for Jace's permit. She pulled it free of the folder and joined Hemingway at the wall of fame. They stood, silent, staring at his picture where he stood in front of the *Trapper John*, traps, lines, and colorful buoys surrounding him on the dock.

Josephine studied Hem's profile. Those serious eyes surrounded by a road map of lines held many stories, experiences, and heartaches. The thin, drooping skin twitched, and the whites glistened with moisture. "The world is a fine place and worth the fighting for, and I hate very much to leave it."

Before she could ask for more particulars regarding his comment, he sighed and faced her, his jowls swaying with the movement. "Earnest Hemingway. My favorite."

Ah.

The brain was a complex organ.

Josephine glanced at the photo again. Trapper John. Was that his name?

She grasped his elbow. "John?"

His eyes lit with clarity.

"We'll hate very much to see you leave it."

Hemingway frowned. "Leave what? I just got here."

Well, she'd tried.

"Never mind. Here's a look at Jace's permit to prove he has legal grounds to the mooring. See?" She pointed to a few areas on the document. "The *Hiley Mae II* belongs to Jace McClintock, and he paid to moor in #7."

Hemingway looked it over, then shook his head. "Why'd you let that baby-faced fella have your boat? It should stay in the family."

She started to explain that the boat had never been in her family. That it had been Seavey McClintock's since she and Jace were in diapers and now Jace owned it, but too many details would just confuse him further. In the name of tradition, boats were usually passed down the generations, but not always. Hemingway was the type to make his boat a member of the family and would view a sale as betrayal. Sure, he'd sold the *Trapper John* when he'd retired, but his only son was a nuclear engineering genius and wasn't even stateside. He'd had no fisherman to pass the boat down to.

The office door opened, and Grantley stepped in, wide-eyed. "I'm so sorry. I was elbow-deep in this essay I'm writing for physics class that's due tomorrow, and I didn't hear him leave the house."

Dark circles marred the twenty-something's otherwise flawless face. Caring for a grandparent who was prone to wander, while trying to graduate college early with a degree in molecular physics was taking its toll. Her dad's job engineering a new pipeline in Africa should be completed by the end of the year, and when he returned, Grantley could cease her online classes and return to school, and he could decide about Hemingway's future care.

"No worries," Josephine said. "We had a nice visit."

Many in the town had promised to help with Hemingway while his son was gone, but now Josephine wondered if they were doing enough.

"Thanks." Grantley smiled at Josephine. "Ya hungry, Grandpa? Let's grab lunch."

He complied and followed her to the exit. She wrapped her hand around Hemingway's arm. "Eww. Grandpa, why is your arm wet?"

Good question Josephine didn't want to know the answer to. The door closed behind them.

Bomb officially diffused. Another Granite Harbor crisis averted. She was finally proving her worth.

# TWELVE

Jace slapped his new sternman's back. "Wicked good haul."

Cooper Jennings had retired from a transmission manufacturer in the Midwest and recently moved to a home on the outskirts of Granite Harbor with his wife, a retired teacher, and their fur babies, as Cooper called them. When it came to lobstering, the man was greener than spring grass, but he was a fast learner, a hard worker, and loved being on the water.

Jace refilled the mesh bait bags while Cooper continued to remove bugs from the pots and measure them before deciding if they were keepers or shorts. The process was painfully slow compared to the pace Jace was used to, but he didn't mind. The teaching process kept him busy enough he didn't think about things he wanted to forget. Market price was great right now, making it hard to be down.

Rope had tangled around one of the traps where Jace hauled them to the surface faster than Cooper could empty and stack aside. They worked together to untangle the knot.

Cooper rubbed his chin with the sleeve of his sweatshirt. "You ever lose a buoy? Or a trap? What happens then?"

Jace's cut rope sprang to mind, killing his good mood. Caleb and, most recently, Nick had experienced the same, and Joey had ensured them a thorough investigation. He'd keep that to himself for now. A trap war could get dangerous and best not scare away his new sternman until he had further proof war was declared.

Jace shrugged. "Not often, but it happens. The rope will get cut in a rudder or a buoy separated somehow. It's called a ghost trap. If you ever go diving, you'll spot some on the ocean floor covered in algae and sea squirt."

"Sea squirt?"

Flatlanders.

"A crusty organism that filters bits of food from the water."

Rope untangled, Jace stacked the trap and worked on another.

The boat dipped and swayed. Jace leaned over the side and peered around the bulkhead. White tracks from another boat's wake reached them. An older Pulsifer-style diesel with a faded green bottom headed northeast in the gulf. Strange seeing an unmarked boat like that this far out and heading farther. Only small vacant islands laid that direction.

Unmarked. The culprit for the cut ropes? Why else have an unmarked boat?

He shouldn't jump to conclusions, but the situation had them all on edge.

He'd report the boat to Joey. Then she'd be aware in case she needed to call the Coast Guard for backup. Besides, he wouldn't mind an excuse to talk to her again. The last few days they'd only seen each other in passing, and every time it had brought up the sense of rightness he'd felt the night he'd walked her home. One of the longest conversations they'd shared in years without pride or their competitive natures taking over.

"Everything okay?" Cooper pointed to the other boat fading quickly on the horizon.

"Yeah, sorry. You done?"

"Believe so."

"Step back, then. I'm takin' off. Don't let your feet get tangled in that rope. You'll go overboard and never come back up."

Cooper jumped back from the pinkish coil. This wasn't the first time Jace had warned him, but he'd continue to warn him until Cooper performed the job like a pro.

The engine revved and they moved forward. Cooper tossed the first trap overboard. The momentum of the boat uncoiled the rope and sent the connected traps into the water, one every few seconds until the stack was gone.

Jace smiled at Cooper's amazement. He worried how the man would fare on the water through the winter when the wind threatened to lash the skin off his face and all his extremities were numb by the time they reached home. If Cooper made it through, he'd earn the title of a true sternman.

They continued hauling pots for a few more hours, then pointed the stern toward Granite Harbor. The sky was darkening with moody clouds, and Jace had learned the hard way years ago not to trust anything other than clear skies and sunshine and even then, one should be cautious.

Light rain fell in a steady rhythm by the time they pulled up to the dock. *Hook, Line, and Sinker* was pulling away to their mooring. Lauren scrambled at the scales. Gerry Matthews cut through the water on his dory, making quick work of the journey from his fishing boat to shore.

Cold water pooled in Jace's hair and trickled down his face. He'd offered Cooper his hooded slicker when the rain started. No sense in the man getting sick. Jace would unload, collect his pay, and warm up in a hot shower.

Crates of lobster collected on the dock as they unloaded and waited for Lauren to finish weighing Nick's haul and loading the crates into a semi that would go to the co-op. This was one of his biggest hauls all season and should be worth around eight hundred. Perfect timing for the overdue student loan bill looming on his kitchen table.

Nick waved and Lauren walked to the *Hiley Mae II*, duck boots squeaking on the slick dock. "Wicked haul," she said, grabbing one side of the crate while Jace grabbed the other. "Now I know why you're the last one back."

Together, they moved the crates to the scale. Cooper hosed the boat deck. Thunder rolled in the distance. The storm was offshore and probably wouldn't amount to much inland except a good, cold soaking.

Several minutes later, the crates had been weighed, emptied, and returned. Lauren jotted his info on a pad of paper damp with rain and handed it over. "Hang in there."

Jace frowned. He had no idea what she meant but wasn't about to stick around and ask either. He thanked her for her time, parted ways with Coop, and stepped into Joey's office. He'd moor the boat later.

The office was dry and warm. Joey looked up from her filing cabinet and down to his feet. Water dripped off him, creating puddles on the floor. A mop rested against the wall next to a chair full of ragged towels. She'd been expecting the deluge.

He, however, had not been expecting Hurricane Joey. Polka dot rubber boots, jeans, a flannel shirt under what looked like a grandpa cardigan, kinky damp hair, and black glasses. She must normally wear contacts because he never remembered seeing her in glasses. It was definitely a look he'd like to explore further.

He continued to drip and backed toward the exit. "You want me to come back later?"

She closed the cabinet with her foot and dropped the file on her desk. "I think the damage has already been done."

At her grin, he approached, prepared to tell her about the unmarked boat but decided to make small talk first. Anything to stay longer and absorb this new side of Joey that made his muscles buzz. "Biggest haul yet."

She looked down at his boots again.

"I'll clean it up." He went for the mop.

Joey sighed. "It's not that."

He waited.

"The senate failed to renew trade sanctions with the international markets. Until something is negotiated and the tariffs balance out, prices are down."

His stomach soured. "How much?"

The paleness of her cheeks told him the best thing he could do was walk out the door and light his wallet on fire.

She pressed her lips together. Once. Twice. "Four dollars a pound."

His breaths quickened, and his neck burned hot. "That's less than half of what it's been all summer."

"I know. I'm sorry." She pinched the skin on the bridge of her nose, pushing her glasses onto her forehead.

Sorry didn't pay his bills.

He threw out his hands. "What are we supposed to do? We can't make a living like this."

Market prices were out of her control. So were the decisions made at the senate level. He knew this. He also knew taking it out on her was a jerk move, but he couldn't contain the anger and despair threatening to choke him. It seemed the court system was going to ruin his life one way or the other and every ounce of control he had in his life was slipping.

"I propose we cut supply and force the market upward."

The same experiment she'd touted at last month's meeting. He'd left Boston to live a life he could control. This was not control. This was like playing a rigged game of poker with the last few dollars in his 401k. "What if that doesn't work?"

He ran his fingers through his sopping hair, sending a rush of cold water down his back.

"Then we go to plan B."

"What's plan B?"

"I'm still working on plan B."

This time he said exactly what he was thinking.

She bit her lip.

"You're the harbormaster, Joey. You're supposed to have our backs. We need plans A through Z in everything we do."

Color leeched back into her cheeks. "I do have your backs. I'm working this from every angle. Even at home. Even in my sleep! But I can't work miracles, Jace. I can't sway the politicians or the international markets. Ultimately, market price is out of my control."

Somebody needed to work a miracle because he was tired of his life eroding all around him.

He also needed air.

Before he said anything he'd regret—because he was being an irrational idiot right now—he stormed back to the dock. He heard Joey call his name but kept going. He needed distance, so he wouldn't say or do anything that hurt her. This wasn't her fault. He needed a hot shower to clear his head. He needed time to process a proper apology.

He jumped onto his boat.

"Jace, wait. I've been crunching the numbers and—"

He started the engine. Banged his hand on the steering wheel when he realized the boat was still tied to the dock. He left the cabin to unwind the rope, but Joey had already started on it. She didn't want the dock ruined any more than he did.

She tossed him the rope. Instead of taking the time to loop it and set it out of the way like he always did, he let it hit the platform in a messy heap. When he reached the steering wheel, he saw Joey jump aboard from the corner of his eye. Her boots rolled over the wet rope and sent her flying backwards. Her skull smacked the platform.

Eyes closed, rain pelted her unmoving form.

Jace's heart raced. Her pale face, limp body. . .her health out of his control. . .memories from another time circled to overtake him. His body went cold.

# Thirteen

Rain pelted Josephine's face. Pain pulsed in the back of her head. She moaned. Warm hands cupped the sides of her neck.

"No blood. Do you think you can stand?"

She opened her eyes, but her glasses were covered in rain drops. Though he was only a dark form, she recognized Jace's voice. "Does anything besides your head hurt? Feel broken?"

"Just my skull." She palmed her head. "And my pride."

"I'm going to lift you on the count of three. Ready?"

He counted, and she levitated into the air.

Jace was carrying her. Before she had time to push past the pain and revel in her first time being carried by a man, he lowered her onto a stool in his boat's cabin, safe from the weather.

He released her to close the door, and she instantly missed his touch. She removed her glasses and started shivering. He rummaged through what looked like a large toolbox and pulled out a wool blanket and a First-Aid kit.

"We need to get you warm." He peeled off her wet cardigan. "Do you have on another shirt beneath your flannel?"

"Y-yes." Her teeth clanked together.

"Good." His fingers made quick work of the buttons and peeled it off as well, tossing it into the floor with a plop.

If her brain waves weren't so concentrated on her pounding skull and her freezing core, she might feel violated. But Jace was running in full doctor mode, hunting around for supplies and not giving her body another glance.

He tucked the wool blanket around her in a cocoon, their cheeks almost touching. Rain dripped from his hair and nose. He crossed the loose ends of the blanket under her chin and held it in place. Kneeling, proposal style, he put some space between them and sighed. "I'm so sorry."

Her teeth chattered. "It's not your fault."

Jace put his head down. "Yes, it is."

She wanted to assure him it wasn't, but decided she liked his undivided attention. A little guilt never hurt anyone.

The lines on his forehead grew deeper. "I'd like to probe the wound to get an idea if you need to go to the hospital or not."

Probe the wound? That didn't sound fun.

She twisted so he could more easily access the back of her head. His fingers brushed sections of hair aside as he searched for the bump. Heavenly. She hissed when he found the bullseye. He pressed against the skin, as if trying to determine how large an area they were dealing with. She crammed her lips together to keep from reacting to the pain.

"Almost done." He dropped his hands, and she swiveled to face him.

He opened the First-Aid kit and moved the contents around with his finger until he found a cold pack. After breaking the contents inside the pouch to release whatever it was that made it turn cold, Jace pressed it against the wound.

"Nothing is split or bleeding, but you'll have a good bump."

Light blinded her left eye, then the right.

Where had the flashlight come from?

"Your pupils are dilating normally. How many fingers am I holding up?"

"Four."

"Two."

She started to put on her glasses.

"I'm kidding, it's four."

She knocked her knee into his elbow. The motion yanked the blanket off her leg. He covered her back up, keeping his hand on her knee. "I'm sorry, Joey. I shouldn't have stormed off like that. Shouldn't have gotten angry in the first place."

The agony in those blue depths was endearing. Topaz with copper sunbursts around the pupils. "I know better than to board a captain's boat without first asking permission. The injury is my fault."

He swallowed. "You have my permission to board my boat at any time."

Heat blasted through the vents, warming the cabin. Her body relaxed under his care. Jace was soaked, hair stuck to his head at weird angles, eyebrows a little wild.

She'd never gotten the opportunity to examine him this close before—as a virile man anyway—and found it made him even more appealing. The perfect scholar had a few flaws after all. Like a front tooth that sat slightly forward of the other. One of his earlobes was slightly bigger than the other. And he had a bear of a temper. But they'd always been good at getting under each other's skin.

Only right now, they weren't. Her head injury had broken the barrier between them, freeing the tension. For now. In this moment, they were just a man and a woman. Bodies very close in proximity.

Whoo-boy. She'd hit her head harder than she thought.

"What's wrong?" he asked.

"It's getting hot in here." Yikes. That sounded like a bad pick-up line. Or terrible lyrics for a song.

"Oh. Sorry."

She took over holding the cold pack while he stood and turned down the heat. The windows were shrouded in fog. Another thought she wouldn't dwell on.

Jace leaned his backside against the instrument panel and ran a hand over his face. "What were you trying to tell me before I stormed off like an ogre?"

She grinned, recalling the night she'd called him Shrek.

"Something about crunching numbers. Right before you fell. I promise to listen this time."

She shifted to brace her arm on the instrument panel next to him. Now she could hold the cold pack without fatigue. "I was going to say that you and I have accomplished some great things on our own over the years. I know we've never worked as a team before but maybe if we brainstorm, we can come up with a solution that benefits everyone."

Except she was the harbormaster, therefore she was the one who was supposed to find a solution. Which she was trying to but two was always better than one, right?

"Together, huh? You think we could do it without killing each other?"

She shrugged. "We're already 1-0."

His shoulders drooped. "I'm sorry."

"I'm joking. I'm fine. See? Stop apologizing." She removed the cold pack and shimmied out of the blanket. "I could box you right now."

She stood with her fists raised. Swayed.

His arms went around her waist. She leaned into him, his sopping sweatshirt soaking through her tank, making her cold again. "Slow down, Rocky."

She was eye-level with his chin. His stubble was forty-eight hours away from a full-grown beard.

Don't. Touch.

"You need dry clothes, a hot dinner, and a comfortable place to rest before you go entering any fights. You hear me?"

She nodded, then regretted it.

"When you shower, make sure it's lukewarm. I don't want you getting too hot and passing out." His hand slid down her spine to the small of her back. "If you're not able to hold down your dinner, call me. That's a sign of a concussion, which I don't think you have, but it's possible. You hit pretty hard."

His fingers traced a few inches back up her spine. "No sleeping for at least three hours." Had his voice lowered octaves? "Promise?"

Were his eyes soft and hooded or was she imagining things?

And when had her arms moved to cup his biceps? "Yes, Doctor Jace."

He stiffened beneath her touch. She'd sounded desperate and flirty and pathetic. Heat flashed in her cheeks.

He looked at the still fogged windows. "The rain stopped." He released her slowly, though he kept his hands out, prepared to catch her if needed.

Dang it.

Now that the spell was broken, her head was clear enough to handle her extremities but not her embarrassment.

He handed her the cold pack and wrapped the blanket around her again. "I should get you home."

In her current state of humiliation, she'd rather see herself home. "I can manage. Thanks for the medical care."

The boat's engine quieted. He tucked the keys into his pocket and picked up her wet clothes. "There's no way I'm letting you drive alone. I'll take you home."

She really didn't want him to feel obligated. She wanted the softness between them back. His arms curled around her once more.

He stuck close as she gathered her purse and keys from her office, turned out the lights, and locked the door. She hated to leave a wet mark on his truck seat, but he was wet too, so it couldn't be helped. A few minutes later, they were parked in front of her house.

Jace tapped his thumb on the steering wheel. "Can I see your phone?"

"My—? Okay." She dug the device from her purse and gave it to him.

He hit a few buttons and the phone in the pocket of his dash lit, buzzed, then silenced. "Now you have my number. Call if you need me. Or have any questions."

"Thanks." She gripped the door handle. "I hope me calling you Doctor Jace didn't offend you."

He flinched. "Nah, it's just getting late, and you're hurt, and I still need to moor my boat and. . ."

His two worlds were colliding again, one of them full of harsh secrets she wished he'd confide to her. She reached for his hand, wanting their connection back more than she wanted ibuprofen. And that was badly.

She raised her eyebrows and lifted one side of her mouth. "I'm a good listener."

Jace stared at their joined hands. "It's not a story I'm willing to tell tonight. Sleep well, Joey."

He squeezed her fingers then released her hand, ending the conversation.

"'Night." She wiggled out of the blanket and left it on the seat, unbothered at the use of her nickname.

In fact, she was okay with it if he never called her Josephine again.

He waited until she'd made it inside the house before driving away. She leaned against the door, cold pack pressed to her head, wet clothes balled in her other arm, reeling over the specialized appointment with Doctor Jace. Why had she called him that? If she'd have kept her mouth shut, they might be kissing right now. Instead, she had a date with a bottle of ibuprofen and a bowl of canned soup.

Or had she misread his signals as signals when they were really nothing more than patient care? Maybe he hadn't been toying with her back but had been checking for a spinal injury. And then she'd gone all husky-voiced and flirty. Oh, she was mortified.

She removed her boots and stumbled through the dark house to the medicine cabinet. She could still hear his concern, feel the tenderness in his touch. Was he that gentle with all his patients? If so, she bet he was sorely missed at the hospital.

Something had shifted between them tonight even if she couldn't see past the fog in her brain to decide what it was. Even so, it sent a thrill racing through her. A bit of reckless excitement. Then again, she'd thought that about their relationship before, as teenagers sitting on a rocky beach and once again in her kitchen.

But if his response to her tonight was a taste of things to come, the knock in the head was well worth the trouble.

# Fourteen



Josephine stepped off the ferry and onto steady ground. *Home.* After a summer in the dorm of UMaine's Maritime Conservation campus, she couldn't wait to see her parents, take a hot bath, and sleep in her own bed. The start of her senior year was only two weeks away, and she wanted to savor the last of her freedom before she dove back into her studies.

Before the mundane routine of academic competitions between them began, she wanted to see Jace. All summer long, she'd analyzed the meaning behind his giving her the internship. The sweet and tender way in which he'd offered the gift. Her reaction to it, mentally and physically. So many times, she'd recalled the peacefulness that had flowed between them as they'd sat quietly on the shoreline for over an hour, watching the waves roll ashore, their arms brushing.

Something had shifted between them that day. She felt it as solid as the concrete beneath her sneakers. And how she wanted to explore it. To see if they could be successful at being more than rivals.

A warm breeze blew the scent of Ms. Jean's fabric softener from the clothes hanging on her line. Josephine waved at Mr. Edwards, walking his golden retriever. Ahead, a mother with two small children exited the library. At the stop sign, a hand stuck out from the window of a sedan and waved at Mabel and Maurice, who were watering the lush flowers surrounding their porch.

Josephine truly believed there was no better town on the planet to live than right here. While other kids dreamed of the day they could leave Granite Harbor and move on to bigger things, she dreamed of finding a good job within the community, marrying a great man with whom to raise a family, and never leaving this stretch of coastline.

Hoisting her backpack higher on her shoulder, she headed toward home, dragging her rolling suitcase behind her. Dad had planned to meet her with the truck, but she'd arrived a day early. At the sight of the familiar landscape, homesickness had pushed against her chest and instead of using the payphone by the dock to call her parents and waiting for them to arrive, she'd decided to walk the distance.

A man sitting on a park bench watched her walk past. He was alone. Around the age of her parents, he was muscular and reminded her of a soldier, like her uncle Trey. Though he appeared non-threatening, the intensity in which he watched her gave her the creeps. Staying aware of her surroundings, she picked up speed until she was far enough past him to relax.

The scent of food on a hot grill wafted from Maggie's Diner. What she wouldn't give for one of the cook's specialties, like the Hemingway burger, named after the town legend. The patty was as rustic as the fisherman himself, with chunks of garlic, chopped capers, and a blend of spices that hit the tongue like a profound sheet of poetry. But her pockets were empty, and she didn't fit into the crowd of her peers currently occupying the booths, judging by the familiar vehicles in the parking lot.

For one, they all had the common denominator of popularity and personal transportation. She did not. Though she'd turned seventeen last month, she was the youngest in their class and had yet to get her driver's license. Something she should rectify soon if she wanted to act on her instructor's suggestion of continuing her education by shadowing some of the town's fishermen or the harbormaster. He'd been impressed by her thirst for knowledge and willingness to work.

The thump of her suitcase wheels on the cracked pavement ceased with her steps as Jace exited the diner, tucking bills into his wallet as he walked to his car. Time had certainly made her heart grow fonder. It pounded as she studied the planes and angles of his face where the summer sun kissed. Hair disheveled, the tips more blond now than brown, he looked like he belonged in the cast of her favorite prime time teen drama instead of in a parking lot.

My, my, was he gorgeous.

She retracted her suitcase handle and lifted it for carry, preparing to join him and ask how his mentorship with Doc Greenwell had gone, how he'd kept himself occupied without the ability to pester her—anything he was willing to share—when Alice Underwood dashed from the diner, ran up behind Jace, and threw her arms around his waist. He startled, and she laughed. Josephine's heart burned when he pivoted and threw his arm around Alice's neck, pulled her to his side, and pressed his lips to hers.

Wincing, Josephine turned away from the sight. Her chest ached. Apparently, his gift of the internship meant nothing more than seizing one opportunity over another. While Josephine had lain in bed at night, thinking of what the future might hold for them, he'd been busy making out with Alice.

Her eyes stung. She would not cry. She refused to shed a single tear over Jace McClintock. She was done with that. Wasting her days pining for him simply wasn't worth it.

Familiar insecurity whispered in her ear. She was always the outsider and would never find a place to truly belong.

Guilt took over next. She had loving parents who accepted her as if she were their own, so she had no reason to feel unloved or unwanted. Yet, she did. Her birth father hadn't wanted her. Jace didn't want her.

Maybe, no man would.

She pressed the button on her suitcase handle to extend it to full length. One step at a time, she moved forward down the road, the wheels clattering behind her. The noise caught Jace's attention, and his face lit in a smile when he saw her. He held up one hand in greeting while extracting Alice from his neck with his other.

Josephine swallowed the hope that beat against her from his gesture and kept moving. He took three steps closer, then stopped. His wicked handsome grin fell with his arm when he realized she wasn't going to acknowledge him. To do so would be to admit defeat.

She swiveled and pinned her gaze on the road. Defeat was something she'd never allow Jace to have over her ever again.

# Fifteen

Three days later, the *Hiley Mae II* was tied to the busy dock for inspection with two other boats. The sun was high in the west, but the air was chilly. Fall had taken residence, bringing the scent of wood smoke, decaying leaves, and lots of work to be done before winter.

"Delivery for Jace McClintock!"

The dock quieted. Everyone looked to the man walking down the ramp wearing black slacks, a blue dress shirt, and carrying a bouquet of roses.

"There's your man." Ron pointed at Jace from his crouched position at his stack of traps and grinned.

The man weaved through the quiet crowd to Jace. Quiet because the nosy cretins wanted to razz him for it later.

"Jace McClintock?"

Jace grunted.

"Delivery." Dave, according to the name embroidered above his shirt pocket beneath the Stonington Floral & Gifts logo, thrust the bouquet of red roses at Jace. "You'll want to put these in water right away.

Jace looked over the side of the dock deciding his next move. "You sure there hasn't been a mistake?"

Dave put his hands on his waist. "Nope. The customer gave me your name with specific instructions to find you at this dock at nine-fifteen." He looked at his watch.

Laughter filled the dock. Son of a gun.

Dave nodded. "Have a nice day."

Dodging insults the rest of the afternoon wasn't what Jace would call a good day, but it was coming. Now to figure out who on earth sent him a dozen roses. While he searched for a card, his mind brought up every woman he'd dated in the last few years, but none of them had stayed in contact and wouldn't have known the exact time to find him here. He thought of his buddies in Boston seeing this as a good prank, but they'd gone silent after the malpractice accusation so none of them made sense either.

"Who's got the hots for ya, Jace?" Tilly. Go figure.

Other comments were thrown his way, but Jace ignored them while he opened the small envelope.

*Thanks for caring for my injury.*
*~ 2008 Clam Bake Queen*

Jace threw his head back and laughed. The first bit of joy he could remember feeling in a long time.

He hadn't seen Joey since he'd dropped her off at home, though he'd texted a few times each day to check on her symptoms. The little devil. He'd completely forgotten about her victory in the clam bake pageant. Seems she still held a grudge.

Classic Joey.

"Anybody seen Joey today?" he hollered down the dock. He was going to hear about this charade for days. Now she would too.

A few hoots exploded into the air. A whistle. Jace stepped onto his boat.

"Joey, is it?" Tilly said.

"The harbormaster's sending you flowers?" Ryan asked. "Isn't that a conflict of interest?"

"Why, because you're interested?" The young man better respond carefully.

"Maybe." Ryan shrugged.

Gary tossed a broom to Ryan. "I've seen Josephine eat tougher things for breakfast. Besides, she needs a man who can fog up the windows on his boat."

The man's eyebrows wiggled at Jace.

Jace pointed at him. "I've already explained what that was about. She hit her head and—"

"Yeah, yeah." Gary shrugged. "Doesn't mean we can't have fun with it though."

Nick tossed a coiled rope onto the dock. "I saw her jogging toward Pelican Point about twenty minutes ago."

Jogging so soon after a head injury? He should check on her. That would be his excuse anyway.

The flowers would be fine on his boat for now. He could wait and see her when she came around to inspect in a couple of hours, but truth was he wanted to have her alone. He'd grown tired of their same old dance, and whether he wanted to admit it or not, he was into her. The way she'd curled against him the other night when he'd held her said she was into him too. And when they were together, the chemistry practically boiled over.

Some things never changed.

Life was short. Cliche but true. He wanted to stop thinking, planning, analyzing, remembering, feeling guilty, and just let go.

With her.

Jace drove to the lookout point, keeping watch to make sure he didn't miss her. He waited about ten minutes before she rounded the cliff. Taking his time, he walked down the rocky shoreline. The moment she spotted him, her stride slowed, then picked up pace as she closed the distance.

"Is everything okay?" she yanked out her Air Pods and tucked them in her pocket, panting.

"You shouldn't be running so soon after hitting your head."

She smirked. "Thanks for your concern but I'm fine. I'm not experiencing any of the classic symptoms of concussion and the swelling has gone down by half." She wiped sweat off her forehead with the back of her hand. "Is that the reason you tracked me down?"

He enjoyed the glint of mischief in her eyes. "Some man just delivered an embarrassing display of red roses."

She snickered through her fast breaths. "I wanted to express my thanks."

"Publicly? With floral arrangements?"

She stepped back and rested her hands on her hips. Sweat glistened on her forehead. "I thought it was proper, seeing as I never thanked you for forging my application for the clam bake pageant queen all those years ago."

"You won! And received a scholarship."

"I hated every minute of that fluff parade." She pushed the sweaty hair away from her forehead with her wrist. "The make-up, the stage fright, the tight sparkly dress. I hate wearing dresses, by the way. In fact, I haven't worn one since."

She motioned for them to walk.

"You do your fellow man a disservice. You looked amazing in that dress." May as well come out with it.

"Really? Then why did you guys make fun of me?"

He picked up a stone and skipped it across the water. "It was the first time any of us noticed you had a figure. We weren't sure what to do with that."

She turned away and mumbled something that sounded like "asking me on a date would've been nice," but he wasn't certain. Her cheeks were red. From her jog most likely, but he hoped a little from his comment. He wanted to flirt with her. Pick up where they'd left off the other night. He was glad he switched cell carriers so he could text her whenever he wanted. Unwise in his current circumstances, yet hard to suppress the desire all the same.

Joey stopped and stretched her legs. "You'd left for college by the time I discovered it was you who pulled that stunt. I've been waiting for the perfect time for revenge. I thought the flowers fit the payback nicely. That, and nominating you the lobster trap Christmas tree elf."

Her attempt at a villainous laugh was mighty cute.

"Revenge successfully completed. No more duplicity. Deal?" He stopped and held out his hand. She considered it with a twist of her lips. Then she slid her sweaty palm against his.

"Deal. Unless we're in on it together."

Together. He liked that.

Jace released her hand long enough to grab it with his other. He entwined their fingers and continued walking. He waited for her to pull away. She didn't. Her hand tensed for only a moment, then relaxed. He caught her goofy smile from his peripheral vision.

He wasn't sure what had contributed to his boldness to-day—the salty air, the coming seasons, opposition weighing his shoulders. or his daily reminder of how fleeting life was—but he wasn't complaining. Best part, neither was she.

"About the elf thing—all the guys except Nick and Tilly are harvesting this winter, and they've rented out their traps. Where am I supposed to find enough to make a fifteen-foot Christmas tree?"

"Hmm."

He stayed quiet while she considered this, enjoying the feel of her skin against his, only the sound of their feet on the rocks and the waves lapping ashore. He'd describe the feeling as content. Something he hadn't experienced in a long time.

"There's a bunch of old wooden traps in the boathouse you can have. They're not in perfect shape but should hold up for one season as a display. I planned to throw them out when I cleaned anyway. You're welcome to them."

"How convenient. You get your boathouse cleaned out and your Christmas tree at the same time." He bumped into her and winked.

"I'm a very intelligent woman."

"Yes, you are."

She bumped him back.

As much as he wanted to do this all day, he needed to backtrack to his truck. "I hate to leave but a strict harbormaster is set to inspect my boat in a couple of hours, and I've still got some small repairs to do."

She raised her chin like a soldier. "You'd better get to it then."

"Can I give you a ride back?"

"No, thanks. I need to finish my run. I'm not as active now that I have a desk job. Gotta keep my girlish figure."

"There's not a thing wrong with your figure." He studied it one more time to prove his point. This time she definitely blushed. Something he'd never seen Joey wear before.

She shook her head.

"What?"

"We've tortured each other for so long, I don't know what to do with this." She wagged a finger between them.

"Enjoy it."

"I am."

"See you at eleven." He let go of her hand.

"I'll bring the key to the boathouse. You can clean it out whenever it's convenient for you." She grinned.

"You're trusting me with the harbormaster's keys?"

"I trust you." She walked backward a few feet. "Because if you do anything to betray that trust, your boat is going to look like a float in the Rose Bowl."

"Yes, ma'am." He gave a mock salute and started for his truck.

"Jace?"

He turned.

"It's really good to have you home."

For the first time since his return, he was glad to be home.

If anyone would have told Josephine that she'd lay down her hatchet and truly befriend Jace—not just befriend but hold hands with him!—she'd have laughed them to scorn. But she had and the high school giddiness of it all still flowed through her a week later.

To her dismay there had been no more handholding, but there'd been plenty of camaraderie, text messages, flirty glances, and knowing smiles. Without being spoken aloud, neither of them knew quite what to do with this new. . .whatever it was. The sheer wonder and unsteadiness of it all was like climbing Mount Katahdin in record speed.

She pushed away the negative thoughts and wrote the appropriate numbers with her chalk against the vintage green board on her office wall. She'd contacted the co-op and other local harbors, who'd discussed it with their fisherman and, together, they'd decided to cut the supply. The wholesaler had willingly worked with them and compromised to meet in the middle. The agreement wasn't perfect but tolerable. It would keep the lobsterman in business and throw a small wrench into the government's grinding wheels.

Her next task was discovering who the culprit was behind the cut ropes. Three lobstermen had fell victim, though no new reports in the last two weeks. She'd spoken with other area harbormasters and they, too, were experiencing random vandalism.

Together, they'd filed a report with the Coast Guard, and all were on the lookout.

A boat chugged to the dock, and she leaned against the window for a better view. Not Jace. She needed to stop doing this. She'd worked for years without looking to see if every boat was Jace's. She'd grocery shopped for years without glancing at every customer to see if they were Jace. She'd paid her bills and cooked dinner and gone to sleep for years without being distracted by daydreams of Jace.

And with one walk along the shore, palms kissing, she'd turned into one of those pathetic heroines from a romance novel.

The door opened. "Delivery for Joe Rockwell."

Mail carrier Troy Bennett entered holding a petite box, a newspaper, and a stack of letters. The man was a dead ringer for Mr. McFeely from Mister Roger's Neighborhood. Voice and all.

"Thank you, Troy." Josephine reached for the items.

"I'm teasing about your name, of course. I know you aren't Joe, but that's what the letter says." He tapped the transparent window box on the envelope.

Sure enough, the letter gracing the top of the stack was addressed to Joe Rockwell. Why was she surprised? Unless she was met in person, everyone assumed Joey equaled male. The very reason she'd always hated the stupid nickname Jace had stuck her with in second grade because she was a tomboy.

Well, she wasn't a tomboy anymore, she was a woman. And finally—*finally*—Jace had noticed. Now, her nickname on his lips sounded more like an endearment than a barb. Cue the high school giddiness again.

"Sign here, please." Troy held out a peach-colored form for her to sign to accept the certified letter. Familiar with the process, she signed her name, and they traded papers.

Troy adjusted the mail bag slung over his shoulder. "Enjoy your day."

"You as well." Josephine followed him into the crisp outdoors. She tucked the rest of the mail against her like a football while she opened her copy of the *Bangor Times* to glance through the headlines. Though reading a newspaper was old-school for her generation, she liked to keep up on current events. Internet connection was sketchy sometimes and she hated reading long articles online, so she preferred a physical subscription.

A buoy bell clanged, and she glanced over the harbor, her sight resting on the *Hiley Mae II*, moored and bobbing in the water. How had she missed Jace? When had he returned? Why didn't he stop in and see her?

Stop it, Josephine!

There was a line between attraction and obsession. She would not cross it. Even if she'd waited years for his laser-focused attention to land on her.

She stepped back into her office, determined to think of anything but Jace. The mail landed on her desk and disturbed the sticky notes attached to the bottom of her computer monitor. She settled onto the chair, one foot curled beneath her, and opened the newspaper.

A new music venue had opened in Portland. A teacher's union was fighting for higher pay. The Washington County animal shelter was getting a new addition. A Boston doctor was being sued for malpractice.

A fuzzy black-and-white picture of a man who looked like Jace, wearing scrubs and a stethoscope curled around his neck, rested beneath the headline. She held the newspaper closer. That was Jace. She stopped breathing. An odd sense of awareness prickled her body as she read the small print.

Jace, accused of malpractice?

A three-year-old girl—dead.

Nausea rose in Josephine's throat. She took a deep breath, then swallowed.

That was why Jace had returned home. Why he'd gone back to lobstering when his passion was in medicine.

According to the article, the court date was scheduled for December twentieth. Right before Christmas. No wonder he'd been furious that she'd foisted the responsibility of building the lobster trap Christmas tree on him. He had enough going on and was probably trying to fly under the radar.

She collapsed against the back of her chair, reeling. She hadn't heard any such rumors around town. If anyone had known, the news would already have been out. It wouldn't take long now though. Not many read a physical newspaper nowadays, but most folks kept up with local news. Occasionally when something big happened in the northeastern region of the country, the *Bangor Times* would syndicate an article from a larger publication. All it took was one person in Granite Harbor besides herself to see this article and by dinnertime, everyone would know.

And the television news? She was surprised local reporters hadn't covered it already. This was going to get out and humiliate Jace.

Why hadn't Jace been honest with everyone from the start?

Guilty or embarrassed?

She sighed and rested her head in her hand. Awful timing since they'd just started some semblance of a relationship. Malpractice? That wasn't Jace. He was careful and precise cutting his steak, for crying out loud. Negligent medical treatment?

It just didn't add up with what she knew of him.

Being accused of something didn't equal liability. In fact, knowing what she did about Jace, this whole thing had crushed him. That knowledge was more in sync with his behavior since he'd returned home.

She would wait for him to tell her. If they were going to proceed into something more than rivals, they'd have to trust each other. Despite their years of taunting, she did trust him. Now, she'd have to practice patience.

Once word got out, how would the community react? What would they think of their harbormaster dating a man accused of murder?

# Sixteen

Joey had roses delivered, and now Jace was returning the sentiment by delivering a wounded, and very mean, feral Maine Coon that had to weigh close to twenty pounds. It wasn't doing any harm in the boathouse, but once Jace noticed something had attempted to rip one side of the tom's head off, he'd decided the animal was getting medical attention whether it wanted to or not. Jace wasn't a vet, but he knew the cat would need sedated before anyone could touch it safely.

With every step, the cat growled inside the live trap, growing louder like a siren until it was shrill enough to wake the dead. Then it would start over at the lowest octave again. Jace wasn't trying to inflict torture, but he had to find Joey and take this cat to the vet.

Ron rounded the boat yard. "What is that hellacious noise?"

Jace gave a brief version of the story. "You seen Joey?"

"Office. She's been acting weird today though. All—I don't know. Mooney? Say, you wouldn't have anything to do with that, would ya?" Ron smirked.

Good to know. It was the first time he'd ever been able to make her feel anything for him other than disdain. "Not a thing."

Jace kept walking, as the awkward way he had to carry the trap to keep from getting clawed was causing his arm muscles to burn.

Ron hooted. "See ya 'round, lover boy."

Jace rolled his eyes. The cat hissed at Ron as they passed. "Good, kitty."

The animal sounded the siren again. Several people on the dock, including Joey, stopped their tasks at his approach.

Jace raised the trap. "Special delivery for Miss Josephine Rockwell."

One side of her mouth twisted.

He stopped in front of her. The cat lunged, and she jumped back. Jace maneuvered his hold to keep from dropping the trap. "Your intruder."

"What happened to it?"

"No idea. I need to take it to a vet."

"My delivery was way cooler than yours."

"In the eye of the beholder. Come with me?"

Her color brightened. "Give me ten?"

She was already backing away. "Meet you at the truck."

He got the cat settled in the bed and maneuvered a spare tire beside it so the trap wouldn't slide around. The nearest vet was in Stonington. It would be a long, painful ride for the cat but too short a time with Joey. Now that he'd catapulted over the line from enemies to possible relationship territory, he was ready to explore and wanted time to do it.

Joey joined him at the truck a few minutes later. She wore a green jacket from Bean's over a gray shirt and jeans. The end of her ponytail had tangled in the hood but before he could react, she pulled it free. He'd intended to open the door for her but, again, before he could react, she'd climbed inside the truck and was connecting her seatbelt.

Miss Independent.

Jace started the truck and drove west toward Stonington. He gave as many details about the cat as he could and that was limited. "What do you think tore him up like that?" she asked.

"Can't say. Whatever it was had vicious claws."

"Or teeth."

"I'd say the attacker was too large to follow it into the boathouse through wherever it enters and exits from."

She swiveled to look through the back window. "That's a huge feline."

"Let's see what the vet says, but I'd prepare to make a call to the DNR."

She faced the windshield and nodded.

"I want you to be extra careful if you have to make any trips out there." He took his eyes off the road long enough to glance at her profile.

"Concerned for me?"

He heard more than saw her smile. "We've had our differences, but I've never wished you harm, Joey. I mean, Josephine."

"You've never called me Josephine unless you're being sarcastic, and hearing you say it sounds weird."

"Does this mean I can call you Joey?"

"You have been, and yes."

He held out his palm. She accepted.

"This doesn't mean I've forgiven you for branding me with the boyish name, though."

"Of course not. Wouldn't want that."

As much as he wanted to keep driving and enjoy the feel of her hand in his, they'd arrived at the vet's office.

Situated on the outskirts of town, the facility was easy to access and offered a great view of Moose Island. Joey went in to explain the situation while he retrieved the hissing cat and carried it inside.

They were asked to sit in the waiting room while they waited for an exam room to open. When it did, the veterinarian introduced herself as Katie, then walked around the table to get a look at the animal who loathed humanity.

"You found him like this?" Katie asked.

"Yes," Jace said. "I have no idea what happened. It looks like a fight with another animal to me."

"It appears that way, but I won't know for sure, or the extent of his injuries until I've had a chance to examine him." The cat thrust his paw at the cage, claws bared, and howled. Katie leaned casually against a countertop. "He'll need full sedation in order for me to do anything."

Jace didn't blame her.

"Since it appears to be a stray, I have to ask." Katie addressed Jace. "Are you taking financial responsibility for his care?"

"I will," Joey said.

Katie stepped toward the door. "I'll start with sedation and an exam, then call you with my findings. From there you can decide how far you want to go with this. If surgeries are needed, I can contact the humane society and see if they're able to help. Sometimes folks are willing to step in with donations."

"Sounds good. Thank you, doctor." Joey shook the vet's hand.

Thank you, doctor. Three words Jace had heard often. Words that carried weight. Sometimes the weight of relief, sometimes the weight of uncertainty, sometimes the weight of grief. But he'd always been the one to bridge that gap between patient and diagnosis. Until he'd failed to save a little girl's life.

"Jace?" Joey gripped his elbow.

The heaviness that cloaked his body whenever he returned to that night bared down on him now.

"Where'd you go?" A V formed between her brows.

Katie had left the room with the cat.

Jace shook his head to clear his thoughts. "Sidetracked. Sorry. Are we ready?"

"For now."

Jace held the door for her and followed Joey to the counter where she paid for the office visit. He felt like a jerk not paying, but it wasn't his pet, and his income was too unsteady. Truth was, he missed doctoring. He missed the pay, he missed the atmosphere, but most of all, he missed helping people. Whether it was his calling or not, he couldn't chance being responsible for any more lives.

The short trip back to his truck was like wading through wet concrete. He needed to shake the darkness and go on with the day. He needed a distraction. Joey climbed in beside him and smiled, attempting to lift his mood.

Joey was a good distraction. "Hungry?"

"Always."

"Pizza?"

"Meatlovers."

"Done."

Pizza came in the form of a convenience store's kitchen, but the food was decent, and they sold a good variety of drinks and snacks. He paid this time, then drove two streets over so they could watch the boats sail past while they ate. The heater whirred quietly at their feet.

"Thanks for rescuing the cat." Joey claimed a slice of loaded pizza. "Once the boathouse is cleaned out, I'll figure out how he got in and remedy that."

"Speaking of." Jace piled three slices on his paper plate. "Those lobster traps, they're antique. You can't just throw them out when Christmas is over."

"I can't throw them out because they're old?"

He popped a chip in his mouth and chewed. Swallowed. "They hold some kind of significance."

"Like what?"

"I don't know." He'd noticed the oddity, but the cat had interrupted his inspection, and he hadn't had time to consider it. "There's a buoy attached to each trap, and each buoy is different."

*And?* her face said as she chewed.

"A buoy is a fisherman's signature. I think those buoys represent who each trap belonged to."

"If they were so important, why are they piled in the boathouse, disintegrating?"

"I don't know. But I do know that traps like that haven't been used in decades. And I'm not talkin' a few. I'm talkin' many."

"How many?"

He tapped his finger on the lid of his cup. "Maybe. . .thirties, forties?"

They were silent for several minutes.

It was amazing how comfortable he was with her, even in the quiet. Not like other women he'd dated who felt the need for constant conversation. He also liked it when she talked. Her discussions had meat, not insignificant chatter. Joey was comfortable in her own skin, confident in her abilities, and he admired her for it.

How different would things have been had they made peace sooner?

Joey wiped her mouth with a napkin. "We both agree they're old. The fact that they're old doesn't mean they hold special significance."

"Everything old holds special significance—people, buildings, stories."

"Agreed. I only meant that it's plausible the traps were stored in the boathouse, for a non-significant reason, forgotten, and never cleaned out."

Jace collected the trash as he talked. "Why would generations of harbormasters—who are the only ones with access to that boathouse—leave them in there if they weren't important?"

She took one last sip of her drink and tossed it in the bag he held open. "Because all of the past harbormasters have been men. And we all know men don't declutter."

How he'd like to kiss the tip of her sassy, scrunched nose. "Are you stereotyping all men?"

"No more than you're stereotyping all things old."

He opened his mouth to reply, but all he could do was laugh. "Touché."

"Thanks for lunch." She reached for the bag. "I'll throw it away."

"Oh, no." He opened his door and stepped out. "I'm not falling into your stereotype."

She shook her head, smiling.

Leaving his door open, he deposited the sack in a nearby trash-can. It wouldn't be long before the gloom of winter would be upon them. For now, the trees were a kaleidoscope of color. A few tourists would flood the east coast for two short weeks, and then all would be quiet until mud season next spring.

He returned to the truck. Joey sat with clasped hands between her knees, shoulders hunched. "You cold?"

"I get cold easily."

"You're a woman. All women get cold easily."

"Now who's stereotyping?"

He winked. Now that he knew that about her though, he'd remember it.

Heat blasting, he drove back to Granite Harbor. Joey remained quiet, staring out the window, as if she had something on her mind. He wanted to ask but didn't want to push anything too far too soon. "I've been thinking. I'll use the traps for the Christmas tree, but before we throw them out, I'd like to see if anyone knows anything about them."

"Since it's so important to you, I'll check around too."

"Thank you." Sweat beaded at his temples. His feet were on fire. "Warm yet?"

She turned the dial on the heater to Off. Propping her feet on the dash, she leaned her head back, closed her eyes, and smiled.

Content. Happy.

Two emotions he wished he could experience simultaneously again. With her at his side, he was getting closer.

# Seventeen



Josephine sat cross-legged on the couch and reached for her laptop and pumpkin spice hot chocolate on the coffee table. Halloween was less than two weeks away which meant it was time for all things pumpkin flavored in her life, despite years of Dad's teasing that it wasn't acceptable until November first. The fireplace, surrounded by white pumpkins from the Thomas Farm, crackled from the small logs she'd set ablaze to knock the chill from the room. The only thing that could make the space cozier was Jace, but the slow pace of their relationship hadn't brought the doctor around for a house call.

Now, she knew why. She opened the laptop where she'd tucked the newspaper clipping between the screen and the keys earlier in the day. She skimmed the article for the hundredth time. Had anyone else in town seen this? She wondered how many in their small community, if any, subscribed to the larger publication.

Despite her better judgement, she ran a search on Jace's name but all it did was bring up genealogy websites and one's offering her public information if she was willing to pay a fee. Her next search on Boston Medical took her to the hospital's website with pages of the services they offered and testimonials from pleased patients.

After a long, soothing sip of chocolate, she decided to search for Jace's full name followed by Boston and the words malpractice suit.

Bingo.

She stared at the screen, unable to shake the feeling that by clicking and reading she was somehow betraying Jace. Silly, really. After all, it was public information, and it wasn't like she was digging for details so she could gossip. Still, she should probably wait for Jace to tell her himself.

But what if her knowing could help him somehow? She could better defend him if word got out. She could still wait for him to reveal it in his own time, and until then she'd know how to silently support him. Of course, there was a possibility that what she found would make her want to end it with him altogether.

She rubbed her forehead and blindly stared into the leaping flames of the fire. Was that just an excuse to quell her curiosity?

What if Jace never offered to tell her?

With a deep breath, she clicked on an article from the *Boston Times*. A picture of Jace being escorted from the hospital by two men in black suits filled the corner of the screen—shoulders slumped, forehead marred with frown lines, eyes angled away from the camera. Grief and mortification were stamped on every inch of him, and her heart sank.

*Pediatric doctor Jace McClintock was escorted from Boston Medical yesterday on charges of malpractice after the death of a three-year-old girl. When asked for a statement, the hospital's president Jonathan B. Whitcolmb said, "This accusation is being fully investigated. We pride ourselves on providing the best care to our patients at Boston Medical. Doctor McClintock is one of our finest pediatric doctors and has never given us reason to doubt his abilities. Rest assured, if the accusation proves true, we will resolve the issue accordingly, but also keep in mind, an accusation does not prove guilt."*

*This paper has since learned from an anonymous source that Doctor Jace McClintock was put on unpaid leave until the matter is settled in court. A request for a statement from the doctor was denied.*

The article went on to provide a few other links to articles regarding the case, but Josephine closed her laptop. Tears burned the backs of her eyes. No wonder Jace had come home so broken. He'd always held a passion for serving others and losing a patient—a child at that—must've been devastating for him. And the scar on his reputation. . .

Now she understood why he'd wanted the harbormaster position and why he'd been so rattled by the fledgling market. By creating a life here, he must have no intention of returning to doctoring. He had to make an occupation of lobstering, which he hated.

This certainly complicated things.

She returned the laptop and mug to the coffee table, her appetite for the evening indulgence gone. Complication had never stopped her from going after what she wanted before, and it was clearer than ever how badly Jace needed a friend. A support system.

No matter what the reporters wrote or the who's and why's of the article, she knew Jace was a man of integrity. Now if he could just convince a jury.

"Word around town is you've been spending time with a certain harbormaster you've always loved to hate."

Jace glanced at Dad from the driver's seat and bobbed his shoulder. "Nothing happens around this town that everyone doesn't know about two hours later." He was just thankful that word of the malpractice accusation hadn't found its way up the coast yet.

When it did, it would hit swiftly and deeply.

"Glad to hear it. I've always thought that girl would be good for you. Don't screw it up."

Jace might be offended if it wasn't for the teasing smirk on the man's face.

"Seriously. Don't." Dad patted his arm.

"I'll do my best." Dad's color had improved since Jace had found another sternman. More rest and less use of his back was helping. He hoped the ten hours to Boston and back wouldn't aggravate Dad's condition. The very reason Jace insisted they stay in a hotel tonight to break up the trip.

"Tell me again why you want to give up heaven on wheels to buy my rattle-trap truck?" Dad adjusted the knob for the heated leather seat and wiggled against it like a cat on a blanket.

"It's not practical anymore, and the dealership is willing to pay me a thousand dollars more than what I owe." The one thing in

Jace's life he wouldn't be indebted to any longer. "Like Miss Janie said, for Granite Harbor it's 'putting on airs.'"

"Bah, that woman has an opinion on everything. And states them, even if nobody asks."

Jace turned onto the main road heading out of town. "By the way she was looking you up and down at church last Sunday, I'd say she has an opinion about you she'd like to state."

"We weren't talking about my love life. We were talking about yours."

"There isn't much to talk about."

"Here neither."

"I guess that makes us the most eligible bachelors in Azure County."

Dad raised his fist, and Jace bumped it with his own.

Silence settled over the car as Dad closed his eyes. Jace pulled into a gas station at the crossroads and parked next to one of the two pumps. The building was outdated, and the pumps were as slow as the maple syrup drips in February, but it was best to fill up now. He wanted to get to Boston with plenty of time to make the transaction and treat Dad to a steak dinner at Abe & Dooley's. Not that Jace was excited to return to the city and its memories. He hated to spend the extra money on fine dining and a hotel, but Dad deserved it. He hadn't pried into the hard things when Jace returned home and had basically passed his life's work to Jace at a very steep discount.

It was the least Jace could do.

He zipped his hoodie as far as it would go while he waited for the gas meter to climb. The days were getting colder, the wind harsher. The scent of pancakes and bacon drifted across the road from Maggie's Diner. His stomach grumbled, and he wished he'd eaten breakfast.

A commotion caught his attention in the diner's parking lot. People filed out of the entrance and began pacing, some on their phones. Jace squinted. Was that woman crying? The pump clicked off, and Jace hung the nozzle back up and pushed his gas flap closed.

Someone yelled his name.

He looked around. A man wearing an apron waved his arms and looked both directions before running across the road. "Help, Jace! Maggie's granddaughter is turning blue."

Harold, Maggie's loyal cook.

The panic on the man's face made Jace's blood turn to ice.

"Jace!" Harold was panting by the time he reached the car.

Dad opened his door, got out, and waited for Jace to respond.

"I. . .is she choking?" Jace's heart slammed against his ribs.

"No, I don't know what's wrong."

Run!

Except he couldn't. The judge had made it clear he wasn't allowed to practice any form of doctoring until the case was settled in court. He could go to prison if he did.

"Have you called 9-1-1?" Jace took a step toward the diner but stopped.

Harold nodded. "Yes, but you know how long it can take for them to get here from Stonington. You've got to help her."

Jace wanted to slam his fist into the car. He wanted to help the child, but he couldn't. If he did and she didn't survive, he'd never see the outdoors again unless it was in the confines of electric razor-wire fencing.

"Jace!" Dad yelled, throwing his hands up.

Oh, God, what could he do?

He couldn't let the girl die.

Jace swallowed. "Tell me everything you know."

They jogged across the road as Harold relayed what the girl had ordered before she started changing color. If she wasn't choking, it was likely a food allergy. Jace ordered Harold to keep going, and he turned and ran back to his car. He'd planned to wait and clean out the glovebox and console when he got to the dealership, so his First-Aid kit would still be in the car. In it, an EpiPen.

"Open the glovebox," Jace yelled to Dad standing by the open passenger side door. By the time Jace got there, Dad already had the First-Aid kit in his hands.

Jace grabbed it and sprinted across the road. The crowd in the parking lot blurred as he passed and ran through the door Harold held open. His eyes darted around the diner. Maggie was hunched over a body lying on the floor littered with small scraps of food. Something was burning.

"Is she choking?" Jace managed through labored breaths.

The woman shook her head, tears streaking down her red cheeks.

"Go check the grill before the place burns down." Jace dropped to his knees beside the girl. Giving Maggie a job would get her out of the way and keep her busy enough to not break down.

Terror squeezed around Jace's neck as the girl struggled to breathe. Her swelling skin was turning a purple tinge, her arms and legs wiggled, eyes bloodshot. Jace sent up a prayer that he wouldn't make the wrong decision this time. That the actions he took today would save a life, not take one.

Sweat rolled down his temples. Jace yanked open the First-Aid kit and rummaged for the EpiPen. *Please don't let it be expired.* Twisting the cap to engage the needle, he grabbed the girl's thigh and jabbed it through her jeans into her flesh.

*Don't let me be too late.*

He felt for a pulse on her wrist and counted. Each second that passed brought more color to the girl's cheeks. She slowly relaxed and was taking tiny breaths by the time sirens sounded in the distance.

Jace wilted in relief.

Within seconds, the EMTs were taking over and Jace did his best to answer their questions, one arm around Maggie to help prop her up as much as himself. While they loaded the girl into the ambulance, Harold approached, wringing his filthy apron. "I'll clean up and shut down for the day. You go on with Lizabeth."

Maggie was shaking so badly Jace wasn't sure she'd be able to climb in with her granddaughter. "She's going to be fine, Maggie," Jace said, helping her toward the ambulance. "They'll take good care of her."

He said the words for himself as much as for Maggie. "She's going to be fine."

The small crowd thanked Jace with back slaps and words too kind for what he deserved. Dad waved at him from a parking space at the edge of the diner parking lot. It seemed to take Jace a year to reach the car his legs were so weak. "You okay, son?"

"Yeah." Jace's voice was raspy. He got behind the wheel and relished the warmth of the seat. Dad got in beside him. Emotions burned the backs of his eyes, but Jace forced himself to reverse the car and drive toward Boston.

Dad rambled about something, but Jace wasn't listening. He just stared at the road ahead and tried to process all that had happened. With each mile of blacktop they covered, Jace began to slip.

"Son, pull over."

Jace obeyed. Tears pushed from the corners of his eyes and his breaths came hard. He'd saved her life. She was going to be okay. His hands trembled.

Why hadn't he been able to save Arabella's?

Dad clamped a hand on his shoulder. "You did good, son. You did real good."

Jace was sobbing now and mortified to his core. Dad rubbed his arm and waited for Jace to get it all out, the way he'd done for months after Jace's mom had left them when he was five. Scrubbing his face, Jace took a deep breath and composed himself. "Sorry."

"No apology needed." Dad patted Jace's hand. "You finally gonna tell me what happened in Boston?"

Jace rested his head against the seat. A car slowed and drove around them. "It's a long story."

Dad nodded. "We've got a long journey ahead."

It was time. He'd waited far too long already.

Jace looked into his mirrors then eased onto the road. By the time they reached Boston, he'd told Dad everything.

# Eighteen

*Sixteen years earlier*

Joey wouldn't talk to him. She wouldn't even look at him.

After all his effort to make sure she received the summer internship, this was his reward.

Jace grabbed a lunch tray and pushed it along the metal bars, grabbing a chicken patty sandwich and fries from under the warmer as he went. What had set her off? That day on the beach, when he'd told her he was taking the mentorship with Doc Greenwell and giving her the internship at UMaine, she'd been elated. So much so that she'd pressed her soft body against his in an embrace he thought he'd never receive. An embrace he'd hoped to recreate many times over, but she was avoiding him like a slacker did homework.

He added a fruit cup, Coke, and two cookies to his tray then paid the lunch lady at the cash register. He sat next to Ben and Lamar and three girls from the junior class.

Joey sat at a corner table across the lunchroom by herself, sipping a carton of juice, reading *Lord of the Rings*. A foam bowl lay on its side on her tray. She must've chosen the chili. Her hair was knotted on top of her head as if she'd gotten ready in a hurry this morning. She turned the page, then rubbed at her eyes. Yawned.

When their gazes connected, she frowned and held the book higher to cover her face.

Jace sighed and pulled the peanut butter sandwich he always brought from home out of his sweatshirt pocket and took a bite.

She'd been weird around him ever since she'd seen him with Alice. Was that it? Was she jealous? Because that would be awesome. But then that didn't make any sense. He and Alice had split three months ago. Wouldn't that have fixed her envy?

He shoveled in half his sandwich. Girls. He'd never understand them.

Jamar elbowed Jace's arm. "I'm not going. Are you?"

"To what?" Jace asked.

"Have you not been listening?"

"No, sorry." Jace popped a fry into his mouth.

Braylee pulled out the chair across from Jace and flopped onto it. "The Clam Bake Queen pageant. Aren't you coming to support your friends?"

She batted her eyelashes in a fake, sarcastic manner.

That's why he wouldn't exactly call the girls sitting at this table friends. More like acquaintances he sat with occasionally because Jamar was dating Amanda.

"It's three weeks from this coming Saturday." Amanda pushed her half-eaten tray to the other side of the table. "I'm officially on a diet."

Jamar picked up her tray and stacked it on top of his empty one. "Well, I'm not. So, I'll eat any food you don't want from now until then."

Jace chuckled. Jamar consumed twice the food Jace did on a normal day.

"I saw the most gorgeous dress I'm saving for." Braylee went on to describe every inch in mind-numbing detail. Jace's gaze flicked to Joey, and he wondered if she planned on entering the pageant.

"The winner gets to ride on a special float during the Clam Bake Parade, and they get the privilege of plugging in the lights at the Christmas tree ceremony on the docks." Amanda pulled the elastic band from her hair and scooped the strands in her palm to make a ponytail. "Entries close next week."

No way was Joey planning on entering then. If there was one thing she hated, it was attention. Especially his. Though he'd love to see her in something besides jeans and a sloppy flannel. Like maybe something tight and slinky.

"When did you say the deadline entry is?" An idea formed in Jace's mind. One Joey would absolutely hate him for.

Jamar snickered. "Why, are you entering? I bet you'd look great in a low-cut gown."

Everyone laughed.

Jace shook his head, not amused. He was going to enter someone, though. Someone beautiful who worked hard and deserved the scholarship that came with winning. Someone who deserved some extra attention. And when Joey won, he'd be there to show her just how special she was to him.

# Nineteen

Her office computer didn't hold records older than 1986, when Granite Harbor decided to put away their Royal typewriter, complete with suitcase, and jump into the twentieth century. She knew this because it was sitting on a shelf in her office's storage closet with boxes dated as far back as 1965. The filing cabinets she used daily only held records from the last decade. The previous two harbormasters knew nothing about the traps when she'd called and asked, and all the harbormasters before them had already passed away.

Josephine had hit a dead end and would more than gladly say she'd tried and move on with her life. Except that she wanted to please Jace. The traps had piqued his curiosity. The traps were a good excuse to text or call or hunt him down when she missed seeing him. The trap mystery might be a good diversion for him as the holidays, and his court date, approached. Except, the gravity of his situation would make any celebrations difficult.

After walking the dock to inspect for weak areas and patrolling the harbor, she put up her "gone for the day" sign, locked her office door, and drove to the Granite Harbor Public Library.

Like town hall, the library was established in a house once built by a founding father. Fiction was shelved on the main floor, while non-fiction was shelved on the second. Each floor had a room for silent reading or studying by the gas fireplaces, a room with pocket doors for meetings, and a restroom. All within the house were loved and cared for by Mrs. Fletcher, the world's most dedicated librarian. Dedicated as in, if you ask Mrs. Fletcher a question, be prepared to stay until closing. She wouldn't rest until she'd found the answer.

Josephine was taking a great risk by approaching Mrs. Fletcher with her request. Jace had better be worth it.

"Well, hello, Josephine Elaine Rockwell." Mrs. Fletcher stood from behind the circulation desk and straightened her glasses.

Sweet Mrs. Fletcher, the only person on the planet besides her parents who called her by her full name. She was also a certified genealogist and couldn't help herself, Josephine supposed.

"Hiya." Josephine smiled.

"Are you here for Clive Flemming's latest release, starring Fannie Reynolds as harbormaster?"

"Um, no. Though that does sound intriguing." Josephine rarely read books anymore. Magazines, short online articles, and local harbor newspapers were more her speed nowadays.

"Oh, it is. I read the book in two days. Fannie was a side character in his last series, so it's nice to see her have her own story. It all starts with a dead body found on the dock and—"

"Actually, Mrs. Fletcher, I would like to read that. Will you hold it for me? I'll check it out as I'm leaving." Because if Josephine didn't, not only would Mrs. Fletcher spend the next twenty minutes telling her every detail of the entire book, spoiling the plot, but she'd never get to what she came for. "First, though, I wondered if you store boat records here from the forties and fifties. I've checked my entire office, but the records I have only go back to '65."

"Hmm. No, we don't have any boat records here. What information are you needing to find, and why would you think that information would be in boat records?"

"I'm trying to find record of Granite Harbor's fishermen and their buoy patterns from those decades."

"I'm sorry, but the closest thing we would have to fishermen records would be articles from the Seaside Press, a newspaper once published right here in Granite Harbor but shut down sometime in the eighties, I think. We have their issues stored on microfilm upstairs if you'd like to go through them. They go back to when the town was founded in 1879."

While Josephine didn't want to spend the rest of the day cozied up to a microfilm reader, what other option did she have? She hadn't seen or heard from Jace since their pizza date three days ago and rumor had it, he and his dad had gone out of town. While she wanted to be that woman who didn't wait on the man to always make the moves, she was that woman.

"What's wrong, dear?" Mrs. Fletcher's bifocals magnified her watery eyes.

"What do you mean?"

"You sighed."

Josephine smiled. "Nothing, just taking in the smell of books."

The woman clamped a hand on Josephine's arm. "It's my favorite too!"

She followed Mrs. Fletcher up the stairs to the microfilm reader where she waited for the librarian to retrieve the appropriate reels.

It took fifteen minutes of listening to Mrs. Fletcher hum "Yankee Doodle" before the machine was loaded and running.

"Here you go, dear."

"Thank you, Mrs. Fletcher."

"See that phone over there?" The librarian pointed a bony finger at the wall. "When you're ready for another reel, let me know by picking up the phone and dialing 0. I'll come up and swap them for you."

"Great."

Biting her lower lip, Josephine settled in the chair and began scanning articles starting in January of 1940 that were like x-rays of the newspapers. Thank God for the invention of the internet.

At first, she took the time to read any headline that caught her attention—the premiere of Gone With the Wind, Winston Churchill's acceptance as Prime Minister, Hitler's invasion of western Europe. She quickly realized she'd be here for days if she didn't stick to her subject, so she concentrated on articles directly related to Granite Harbor.

In 1942, the town received its first traffic light, and the P.C. Ship Company started building boats for the military. The summer of 1943, the area fishing industry was surviving on either older men or able-bodied women. August of 1943, a small boy named Johnny Tucker took the record for an eighty-pound Atlantic Cod with the help of his cousins.

She squinted at the screen. Johnny Tucker. Was he Trapper John? The boy in the grainy black-and-white photo did resemble Hemingway with his mussed hair and wind chapped skin. A mixture of innocence, temper, and mischief reflected in his eyes. Still did. She took out her phone and captured the picture to show Jace.

Article after article flashed before her. A few she paused to read, others she passed over. Mrs. Fletcher checked on her, informed Josephine she could print from the machine for twenty cents a sheet, and then warned her they'd be closing in an hour.

Was it really four o'clock? Who knew microfilm could be so entertaining?

September of 1945 declared the end of World War II. Page after page listed local casualties, organizations that were helping to recover the war efforts, and ways locals could volunteer to help. Even the iconic V-J Day photo of the celebrating sailor kissing the woman in Time Square had made its way into their little newspaper.

Josephine's hopes of finding information related to the traps in the boathouse were sinking in tandem with her aching backside. She was nearing the end of the reel and would have to come back another day to scour the last half of the 1940s.

Skim headlines, turn the page. She was working on autopilot when a photograph blurred past her seconds too late. Jerking to attention, she went back a page. December 7, 1945, was Granite Harbor's first town-wide Christmas celebration marked by a pyramid of lobster traps.

*Exactly four years after the attack on Pearl Harbor, Granite Harbor honored their fallen with a gathering that knit many grieving hearts for the upcoming joyous and difficult holiday. "Christmas, without my boys, will never be the same again."*

*These words spoken by Nancy Brooks communicate the feeling of almost every family in town. Some of our boys were brought home to us, while some will never return. Either way, they will forever be in our hearts.*

*Jack Smith, who lost his son during the battle of Iwo Jima, knew that now, more than ever, the first Christmas after war's end, the community needed one another. He decided since many of the fallen had come from generations of fishermen or had been fishermen before enlisting, a memorial featuring one of their traps or nets stacked into the shape of a Christmas tree would create a much-needed symbol. "The fallen are now in the arms of our Creator, who was born long ago," Smith said. "These mothers are not alone in their grief. Mary also knew what it was like to raise a child only for Him to be killed by hatred. But that soldier rose again, and though our lives will be forever changed, we can take comfort in knowing our boys are waiting for us, and we'll see them again."*

Josephine's vision blurred, and she blinked the moisture away. Those old traps in the boathouse represented lives lost. Lives of many of their ancestors. And it seemed they were forgotten.

A shiver stole through her, and she rubbed her arms.

Without reading the rest of the article, she printed out the remaining pages of 1945, checked out the Clive Flemming book she had no intention of reading, and asked Mrs. Fletcher if she knew anything about that memorial service.

"I had no idea." Mrs. Fletcher lifted her glasses to read the printed article, then rested them back on her nose as she returned the stack of papers to Josephine. "This is fascinating. I'd always heard the New England tradition of making lobster trap Christmas trees started here, but I didn't know this was how it began. You say the traps are still around?"

"They're in the boathouse."

"Fascinating."

"I wasn't sure what to do with the reels of microfilm. I left them there."

Mrs. Fletcher flapped her hand in a shooing motion. "I'll get them, no worries. I'll see what else I can dig up. If I find anything, I'll let you know."

"Thank you."

Josephine left the library as dusk began to fall. How sad that stories and events so vital to a community got lost over time. Things like that should be better documented. Be taught. Be remembered.

She drove to Jace's house. His truck was parked in the driveway and a lone light shown through what she guessed to be the living room window. Hopefully, he was back from his trip. She knocked on the door, shivering as the wind kicked up. A series of storms were supposed to bring a drop in temperature. She should have dressed warmer.

What felt like several minutes passed, and she knocked again, louder this time. Maybe he wasn't home and had left the light on to make it appear as if he were. If he didn't answer soon, she'd go home. Hunger gnawed at her insides. A warm fire and a Yellowstone marathon sounded better by the second.

The door swung open and blessed heat rolled over her. Jace stood in the doorway, hair damp, wearing a soft-looking henley and sweatpants. Barefoot.

Yellowstone could wait. She'd struck gold right here.

"Hey." He grinned. "Come in."

He stepped out of the way.

It was good to see him smile. She entered and immediately noticed the outdated decor. Dark wood paneling on the walls, maroon carpet, and a ceiling fan that screamed 1980s.

"Nice surprise." He closed the door behind her.

Was it?

Good.

"I found something." She held out the rolled-up papers.

He stepped closer to retrieve them and a masculine, inviting scent rolled her way. Something bold yet not overpowering. Like an Irish spring. Whatever that smelled like. She didn't care. She'd missed him, and with all she knew now, she wanted to wrap her arms around him and tell him she supported him in every way.

"What's this?"

"An explanation for the traps in the boathouse. I found it at the library on microfilm. Apparently, we used to have a town newspaper called the *Seaside Press*. You were right. They're not just old ordinary traps."

She briefed him on her findings, then gave him time to skim the article. All the while, she did her best not to concentrate on how comfortable he looked or how delicious he smelled because those thoughts were warming her up quick.

"Wow, that's something," he said, shaking his head.

"I know, right?" Brilliant response but it was better than kiss-me-Jace-before-I-explode.

His gaze connected with hers. "You're welcome to sit down."

He gestured to the ugly couch.

Yeah, that probably wasn't the best idea. She might lose her resolve, make the first move he wasn't ready for, and ruin everything.

"Thanks, but I need to get home. I just wanted to tell you in person what I found."

"I'm glad you did."

Without taking his eyes off her, he rolled the papers and held them out. Her heart pounded, and she was afraid if she opened her mouth to speak, he'd hear the thumping. But the longer he stared at her with heat pooling in those blue depths, the harder her blood pumped.

"We should do something about this." His attention slid to her lips.

She totally agreed. "Like what?"

His gaze slid up to her eyes again. "We should find out who the traps belong to and honor those men again."

Oh, that.

She swallowed. "And women. There were a few nurses among them."

"They need not be forgotten. What do you say, Jo? Work on this with me?"

If it involved being with him, she'd say yes to almost anything. "I think it's a great idea."

One corner of his mouth hitched in satisfaction. He was affecting her, and he knew it. Found it amusing, in fact. He was waiting on her to crumble first, but he'd underestimated his old rival.

She shoved her raging hormones aside—sorry, girls!—pretended indifference, and shrugged. "Well, I'd better go."

Before she let him win and jumped into his strong arms.

He chuckled and inched forward, bending to kiss her forehead. His warm lips lingered on her skin. 'Night, Joey."

His breath whispered against her skin, sending delightful pulses of sensation down her body.

"Goodnight," she squeaked and headed for the door. His laughter followed her into the cold night air. Arrogant man.

She hurried to her car. If they kept this up, there'd be enough electric charge between them to light up every Christmas tree from here to San Francisco.

# TWENTY

Jace rubbed sleep from his eyes and opened the door to Maggie's Diner. He needed coffee. Now. Slumber had been slow to come after Joey left his house last night. The way she'd looked at him with such heat, such longing—he'd come close to kissing her. And he was certain she'd welcome it. He'd lain awake late into the night reminding himself they needed to take things slow. Their competitive natures blended with their chemistry and years of denial might spontaneously combust otherwise.

And now that he'd confessed his burden to his dad, a part of him felt free to play with the science. First, he needed to tell Joey.

"Hiya, Jace." Maggie burst from the kitchen's swinging doors carrying a loaded tray of steaming food. "Sit wherever you like. Be with you in a minute."

"Just coffee to go. No rush."

She winked at him and continued toward her waiting customers.

The diner was quiet this time of morning. Hardly anyone except the fisherman were awake, dressed, and ready for a hearty breakfast before heading out onto the cold water. Jace wished he had the luxury. His breakfasts consisted of a microwaved frozen breakfast burrito and whatever blend of coffee was on sale at Johnson's Grocery. Today, he was splurging.

Jace sat on a tattered stool at the counter and waited. He would've been on the water an hour ago, but as the sun delayed its rising, he adjusted his work hours. No sense hauling in the pitch of night any longer than necessary.

Maggie placed a tall foam cup in front of him. Steam escaped the mouth hole of the lid. "Careful, it's fresh and hot."

"Will do. Thanks." He pushed two dollars her way.

"This—" she pushed his money back and pulled a clear plastic container from beneath the counter—"is on the house."

An iced cinnamon roll the circumference of his hand and three times as thick lay inside. His taste buds rejoiced. Her cinnamon rolls were famous all along the coast.

"You don't need to do this, Maggie."

"It's nothing compared to what you did for Lizabeth."

Jace shook his head, emotion welling his chest. "Right place, right time."

Maggie covered his hand with hers. "Right person."

Oh, how he missed helping people.

He thanked her for the roll and coffee and escaped to his truck. The memory of the girl's stiff little body and the fear in her eyes was all too familiar. Too haunting to relive. But he'd known what to do and the fulfillment that flooded his chest knowing he'd saved a life gave him some peace. Why he hadn't known how to help Arabella, he'd never understand.

Or forgive himself.

He'd taken an oath to preserve life. To remember that "warmth, sympathy, and understanding may outweigh the surgeon's knife or the chemist's drug." It was his calling.

But saving one child's life after being responsible for taking another didn't balance the scales. Not to him. He may have had sympathy and understanding in spades with Arabella, but it hadn't been enough.

The fact that Doc Greenwell's offer to partner and then transfer the practice to Jace upon retirement taunted most of his sleeping hours didn't matter. It was over.

And if a jury found him guilty of malpractice? Then, his entire life was over.

He got to work, hauling pots, making polite conversation with Cooper, and tried to forget how his life had turned upside down.

Jace's phone screen lit with a text as he neared Pelican Point. Joey.

> *Vet called. Cat needs picked up. On my way to investigate squatters on an illegal campsite. Can't reach my parents. I paid the bill over the phone. Can you get the cat? Please?*

Jace considered his words before replying.

> *Only if you'll let me bring you dinner too.*

She didn't respond right away, so he left his phone on the instrument panel and continued working. He'd pick up the cat whether she agreed to dinner or not, but this way maybe he could gauge how she saw this thing between them.

Forty minutes later, he checked his phone before moving on to the next area.

> *Only if you promise to stay and eat with me.*

He smiled.

> Six?

She replied with a thumbs up emoji.

Dinner and a cat. Not the most romantic date. In fact, it sounded like one of those cheesy romance movies on TV he skipped past while channel surfing. Those guys always got the girl though, so he'd show up at six with takeout and Granite Harbor's meanest cat.

As promised, Jace knocked on her door at precisely six o'clock, wearing a puffy coat over a Red Sox hoodie, dark jeans, and smelling like heaven. Or was that chili?

He held up a Johnson's Grocery bag that said *Have a Nice Day!* She took it and gestured for him to come inside. "What should I do with your royal highness?"

Jace lifted the pet carrier.

The royal highness growled at her from inside the cage. "Anywhere for now."

Jace set the cage between the couch and the fireplace. Close enough for warmth, far enough away to not overheat. She hadn't really thought about feline accommodations as crazy as the day had been. She planned to adopt him out and hoped it wouldn't take long to find him a nice forever home.

"How'd it go with the campers?" he asked, following her into the kitchen.

"I got to read my first citation. Let's hope I don't have to do that very often."

"Hoping."

She placed the sack on the table and spread out the contents, suddenly wishing she'd dressed nicer than her black leggings, tunic sweatshirt, and fuzzy socks. But she was comfortable after an exhausting day, so she'd get over it. "A single mother with three kids. She lost her job and their home. A family member gave them the old camper. Their car looked rough too. Sounds like they've been living that way since spring. The kids aren't in school, and she barely has enough money to feed them."

Jace removed his coat and draped it over the back of a chair. "That's awful."

"I can't imagine. I hated having to explain to her that by law she could no longer camp there. But I was able to contact the Hope Center for Women and Children in Bangor. They had an opening and thanks to them she'll now have a place with running water and proper beds, and they'll all enjoy three healthy meals a day. Plus, the citation will alert the proper authorities which should keep the kids in school. The school districts in Bangor have great food and clothing programs for families in need."

"That's great. It's a good thing someone reported them then." Jace removed the lids from the foam containers. How is she going to afford gas all the way to Bangor?"

Josephine blinked.

"You filled her up, didn't you?"

If he didn't stop looking at her like that, she might throw herself against him before they ever had their first official date. She peeked over his shoulder to distract herself. "Chili? Oh, I love chili."

"I know."

"And how is that?"

"I heard you talking about it in Mr. Ely's chemistry class. You were telling someone that chili is your favorite food and one day you wanted to travel the country so you could eat chili from every region."

She blinked. "You remember that?"

His neck turned adorably red. "I have a memory like an elephant. Don't be too impressed."

Oh, but she was. She wanted to ask what else he remembered about her, but his hand shooed her toward the food, so she let the subject drop.

Except that would be out of character for her.

She retrieved the peanut butter, bread, and a butter knife and added it to the table. "And I remember you have an unhealthy obsession with peanut butter sandwiches."

"Peanut butter isn't unhealthy when eaten in moderation."

"You brought one with your lunch every day, no matter what main course was served in the cafeteria. Even pizza." She gave a dramatic shudder.

"I was a growing boy. I needed the protein." He pulled out a chair and sat.

"And I needed the chili."

"Then we make a good team." He tugged her closer by the pinky and rubbed his fingertips up and down her arm.

Flirting was way better than dueling. They should have done this years ago.

She took the seat next to him at her small round table for four. The only action this slab of wood got was when her parents came over for a meal or the occasional holiday. She always ate on the couch in front of the TV. The fact that the furniture led a solitary life had never bothered her but using it to enjoy a meal with Jace felt as natural as breathing. She doubted the table would hold such insignificance to her again.

While they ate, they talked more about the traps in the boathouse and brainstormed how to find more information. She told him Mrs. Fletcher had agreed to help with research and how she'd talked Josephine into checking out the newest Clive Flemming novel.

"That was a good one." Jace popped the last bite of pre-packaged chocolate chip cookie into his mouth and chewed.

"You read it?"

"It's been on the bestseller list for weeks. Don't you read anymore?"

"Not really. Not books anyway."

"You were rarely without your nose in a book."

She shrugged. "I'm a woman. Our interests change with age and experience."

"And moods."

Her mouth fell open in mock offense. "True." She giggled. "If you think I should give the book a try, I will."

"It might be helpful in case you ever have to deal with any government conspiracies or dead bodies on the dock."

She put her head in her hands. "Don't jinx me. The idea that we may be on the verge of a trap war scares me enough."

He tugged her hands down and held them in his own. "How's the investigation going?"

"Any area harbors who've experienced issues have reported it to the Coast Guard. They're patrolling but that's all for now."

"Thanks for watching out for us." He rubbed his thumbs against her knuckles.

Jace opened his mouth to speak then shook his head and closed it again. Finally, he said, "What do you plan to name your new pet?"

"I'm not keeping the cat."

"Are you going to release him back into the wild?"

"I wouldn't consider Granite Harbor *the wild*, but no, I plan to find a family who will adopt him. Unless you want to keep him."

"Can't."

"Why?"

"Allergic."

She leaned closer. "Really? Why didn't you say anything about it when I asked you to pick him up then?"

"It's different transporting a cat versus it living in your house."

"What happens when you're around a cat too long?"

"The usual. Itchy eyes, nausea, seizures."

"Liar." She tugged her hands from his.

He smiled and leaned even closer. "I'm willing to come over and help you take care of him until you find him a home, though."

She leaned back in her chair, feigning indifference, though her whole body tingled with want. "Nope. Not chancing you seizing."

"What about the days you have to work long hours?" He rubbed his thumbs across her knees.

"Too risky."

"You don't want me coming over anymore, do you?"

"I don't want you dropping dead on my floor."

"Would you miss me?"

"Well, yeah. Who would bring me chili?"

He stood. "All right, then. The cat's all yours."

"How generous of you." She took his offered hand.

"I'm a very generous man." He guided her against him and wrapped his arms around her back. Ever so slowly, his face lowered toward hers.

Joey's pulse raced. She'd spend many hours over the years daydreaming of such a moment with him but never thought it would actually happen. Now he was going to kiss her, and it would be amazing.

His warm lips skimmed the corner of hers and pressed against her cheek. "Sleep well."

He pulled away.

She wanted to slap the wicked satisfaction off his face. And then show him what he was missing.

All she could do was stand dumbfounded and watch him walk to the door, every nerve in her core sizzling in anticipation and throbbing with disappointment.

Fine. He wanted to challenge who could hold out the longest? She could do that too.

"See you around." She waved her fingers.

He threw up his hand and winked before he closed the door behind him.

She sucked in a frustrated breath.

Whatever. She had a cat she needed to get comfortable anyway and more western drama to binge watch. And yet all she wanted to do was chase after Jace and make her fantasies reality.

Instead, she approached the pet carrier and spoke in a soothing tone. "How're you doing, boy? You've been through a lot, haven't you?"

The big cat's growl was low and only lasted a few seconds. At least she was making progress. Or maybe it was the pain meds dulling his anxiety.

"I'm glad nothing major was wrong. Just some fluids, laser therapy, and a few stitches. Would you like some water?"

She didn't have any cat food. She'd have to pick some up in the morning. And a cat bed. And a litter box. Oh, boy, this was getting complicated. And expensive.

Rowboat was a tabby she'd had growing up, named by her dad because he'd discovered it sleeping in his rowboat tied to the dock and brought it home. Since Dad was notorious for never getting rid of anything, she wondered if he still had the cat house he'd built.

It was nine o'clock. There was a small chance he'd still be awake.

She tapped his name on her phone screen and listened to the ringtone. After three rings, Dad answered.

"Hey, sorry it's late. Do you still have that cat house you built for Rowboat?"

"Huh?" She could almost hear the fog clearing from his sleepy brain. No doubt he'd dozed off in the recliner while watching TV the way he did every night. "Uh, yeah. It's in the barn."

"May I have it? At least for a while?" She told him about Jace finding the cat in the boathouse, the vet, and her current predicament.

"It's all yours. One less thing in there collecting dust."

"Thanks. You aren't in the market for a cat, are you?"

"No. Moby's enough trouble."

"Moby's ancient. All he does is sleep."

"I know. I'm not looking for a pet more needy than that."

"I had to try."

Dad yawned. "I'll pick up some cat food and other supplies for you too. I've got to run into Bangor in the morning to pick up the new bathroom sink your mom ordered. I'll stop by the pet store while I'm there."

Dad was many good things, but his strongest quality was provider. "You're the best."

"So are you, kid. Love you."

"Love you, too."

The screen on her phone faded to black and she stared at her reflection in the dark glass. Her birth mother had died in a car accident when she was six months old. Her birth father hadn't wanted her and gave up custody. Josephine had struggled with that knowledge many times growing up and it had affected her confidence and brought a plethora of insecurities. But if a girl had to go without her birth parents, Marian and Holden Rockwell were the next best thing.

# Twenty-One

"Jace? You completely passed your buoys."

Jace shook himself from the brain fog and looked starboard. Sure enough, he'd blown right past them. "Tired, I guess."

He couldn't get Joey out of his head. Now that he'd held her, come close to kissing her—twice—it wasn't enough. He wanted to learn, explore, test. He'd waited years for that privilege. That's why he wanted to take his time and savor it, even if the pace drove them both a little crazy.

And distracted from his work.

"More coffee?" Cooper held a thermos in each hand.

"Thanks." Though the caffeine would do little to suppress thoughts of Joey, at least it would warm his insides.

Jace continued to an open range and turned hard to starboard to reroute them to the buoys. The unmarked boat he'd seen a few weeks ago near Duro Island came into sight. He set his boat to idle and grabbed the binoculars, bringing the boat into focus. No tracks followed the vessel, which meant it was at rest. A diver jumped overboard holding a shovel. What were they doing? Had Joey ever checked into who owned the vessel?

Only he'd forgotten to mention it to her that night. She'd told him about the market price drop, and he'd thrown a tantrum

Then she'd jumped onto his boat and hit her head. Jace cleared a thickness from his throat the cold air created. "There's that boat again."

"The one we saw a few weeks ago?" Steam lifted from the lid of Cooper's thermos.

"It's unmarked."

"And that's an issue." Cooper said it as a statement, but a question lingered. A flatlander wouldn't understand the significance.

"By law, vessels must be registered and marked for identification purposes that way harbormasters and the Coast Guard can monitor for safety. It helps keep unregulated fishing or unlawful activity to a minimum."

And with several cut ropes in the area, an unmarked boat shot to the top of the suspect list.

Duro Island was within visual. What was the diver doing with a shovel? Treasure hunting? Dredging? He certainly wouldn't use a shovel to cut ropes.

And why aground of Duro Island? The only thing on it was trees and a dilapidated cabin built decades ago that was now inhabited by wildlife.

Jace set down the binoculars and reached for the radio. "Granite Harbor this is *Hiley Mae II*, number 5036189, over."

When no one responded, he tried again.

"*Hiley Mae II*, this is harbormaster, over."

"Joey, there's an unmarked boat near Duro Island. Diver with a shovel. Treasure hunting or dredging? I don't know. Over."

Static filled the speaker for a moment. "A shovel? Describe the boat."

"Pulsifer-style diesel. Green bottom, rough shape. I've seen it once before but didn't mention it. Over."

"I'll check it out. Over."

"Jo?"

"Yes?"

"Be careful. Over."

The line was public, and he imagined the other fishermen's snickering and comments. One didn't typically warn the harbormaster to be cautious over radiowaves.

"Aye, aye, captain." Her soft voice filled the speaker. "Over and out."

He didn't like the idea of Joey checking into the diver by herself, but she was a grown adult, and it was her responsibility as harbormaster. He hooked the receiver back onto the instrument panel and finished turning back to his buoys.

They spent the rest of the afternoon hauling pots and scouting for new areas to lower the traps. This took them further into the gulf than the areas they'd been working, as the lobster settled in deeper waters during winter. They just had to be careful not to set the traps in anyone else's territory.

When they returned to the dock Jace asked Cooper and Lauren to take care of the weigh-in while he hunted for Joey. He found her in the boatyard talking to Ted. The moment she spotted him, she paused mid-sentence, and a small smile lifted her lips. Man, she was beautiful. And that smile was just for him. A simple gesture that soothed his hurts, made him think there might still be a little hope out there somewhere with his name on it.

Jace waited until she'd thanked Ted for his time and walked his direction. "How'd it go?"

"The boat was gone by the time I got there." She pulled a knit cap from her coat pocket and slipped it over her head. Pink dusted her nose and cheeks. "I checked the county database, but many boats fall under that description. I doubt it's a local fishing vessel, as it wouldn't have passed inspection being unmarked."

He held the gate for her and then closed it behind him. "I'm glad you're safe."

"Your concern is sweet."

He took her hand and walked toward the dock. "I know you can hold your own, but you're a beautiful female out there alone on a boat confronting a stranger with a shovel who's capable of anything."

"You're as bad as Mrs. Fletcher with your doom and conspiracy plots. You make it sound like a Clive Flemming novel." She leaned into him as they walked, her arm flush against his, and lowered her voice. "As for this beautiful female thing, I'd like to hear more about that."

"I'll gladly go into more detail after I've moored the boat and taken a shower."

A distant whistle and a catcall pierced the air.

Jace rolled his eyes. "And in a more private location."

She stopped and faced him. "Would this be considered a date?"

"It is on my end."

She grinned. "My house. I'll provide dinner this time. Now go home and shower. You stink."

Joey released him and went into her office, giving him one last look before closing the door. Taking things slow with this woman was going to be harder than he'd thought.

Even with her quirky ways, Mrs. Fletcher was the best. Josephine unlocked her house and welcomed the warmth.

"I gave the historical society your number." A rhythmic beeping sounded in the background on the librarian's end. Mrs. Fletcher must be checking in books. "They'll call you if they run across anything, dear."

"Thank you. You've gone above and beyond." Josephine kicked off her boots.

"My pleasure. How's the book reading coming?"

Um. . .

"Good. What I've read so far is well-written."

It wasn't a lie. The back cover description was well written.

"I'm glad, dear. Nothing makes me happier than matching good stories with good people."

"You excel at it." Joey glanced at the digital clock on her stove. "I hate to rush, Mrs. Fletcher, but I'm expecting company any minute."

"Of course, dear. Enjoy your evening."

"You, too."

Josephine ended the call then immediately dialed Ciara.

*Please, pick up. Please, pick up.*

"Hello?" Ciara's voice was barely audible over a screaming baby.

"It's me."

"Hold on a second. I'm going to get Barry." A thump sounded and the screaming grew less intense until it faded. Joey could picture her friend now, sweatpants and an oversize tee, walking that sweet baby boy down the hall to her husband.

A minute later, Ciara returned. "What's up. Haven't heard from you in a while."

"Giving you some space. You've been busy, Mrs. Mother of Two." Josephine sped to her bedroom.

"So have you, Miss Harbormaster."

"Yeah, about that." Josephine flipped on the light. "I have a date tonight with my running mate."

A pause. "Jace? Oh, my goodness, you have a date with Jace McClintock?" Ciara was probably dancing on her tiptoes the way she always did when excited.

Josephine held the phone away from her ear until her friend stopped squealing. "Are you done now?"

"Oh, don't even. You've had a crush on him for *years*. You can't possibly be that calm."

Josephine glanced at herself in the mirror and cupped a palm to her forehead. "I'm not. That's why I'm calling. You're the trendy one. I need fashion advice, and quick. He'll be here any minute."

"Creativity can't be rushed, my dear."

"C!"

Her friend laughed. "Okay. First, take a deep breath. Keep calm and. . .never mind. I can't think of anything clever to pair with the current situation."

"What do I wear?"

"What do you have?"

Josephine threw open her closet door and began rambling articles of clothing.

"Flannels, fleece, and joggers don't count."

Great. That eliminated three-quarters of her closet. She groaned.

"Where are you going on your date? That'll determine what to wear."

"We're dining here."

"Then anything casual would be appropriate. Nice jeans and a trendy top or a nice pair of leggings and a dressy tunic."

"I don't own any tunics. Only long, oversized sweatshirts."

"A longer top then. Make sure the leggings are thick and not faded. Leggings worn so thin they show your underwear are distasteful and will send the wrong message."

"Duly noted."

"And add a cardigan. But no jewelry unless it's a simple pair of earrings. Anything else would be too much for a night in."

Josephine closed her eyes and rested her head on a row of coat hangers. "Why is this so hard for me?"

Something rustled on Ciara's end of the line. "You tell me."

Josephine considered the question. "Because Jace is used to Boston and all the model quality sophisticated women with their designer handbags and shoes. I hate carrying a purse and the nicest pair of shoes I own are Bean boots."

"Listen to me. Jace isn't in Boston anymore. And when it comes to you, those things have never been important to him. You won him over long ago with your intellect, not your fashion."

Long ago. Was that true?

For a while after he'd first left for Boston, some in the community had offered her condolences of sorts, saying they'd thought for sure they'd end up together. That all that competition was a mask for his true feelings. That's why, in a moment of courageous stupidity, she'd taken a bus to Boston to bear her soul. She'd spied him in a corner of the university library whispering secrets and stealing kisses with a voluptuous blonde every time they turned a page in the book they were sharing.

Hidden amongst the stacks, she'd watched them as the room, and herself, grew smaller and smaller. In that moment, she'd known undoubtedly they were different people with different dreams. Where he was meant to go out into the world, her place was in the safe, comfortable confines of Granite Harbor. The place where she belonged but never felt truly accepted.

Josephine looked at herself in the mirror and repeated the montage. "He's not in Boston anymore."

"Nope, and he's chosen to spend this evening with *you*. Not with what's in your closet."

Ciara was right. As usual. If this relationship was ever going to go anywhere, she had to be true to herself and not try to fit into the mold she thought Jace wanted.

"You're right. Thanks, C."

"Always. Now, make sure you call me tomorrow and tell me how it went."

"Will do."

Josephine lowered the phone to hang up when Ciara shouted her name.

"Yeah?"

"Lip gloss and a little mascara wouldn't hurt. Draw some attention to your best features."

"Thanks. Kiss the kids for me."

"Gladly."

Josephine hung up, stripped out of her work clothes, and dawned a pair of thick black leggings, a long white top, and her favorite kelly-green cardigan. If she was going to accentuate her best features, the color made the green in her hazel eyes pop.

A light coat of mascara, some lip gloss, a hair brushing, and a subtle coat of body spray later, her doorbell rang. Her stomach knotted. What was wrong with her? It was Jace. Just because he'd declared this a date didn't mean she had to be nervous and awkward.

Her anxiety bubble burst when she opened the door. "Dad."

"Hey, nugget." He held a fluffy cat bed in his arms. "Forgot to leave this with everything earlier."

She moved aside to let him in, ashamed that she'd been so concentrated on her date that she'd forgotten she had a cat. Where was the little devil?

Dad wiped his shoes on the rug before continuing through the room. "How's he doing? Is the setup okay?"

"I haven't had a chance to check on him yet. Just got home." She followed him to the mudroom.

The door was closed, blocking entry to the rest of the house so the feline wouldn't shred her furniture and curtains. Dad flipped on the light. The cat house was cuter than she remembered, with metal siding and roof, and tiny windows on each side of the door.

"Has it always been this fancy?" she asked, trying to remember.

Dad placed the cat bed in an empty corner. When he stood, purplish blotches marred his cheeks. He tugged on his expanding belt line and said, "They called this morning and said the sink wasn't ready to pick up yet. I noticed the cat house had lost its appeal when I dragged it from the barn, so I used some leftover siding from the house to spruce it up. I have bigger plans for it though."

He held his hands out in a square, as if it were a camera lens. "White gingerbreading, tiny window boxes, maybe a welcome mat."

"Seriously?" She grasped his arm. "I mean, I appreciate it. Don't get me wrong. But he's a cat. I don't think it matters to him if his sleeping quarters have window boxes."

He flattened his lips. "I'm retired and your mom is in the throes of menopause. Trust me, the cat wants window boxes."

"Window boxes it is." She wrapped him in a hug.

Dad kissed her head, then pointed to a shelf. "I put the food up there. Food and water bowl's there." He angled his finger to a petite bench with built in food and water bowls. "Litter box and a few toys on the other side of his house."

"You really are the best."

"I really need a project."

"Where is the spoiled patient?"

"He ran in his house when I turned on the light. I'd like to put his new bed inside, but I'd also like to keep all my fingers. I'll let you handle that sometime after he's warmed up."

"You think he will?"

"I do."

Joey didn't have the heart to tell Dad the cat was temporary after all the work he put in. She glanced around the room. Looks like she was keeping the cat.

"What do I owe you for everything?"

He waved the comment away. "Nothing. I feel better knowing you're not here alone."

She wasn't sure what help a cat was going to be, even if he was intimidating, unless she could train it to attack on command. Dad's concern was sweet all the same.

The doorbell rang.

Jace.

Shoot. She was hoping to keep their new footing quiet, at least for a while, until she'd had time to explore every nuance. For now, she wanted him all to herself.

Dad's head tilted to the side. "Expecting company?"

She took a deep breath, filled her cheeks, then exhaled. "Yes."

The skin between his brows bunched, no doubt from her weird reaction. He went to the door and opened it. "Jace? Uh, good to see you."

Jace's gaze toggled between Josephine and Dad.

"Thanks, Mr. Rockwell. You, too."

Dad waved him inside. "Call me Holden."

Jace nodded. He looked at Josephine. "You look great."

Dad took in her appearance and cocked his head. "Yes, you do."

Josephine studied her socked feet, face scorching. "Thanks."

"Well," Dad said. "I'd better head out. Your mom probably has dinner ready by now."

"Thanks again for everything." She kissed Dad's cheek. It wasn't until he'd backed out of her driveway that she turned from the window and said, "That was awkward."

Jace smiled. "A little."

"Coat?" She held out her hand. He removed it and gave it to her. "Do pancakes, bacon, and eggs work for you?"

"I love breakfast for dinner."

She hung his coat in the hall closet. "Great. Would you mind building a fire in the backyard? It's a perfect night for it."

"Sure. You really do look great." He stepped closer.

She took in his blue long-sleeved tee and athletic pants and shortened the distance between them. "You smell better."

In fact, he smelled delicious. How about they skip dinner and work on getting the whole first kiss thing over with?

He touched his cold cheek to hers, his nose grazing her ear. Her eyes closed. "Mmm. So do you. All that office work had you stinking like paper and ink."

She walloped him on the arm.

He laughed.

"I've worked hard to get where I am."

He pulled her into a playful hug. "I know. You deserve it." He kissed her temple. "Now about those pancakes. . ."

She jabbed him in the ribs, and he flinched. Taking his hand, she pulled him to the kitchen. "The wood is stacked out back. Lighter fluid and matches are in that cabinet. Blankets are in the hall closet."

He mock saluted. "Yes, ma'am."

Thirty minutes later, she carried their loaded plates to the fire pit where Jace had the logs blazing. He'd draped a blanket over the back of each Adirondack chair. Night had fully committed, stars twinkled, and the salty tang of sea air combined with the scent of burning cedar.

He stood when she joined him.

"Mugs and coffee are on the counter."

He took the plates while she settled in a chair and draped a blanket over her lap. Then he passed them back and went after the thermos and mugs. When he returned, she let him settle in and then handed him his plate. She told him about Mrs. Fletcher and the historical society, and her dad's new hobby of micro-home improvement.

"You're keeping him then?" Jace sipped his coffee.

"My dad?"

Jace choked, then coughed. "The cat, smart aleck. Have you named him yet?"

"No, but I guess I'll have to now. Thanks to you."

"You're the one who wanted him out of the boathouse."

"You're the one who made up false symptoms to keep from adopting him."

"I don't have time for a pet."

"I don't either, but with winter at our door, things are slowing down a bit."

"Job rough on you, eh?"

"No, but I haven't been home much. I'm looking forward to a breather."

He set his empty plate on the grass and studied her, mug resting on his knee. "What made you decide to be harbormaster? I thought you always wanted to be a marine biologist or something."

"I did. Until I learned it would require seven to eight years of additional schooling."

"You've never been afraid of academics."

Firelight created both a glow and shadows on his face, drawing attention to his defined jaw. "It wasn't a matter of academics. It was a matter of finances."

"Didn't you apply for scholarships? Grants? The Island Institute has great resources."

"I had no idea how to write for a grant. I did apply for scholarships. One being for the Katherine P. Bowersock scholarship, but someone else was awarded the full ride."

Clarity filled his features. "Me."

She smiled. "You."

He stared into his coffee. "I'm sorry. I didn't know."

"And if you had've? It wouldn't have changed anything."

"I could've. . ."

"What? Given that opportunity up for me also? You wouldn't have. The scholarship board wouldn't have let you, and neither would I." She put her hand over his. "If I didn't express my gratitude back then for giving me the UMaine internship, let me express it now. That was good of you."

"You deserved it more."

She shrugged. "In the end, it all worked out the way it was meant to. Though I'll bleed out after admitting this, you were always the better scholar. You deserved all the awards you received."

He shook his head.

"I used the scholarship money I was awarded and took a few classes through the Institute. Paid the rest of my way to a bachelor's degree. I may not have a master's or a doctorate, but that's okay.

My place is here. I'm happy. You were the one meant to leave this small town and do big things."

He leaned his head against the back of the chair. "And, yet here I am."

Firelight flickered reflections across his lean body. She curled her legs beneath her and propped her arm on the side of the chair, waiting. She'd promised herself she'd be patient and allow him to tell her in his own timing, but it was the elephant in the room of her thoughts, and it needed addressed before the entire town found out. She reached across the distance and placed her hand on his arm. "What happened in Boston?"

Jace closed his eyes, transported to that awful day in the cramped hospital room, alarms blaring, staff scrambling, all eyes on him waiting for instructions. He shook his head back to reality and stared at the campfire, hoping the flames would stop the awful scene replaying in his mind. The ache in his chest was almost more than he could bear.

"I lost a patient. My college roommate's three-year-old daughter."

"Oh, Jace." Tears pooled in Joey's eyes.

"I was too confident in my education. My abilities. I was arrogant enough to determine a diagnosis without further testing."

She remained silent. Shocked or appalled. Maybe both.

Joey deserved to know before she invested her heart in him.

The crack and hiss of firewood spurred him on as he stared unseeing into the flames.

"Brad's into sports medicine, so when his daughter started showing signs of neck stiffness and staring spells and he couldn't contribute them to an injury or see anything on an x-ray, he called me. After an examination and blood work, which came back normal, I diagnosed her with epilepsy. Prescribed her medicine and scheduled a follow-up appointment.

"A week later, her symptoms were worse. I ordered a CT scan that showed inflammation of her brain. Likely, some form of meningitis. I hated to put her through it, but to make a definitive diagnosis, she needed a spinal tap. The procedure went well. While we waited for test results, we administered two forms of strong antibiotics. A few hours later she was gone.

Joey swiped a tear. "I can't imagine how horrible that must've been for you. For the girl's parents."

He leaned forward and rested his elbows on his knees, knocking his coffee mug to the ground. He placed his forehead in his palms. "The test results showed perfect spinal fluid. It was never epilepsy or meningitis. The autopsy revealed a brain parasite."

Joey touched his back, rubbing circles up and down. The gesture would've been comforting in another scenario. "That wasn't your fault."

He denied her statement. "If I hadn't been so confident that she had epilepsy and had done more extensive testing sooner, she might have lived."

"Don't do that to yourself."

He ignored her words and kept plowing. "Brad's insurance company required them to file a malpractice suit. They'll only pay the medical expenses if the court can prove no malpractice was involved. I was escorted out by two guards and the hospital's board of directors."

The back rubbing stopped. "Guilty until proven innocent? How can they get away with that? That's not what our judicial system stands on."

Vulnerability and the horrific memories caused pools of liquid to swell in his eyes. "Their approach is legal. I'm on unpaid leave until my court date on December 21$^{st}$. If I'm proven innocent, I'll resign. There's no way I can go back there.  If guilty. . .well, everything will be taken care of for me in a locked cell."

Her breath hitched. "How can anyone possibly accuse you of malpractice? You took the knowledge you had and made a sound judgment. It isn't malpractice because you're not the all-knowing God. I can't believe this."

Guilt threw him around the boxing ring again and took another punch. "I'm sorry, Joey. I shouldn't be putting you through this. Shouldn't be starting a relationship I may not be able to finish."

He stood, relieved to have it all out yet mortified all the same.

"No." She blocked him from moving forward. "Forget everything else and get the best lawyer you can find. Heck, I'll chip in money if I need to. We've got to beat this, Jace."

We? That sounded mighty nice.

"I have a great lawyer that's provided by the hospital, but I don't know that he'll be enough. Arabella died because I misdiagnosed her. Had I caught the signs sooner, I could've done something. Maybe she'd still be alive."

"It's called practicing medicine for a reason. A misdiagnosis doesn't mean malpractice. Her death isn't your fault, Jace."

"Now that I know it was a parasite, the symptoms are clear. I should've known."

She gripped his forearms and pulled him close, her forehead at his chin. "Don't do that. Hindsight always makes the path clear." She guided his chin down, forcing him to look at her. "I know you. I know you were doing the best you could with the information in front of you at the time. This isn't your fault."

*Not your fault....*

Whatever the case, he'd lost his best friend, his job, his reputation, and most of all, an innocent little girl.

"Don't let this stop you from sharing your gifts with the world. If you're proven innocent, there's no need to resign. You saved a girl's life just last week. Tell the jury that!"

He shook his head. "I can't. I'm not supposed to administer so much as a Band-Aid until the hearing. If so, I'll definitely be incarcerated."

"Think of how many people won't be helped without you."

He tugged his face away. "My reputation is shot, innocent or not. Someone else will have to save those patients."

"What about us, right here? I've heard Doc Greenwell plans to retire next year. Who best to serve and heal this town but you?"

He pulled from her embrace and started back inside. "I appreciate dinner and what you're trying to do. Your support. You've no idea how much. But I'm not going back to doctoring, and I don't ever want to have this conversation again." He turned to face her. "I told you my story so you can make a sound judgment on our relationship. If you choose to end it, I understand. If you choose to pursue it, then the man I am now is going to have to be enough for you."

Her shoulders wilted.

He braced himself for her rejection.

She held his gaze, drawing closer. One arm wrapped around his waist, then the other. Head on his chest, she fit perfectly in the crook of his neck. "Of course, you're enough for me. You always have been."

The bonfire blurred in his vision. That's all he needed to hear.

"Now I have a confession to make." She pulled away enough to look into his eyes. "Your malpractice suit was mentioned in the *Bangor Times* a few days ago. It didn't mention you as a resident here. The picture was fuzzy and it was only a report they picked up from a larger syndicate, but you know how things go around this town. Someone will put it together and word will get out. Be prepared."

He swallowed his shock. "If you knew, why didn't you say anything?"

"I knew you'd tell me when you were ready. I was okay with waiting because I knew you were innocent."

Jace pulled her close, holding as tightly as he could without hurting her. He palmed the back of her head and let tears fall down his cheeks. Her faith in him meant more than she'd ever know. If only they could stay cocooned like this until the storm that was about to hit this town blew over.

# TWENTY-TWO



*November*

Josephine's breath hung in the air in tiny clouds. She'd have to start driving to work and get her extra steps on the treadmill in the evenings. She was a wimp when it came to the cold, even though she'd hauled pots during winter for years and had grown accustomed to going home and defrosting herself every night. This winter, she was going to work in an office warmed by a pellet stove with a consistently full pot of coffee—to which she would gladly share both—and enjoy every moment.

Head down, she rounded the curve on the pathway that led from the dock parking lot to her office and pulled out her keys. The keyring caught on her knit glove and slipped from her hand. She bent to retrieve it. As she rose, the sunrise against the backdrop of colorful boats reflecting the water made her pause. The sight left her in awe every time.

A boat she didn't recognize caught her attention. She squinted to put the object into better focus. An unmarked boat with a faded green bottom was moored to the dock on the other side of the inlet.

The mysterious boat she'd been watching for.

A man with dark hair jumped overboard and onto the dock, then climbed the short ladder that led to level ground behind Maggie's Diner.

Good. The diner was the perfect place to chat.

Josephine entered her office, set the pellet stove to blazing, and then fished papers from the filing cabinet. Within ten minutes, she was at the diner, inhaling the scents of coffee, breakfast meat, and the yeasty sweetness of Maggie's famous cinnamon rolls.

She walked to the counter, ordered the Harbor Special #4, and scanned the patrons. Mertle Gundy, Avery Adams, Levi Drummond, and. . .the flatlander who'd renewed his mooring license last month and left his permit fee on her desk when she'd failed to collect it from him. The one who claimed he wouldn't be in the area for long. What was his name? Nolan? Corbin?

Colin.

It had to be his boat. He matched the description of the man she'd seen jump from the boat this morning, and everyone else here was native. She didn't want to harass the man, but someone was cutting ropes in the area, and Jace had witnessed a diver jump overboard with a shovel from a boat described as Colin's.

She walked to his table, pulled out the chair opposite him, and sat. Coffee halfway to his lips, he paused. Blinked.

"Good morning." She offered a polite smile.

He lowered the mug to the table. "G—good morning."

"I'm sorry to disturb your breakfast, but I had a couple of questions."

His gaze roamed her face. Slowly, as if taking in every detail. Strange and a little creepy. Serial killer or just odd?

"Does the unmarked boat with the green bottom belong to you?" She hitched her thumb toward the dock.

"Yes."

"By renewing your mooring license, you agreed to follow all the rules and regulations of the harbor including article two section A, stating that you must provide your license number on the outside of your boat either through signage or by other visible means."

His haggard features remained placid. Body language calm. His salt-and-pepper hair and short-cropped beard made him look distinguished and older than she suspected he was.

"Okay."

"You didn't indicate on the application that you'd purchased a different boat from the flybridge trawler that was inspected four years ago. Your new boat will need an inspection right away and any failed areas brought to code."

He shuffled the eggs on his plate with his fork. Red threads marred the whites of his eyes. "I won't be around for more than a couple weeks. I rarely moor in this harbor. I'm not sure I'm even keeping the boat when I leave."

"As the harbormaster, I must enforce the rules of the harbor. How'd you come across that boat?"

A lifetime of pain and regret stared back at her, causing a pit of sympathy to form in her gut. All the suspicion surrounding him should have her on high alert, but something about the man also tugged at her.

He coughed into his napkin. "I purchased the boat from Mike Lexar in Stonington three months ago. He'd removed all the markings before the sale. It needs some work which is why it looks rough." He set down his fork. "If you'd have said something about an inspection the day I came to your office, I'd have complied."

Embarrassment burned her cheeks. He was absolutely right. The oversight was on her part. She would normally have done it the day he renewed the license but had been so distracted by Hemingway and his vendetta with Jace that she'd overlooked her duty.

"Fair enough." She placed a brochure on the table and slid it in his direction with her finger. "Here's a list of things I will look for during the inspection. Since the oversight was on my end, we'll call this a consultation. I'll give you a week, and then we'll schedule your inspection. Where are you staying, so I can contact you?"

He ran his tongue over his teeth. "How about we schedule something now?"

That worked too. She opened her phone's calendar and looked ahead to the next week. "Does next Tuesday at two o'clock work for you?"

He nodded.

She tapped her thumbs along the keyboard. "Great. Next on the docket. There's been a report that you've been seen jumping overboard near Duro Island with a shovel. Treasure hunting? Dredging? Explain."

"I'm not dredging."

"Are you treasure hunting?"

He pointed to the papers in her hand. "Are there jurisdictions in the handbook outlining where in the ocean I can drive my boat and where I can't?"

His tone held no disrespect. "There isn't unless you're crossing into international waters, but I'll leave you the laws and consequences on dredging and digging should you need to read over them."

These, too, she slid across the table. "I'll ask again. Are you treasure hunting?"

The grooves along his forehead grew deeper. "I'm not doing anything illegal."

"Then you'll have some kindling to start a fire tonight." She pointed to the papers now in his hand.

His frown jabbed at her conscience. Somehow, she felt like she was kicking him while he was already down, and she wasn't sure why.

"Look, I'm just trying to keep my harbor safe. Someone has been cutting ropes on the lobstermen's traps and it's my job to figure out who. You're not from here, you're captain of an unmarked boat, and you've been seen jumping overboard with a shovel. I can't help but be suspicious."

"Fair enough." His tone sounded genuine.

"Order up for the harbormaster," Maggie called from the counter.

Josephine held up a finger, and Maggie nodded. Then she rested her forearms on the table and softened her voice. "Off the record, do you have ties to this community? Did you used to live here or vacation here? Family members in the area? I'm trying to figure out why you would purchase a mooring license for a spot you rarely use when you're not sure you're keeping the boat after this month."

He turned to the side and coughed. His lungs gurgled. "In case I decide to keep the boat, I wanted to be legal. You have my word, I'm not doing anything nefarious or hurting the ecosystem, and I'm not the one behind the cut ropes."

She remembered the address on his application and driver's license said Ohio, but his dialect was definitely Maine.

Another deep and rattly cough with a wheeze sounded.

"Allergies are little ninjas this time of year." She waited for him to catch his breath.

"I had a life here, once. A long time ago. I come back for nostalgia sake." He swallowed. "May I finish my breakfast?"

The man wasn't on trial even though she'd interrogated him as if he were. He hadn't broken any laws that she could prove—other than his unmarked boat, which was her own fault—and he was certainly entitled to his privacy.

She stood and pushed in her chair. "I'll see you next Tuesday. Have a good week, Mr. . .Colin."

"You, too." He looked out the window. "Joey."

Odd. She didn't remember introducing herself as Joey. In fact, she'd been so focused on questioning him today she hadn't introduced herself at all. She let it go. She moved to the counter where she picked up her order, threw down some bills, and walked the cold path back to her office. Smoke billowed from the pipe on the roof. She smiled. The office should be toasty.

When she finished her breakfast, she retrieved Colin's application. Warner. Colin Warner. Doing the only respectable thing, she Googled him by his name, city, and state, and searched through the list. None of the social media hits were his. She could acquire his public records if she was willing to pay $49.95, which she wasn't. The next matches were genealogy records from 1914, 1948, and 1969.

Yeah, she wasn't getting anywhere.

She walked to the window and looked at the harbor through the foggy glass. Colin's boat was gone. Though he was strange, she couldn't help but like him. There was something about him that seemed lost, and that he was searching for something to make him whole again.

She was familiar with the feeling.

Jace was loading grocery sacks into the back of his truck when his phone vibrated in his pocket. He finished his task, returned the cart, and opened Joey's text on his way to the vehicle.

*Found something! Colin Warner, the guy you reported with the unmarked boat, owns Duro Island.*

Jace halted and stared at the screen. The guy owned the island?

A horn gave a short blast behind him, making him flinch. Jace waved an apology to the driver as he shifted out of the way. He texted back.

*You sure?*

*Are you doubting my Nancy Drew skills?*

IDK

She sent a GIF where a green cartoon monster with one giant eyeball slapped his forehead.

He smiled.

"Jace?"

He looked at the speaker, and his grin fell. Doc Greenwell.

"Hey, Doc."

Doc Greenwell lowered his head, as if embarrassed. His puffy cheeks and jaw folded around the underside of his chin, droopy hound style. "Young man, I owe you an apology. I shouldn't have bombarded you with my request to join me as a partner. In the middle of the road at that. I thought you were simply helping your dad on the boat until you found a place nearby to settle in. I didn't realize your situation." Doc glanced around. Confirming they were alone, he continued. "I'm sorry you're having to go through this."

All the dark secrets of Jace's "situation" played in the man's gray eyes. Great. His skeletons had finally left the closet and paraded down Main Street. "I heard I'd made the paper."

The man adjusted his gold-framed glasses, nodding. "I owe you another apology. I know the gravity of a malpractice accusation, but it didn't make sense that a young man with your talent would come home to fish. I called an old colleague at Boston Medical and asked a few questions."

Jace would've been less shocked had Doc walked through town naked.

Doc Greenwell threw his palms out. "I didn't ask for gory details, but I needed to understand. What I want *you* to understand is we're human. As medical professionals, we make mistakes just like everyone else. And no one at that hospital blames you. My old colleague confirmed it. You're missed, and they want you back."

Jace shook his head and reached for the door handle.

"You did the same thing for that little girl I'd have done."

The fine hairs on the back of Jace's neck stood at attention.

"You should give your former superior a call sometime. Talk it out. Pray about it before you give it all up." He clamped a hand on Jace's shoulder and gave it two firm pats. He moved several feet in the opposite direction and then turned to Jace again. "If you decide you can't go back there, my offer still stands."

Doc walked into the store, leaving Jace clinging to his truck with one hand on the door handle, the other on the bed. His breaths came hard and fast as if he'd just run a marathon.

His buzzing pocket prodded him into the warm cab and behind the wheel. He inhaled and exhaled slowly to subside the panic filling his chest. He rested his head along the bench seat and dug out his phone. Eight texts from Joey.

> *Matlock?*

> *Velma?*

> *Jessica Fletcher?*

> *Come on. You can't deny I have good mystery-hunting skills…*

> *I found the clue to our lobster trap mystery.*

> *Hello?*

*Did I lose you?*

*Maybe, I'm not so good, then. (winky face emoji)*

He'd laugh if he didn't know the whole town would look at him differently from now on. If the offer of unfulfilled dreams Doc presented to him wasn't mounting in his throat against the pressure of guilt and grief and utter shock. One thing was for sure. Joey was always a great diversion. He tapped his thumbs along the keyboard.

*Call you when I get home.*

He tossed his phone onto the seat beside him and started the engine. The screen lit with a thumb's up emoji.

Jace drove home, carried his groceries inside, and put them away before he collapsed onto his couch, spent. He popped in his ear buds and turned on his phone. He wasn't a drinking man, so Joey would have to be his shot of whiskey tonight.

"There you are." Her sweet voice purred in his ears. "I was getting worried. You almost had me channeling my inner Colombo."

"Colombo, I know. Velma, I know. Who's Jessica Fletcher?"

"Murder, She Wrote. The old TV series."

"No clue."

"I have a thing for vintage television. Hey, I just realized she shares a last name with our town librarian. Maybe that's why she, too, loves a good mystery."

He laid down and got comfortable, ready to change the subject from old ladies to themselves and pretend he didn't have a court-date approaching. "What else do you have a thing for?"

"Hmm, let's see. Chocolate chip cookies—homemade not store bought—chili loaded with sour cream and corn chips, and an ice-cold Moxie on a hot summer day."

"Too cold."

"The Moxie?"

"Your interests."

"Oh, then let me try again. Picnicking at Sand Beach, shopping in Freeport, and binge-watching Hallmark movies."

"Still cold."

"Okay. Studying super hard to beat the guy ahead of me in pre-calc, getting revenge on said guy years after he started the war, and roping said guy into minion work like rescuing cats and building Christmas displays."

"Getting warmer."

She giggled. "Holding hands with said guy and snuggling with said guy by the fireplace."

"And?"

"That's it. That's as far as we've gotten."

"Can I come over?"

"Now? It's almost eight o'clock."

"What are you, old?"

"No."

"Can I come over?"

"Why?"

"Because I really want to kiss you right now."

Her breath hitched.

"I guarantee you'll have a thing for that too." He could imagine the pink blossoming in her cheeks.

She breathed a laugh. "I guarantee I will too, but I don't think it's a good idea tonight."

"Why not?"

"Because. . .once I step off that ledge, my feet may never touch solid ground again."

"Then I'll carry you."

A pause. "You're very persuasive, and though I'd love nothing more than to open my door to you, I think we both should stay put and get some sleep."

"You'll be able to sleep now? I won't."

"Good to know. However, we both have an early start tomorrow, so I'm going to say goodnight."

"What are you doing early?"

"If you must know, now that I've discovered Colin owns Duro Island, and he's been seen performing suspicious activity, I'm going to go check things out."

"You're not going out there by yourself."

"And who's going to stop me?"

He hesitated, choosing his words carefully. "No one is going to stop you, but I'm going to go with you."

"No, you're not."

"Why?"

"You have to work."

"I'll haul on Friday. You know as well as I, this time of year one day won't make a difference."

"What about your sternman?

"I'll let him know he can sleep in tomorrow. He'll be thrilled."

"I love that you worry for my safety, but I'm the harbormaster and protecting these waters is my job regardless of the danger.

I'm perfectly capable of holding my own and getting myself out of perilous situations, should I find myself in one. You're going to haul tomorrow, and I'm going to Duro Island. We'll meet for dinner."

They would. But he was also going with her whether she liked it or not. "I'll bring the coffee. Sleep well, Matlock."

He ended the call before she could protest and texted Cooper to let him know he had tomorrow off.

The man didn't argue.

As predicted, Joey had taken his mind off earlier events enough to shove them from the forefront of his mind. His tired muscles relaxed into the cushions. Covering his eyes with his arm, Jace concentrated on thoughts of Joey and drifted into sleep.

# TWENTY-THREE



The kelly green dress cascaded over her hips in a silky waterfall. Josephine had never worn anything so fine and likely never would again. She'd come home from school two weeks ago, furious that someone had signed her up for the Clam Bake Queen pageant without her knowledge. It had taken Mom all of two seconds to beam like the sun, strangle Josephine in a hug, and nearly deafen her with the excitement. She'd rarely seen Mom *that* happy and didn't have the heart to crush it. It would look good on a college application, so whatever. Mom had driven her to every formal wear shop in an eighty-mile radius for two days until they finally found this sparkly chiffon masterpiece.

Josephine had to admit, the way she looked had been worth the pain.

She examined each angle in the mirror, then tilted to get one last look at the back that draped low between her shoulder blades. Her nerves rattled like an empty tin can tied to a car bumper. She knew how to study. She knew how to work hard. How to fish. She did not know how to be appealing, confident, and extroverted.

If they'd have only told her what interview questions they were going to ask ahead of time, she'd have memorized perfect answers.

Try as she might, she couldn't recall a single response she'd given during that round.

She pressed a palm against her stomach. The active wear round had gone well, at least. Time would tell with the interview portion. If she could survive the evening gown competition, she had a good chance of winning a scholarship she could use at the Island Institute. To enroll in the spring, she *needed* that scholarship.

Music blared from the stage, and Ms. Creighton instructed them to line up off-stage in their correct positions and prepare to walk onstage the way they'd practiced. The curtains peeled back, and the MC announced the next portion of the competition.

Mazie took her place behind Josephine and squealed in excitement. Alice slid in front of Josephine, her gaze drifting up and down Josephine's dress, lip curled. Nothing like being sandwiched between two snobs wearing purple.

The instant her feet hit her mark on the stage, the rest of the round passed in a blur. She smiled. She held her chin high, tummy tucked. She even curled her fingers around her hip the way she'd watched the contestants do in the Miss America contests on television when she was a kid.

The entire competition was degrading and yet oddly catering to her ego. She stared into the darkness of the auditorium to combat the intensity of the stage lights and daydreamed about attending the Institute. Of studying marine life and all the ocean's possibilities. Of maybe, one day, becoming a conservationist or a harbormaster.

Her name echoed through the fringes of the white noise.

She blinked. The crowd roared. The other contestants surrounded her, smiling, urging her forward.

She'd won?

Or had she taken her daydream too far?

Before she knew what was happening, she was at the front of the stage with the MC, while Blaire Halloway, last year's winner, fitted the crown to Josephine's head. Crammed the attached combs into her scalp was more accurate.

Youch. She winced and accepted the bouquet of roses.

By the time it was over, the muscles in Josephine's face ached and she feared the spots in her vision caused by the lighting would permanently blind her. She wanted nothing more than to go home, wash the pounds of makeup off her face, twist her hair into a bun, and settle into a pair of sweatpants and a tee. Finish reading her Agatha Christie book. Grabbing her purse and bag, she strode from the dressing room.

At least she could say she'd driven home in style.

Her parents waited for her in the hallway. Mom bear-hugged her for the twentieth time. "We're so proud of our girl!"

"Thanks, Mom."

When Mom released her, Dad came in for a side-hug. "You were the prettiest one up there."

Josephine rolled her eyes playfully and waved off the comment. Whether any of it was true or not, she was the recipient of the scholarship and she was floating with joy.

Dad kept his arm wrapped around her shoulders as they walked down the hall and around the corner, almost bumping into a group of boys.

Jace, Jamar, and Quintin.

"Sorry, boys," Mom said.

Jace's gaze sharpened on Josephine, then melted downward and slid back up again, appreciation lighting his features. He swallowed.

Hard.

Dad let go of Josephine and patted Jace on the shoulder. "Breathe, son. Breathe."

Jace inhaled.

Jamar and Quintin snickered.

Delicious electricity zinged throughout Josephine's limbs and buzzed low in her belly. Jace found her attractive. That intense focus finally broke the barrier of all the competition and retrospection and saw *her*.

Mom chuckled, slipped her arm through Josephine's, and propelled them toward the exit.

"You guys go ahead," Josephine told Mom. "I'll meet you out there in a minute."

Dad frowned but Mom smiled knowingly. "Come on, Holden."

Mom prodded him outside.

Josephine stood in front of Jace, who still hadn't spoken. "Jace will catch up with you shortly," she said to Jamar and Quintin, who also seemed to be enjoying the view.

Jace raised an eyebrow. Once his friends had left, she leaned close and threw the words he'd said that day to her on the beach back at him. "I see I've rendered you speechless. Hopefully, it won't be the last time."

A wicked handsome grin lifted his mouth.

With a saucy flick of her head, Josephine walked away. Unbidden, she turned to find him still watching. Hope swelled her chest, and she stepped into the crisp night air.

Her mom handed her a jacket, but Josephine turned it down. She'd no need of extra layers tonight. The satisfaction of knowing Jace thought she looked hot kept her warm all the way home.

# Twenty-Four

Jace stood on the dock, hidden by the darkness of pre-dawn. He crossed his arms over his chest for warmth and waited for Joey to emerge from her office. Backlit by the halo of light radiating from the bulb above her door, she exited, locked the office, and started toward the dock dressed in full winter gear. Her independent streak was wicked cute, but her plans for today were about to change.

He waited until she was eight feet away to warn her of his presence. "Do your parents know where you are?"

She jumped and slapped a hand to her chest but didn't scream. Keys jangled as they hit the frosted ground. Her features turned murderous.

Her mouth puckered like a grape left out in the sun right before she charged. "Jace Eugene McClintock," she spat, whopping his arm.

Adorable. "Eugene?"

"Whatever your middle name is—I don't even care right now—how dare you almost give me a heart attack."

He looked her up and down. "You're young and healthy. And should you have a heart attack, I know exactly how to revive you."

He wiggled his eyebrows, grabbed her around the waist, and pulled her close.

She whacked him again.

Her attempt at a tantrum was ruined by the smile that broke through. "What are you doing here?"

"I came to tell you good morning." He kissed the tip of her cold nose. "And to go with you."

"Ugh. I told you I'll be fine on my own."

"Yeah, a lone woman going to a deserted island to confront a stranger we know nothing about and who we suspect is involved in illegal activity sounds like a formula for safety."

She frowned. "First of all, I'm tough. I'll be fine. Secondly, I'm not convinced he's involved in anything nefarious. Innocent until proven guilty. When I saw him yesterday, his boat was void of dredging equipment or anything else suspicious."

"I know you're tough. But when it comes to you, I'm not." He gazed at the vast dark water, unsure why he'd revealed that so soon.

She wrapped her arms around his middle and huffed. "You're infuriating."

"Thank you."

Joey giggled and pressed her forehead against his chest. "Okay, but I'm driving."

He rested his chin on her head, rubbing her back. "I'll agree to that. But we're taking my boat."

She looked up at him. "Why?"

"Because your fancy 27-foot Metal Shark with *harbormaster* emblazoned on the sides would only alert the guy. My boat will be any other boat on the water to him."

"My boat is fast and full of authority."

"My boat is already warmed up, equipped with hot coffee, breakfast and lunch—just in case—blankets, and the best-looking captain you're going to find in these parts."

Her mouth twisted. "Did I mention you're infuriating?"

"Did I mention how beautiful you are in the morning?"

"Nice try."

Jace smiled, kissed her cheek, and led them to his boat he'd tied at the end of the dock. A chilly breeze blew off the water, stirring her freshly washed hair. The lingering scent of her shampoo drove him wild.

"What is your middle name?" She allowed him to help her into the boat.

"Seavey, after my dad."

"Jace Seavey McClintock. I'll have to remember that for future scoldings." She wagged a finger at him. "Mine is Elaine. Josephine Elaine Rockwell. Don't forget it. The town may need that information one day when they erect a statue of me in the park."

Her wry chuckle echoed off the water.

"I'll make sure it says Joey."

"You would."

His wink was lost on her in the dark.

When they were both aboard and inside the warm cab, she shivered. "Oh, it feels good in here."

He turned down the heat. A few more minutes of that and his coat would have to go. "Here." He reached for the two stainless steel mugs on the lip of his dashboard and handed her one. "Fresh and strong."

She tugged off her gloves and shoved them into her coat pockets, then unscrewed the lid and sniffed. "Mmm. Perfect."

He reached to push the throttle, but she stopped him with her hand on his. "Thank you, Jace."

The mixture of gratitude and desire in her eyes tempted him to kill his earlier resolve of taking things slow and press his lips to hers. He reminded himself the outing was work related, and he needed to respect her time on the clock. Besides, once he took that plunge, he wanted to take his time.

"You're welcome. Ready?"

She nodded.

They drove twenty-five minutes northeast and stopped two nautical miles from Duro Island. The sun was still a good half hour from rising and it was a good spot to eat breakfast.

Jace flipped on the light, reached for the stool, and unfolded it for her to sit on. "Blanket?"

"I'm good for now."

He brought out a small rectangular box and handed it to her. "You get first pick."

She gave him a quizzical look then lifted the lid. "Donuts? Are these from Long's?"

"Yep."

"You drove all the way to Long Warf Bakery this morning?"

"I fell asleep on the couch last night and woke up with a crick in my neck. Couldn't go back to sleep, so I spent my time wisely. No big deal."

"Yes, it is. Not only is the gesture incredibly sweet but these logs are the best filled donuts on the planet."

"Is said gesture worthy of a kiss?"

"Hmm. . ." She blushed. Smiled.

"I'll practice patience and wait."

Tapping her chin, her gaze roamed around the box. A minute later, she still hadn't picked one.

"You're imagining what each one is going to taste like before you choose, aren't you?"

Biting her lower lip, she shrugged. "Maaaybeee?"

"I didn't know donuts could be so thought-provoking."

"I'm picky."

He rested his backside against the instrument panel, his arms getting tired of holding the box. "Is that why you're not married yet?"

She tipped her head to the side. "Forever is a long time. Best to be sure I can stand him that long."

Jace nodded his understanding.

"Will I ruin your day by choosing the vanilla cream filled?"

"Not if you'll grab the maple one for me."

"Deal."

He put the box away, grabbed the other stool, and sat across from her. She handed him the donut, and he bit off the end.

"This is wicked good." She licked powdered sugar off her lips.

He concentrated on eating and not the lusty way she ate her food. Otherwise, he'd throw patience overboard and taste her next.

They ate in comfortable silence as the sun crested the horizon. He could do this every morning, fill himself with food and her company. Contentedness settled deep in his bones. A feeling he hadn't experienced in a long time.

"It appears our suspect is staying indoors today." Josephine arched her back to work out the knots. The stool, though comfortable, was getting to her after three hours. At sunrise, they'd circled a wide berth around the island. Colin's boat was moored to the pathetic little dock barely jutting out of the water. They'd settled in an area far enough away to notice the boat leaving but not so close Colin would be suspicious.

Jace turned the volume on the radio down and agreed. "Weather service is saying a light storm around two."

She leaned toward the windshield for a better view. "That means there's a fifty percent chance of full sun and a fifty percent chance of a tsunami."

Jace lifted his travel cup to his mouth and threw his head back. Swallowed. "Out."

He tossed the cup into a duffel bag.

"I ran out an hour ago. I say we head back." After all that coffee she had to pee.

"I say we shanghai the island and find out what he's up to. I don't trust him."

"I appreciate your enthusiasm, but the island is his personal property. We can't trespass just to harass him. I'd have to find proof of wrongdoing and then work with the police for a warrant to search his boat and premises."

He sighed. "I still don't trust the guy."

"In this country we try to live by 'innocent until proven guilty.'" As soon as the words left her mouth, she wanted to slap herself. "I'm sorry. That came out before I realized how insensitive it was."

Jace shook his head. "It's fine."

She curled her fingers around his forearm. "Any updates?"

He shrugged. "Ran into Doc Greenwell yesterday. Apparently, you're not the only one who reads the *Bangor Times*."

"Oh, no."

"I'm surprised it hasn't come out before now."

Josephine rested her head on his shoulder, hating that he had to go through this. He placed his hand over hers and squeezed. "One more hour?"

"One more. Then I need to head back. I have work to do, among other things."

"Like what, raising your feet on your desk and taking a nap?"

She sat up, mouth open. "Is that what you think I do all day?"

"Well, yeah, why do you think I wanted the job?"

"I thought it was because you knew I wanted it."

He scooted in front of her, so their knees were touching. "What you didn't realize is that I really wanted you."

"Liar."

He put his hands out. "Honest."

"What changed?"

"What do you mean?"

"Growing up, you couldn't stand me. You were always doing something to torture me or rub it in when you got a higher grade than me. What changed?"

"It's a kindergarten mentality. If a boy gives a girl too much trouble, it's because he likes her."

"You're saying your meanness was really a sign of affection?" Coulda fooled her.

"Exactly."

"That's insane."

"It's what guys do."

"You weren't being mean to that blonde supermodel you dated in college. Does that mean you didn't like her much?"

He leaned back. "Which blonde?"

"Oh, there was more than one?"

He laughed. "I just mean, which blonde? I don't remember dating a blonde."

"I remember."

"Huh?" Jace cocked his head, waiting.

She rubbed her forehead. She hadn't meant to confess her secret but here it was. "The spring of your freshman year, I went to Boston."

His brows rose. "You did?"

"I wanted to see what city life was like. And while I was there, I may have tried to find you."

He blinked.

"I went with Ciara. We asked around campus until we found someone who knew you. They said you were probably in the library. Ciara started chatting up a guy in an athletic uniform and told me to go ahead."

"And?"

"I found you."

When she didn't say anything else, he put his hands out.

Even now, the memory made her want to pluck the woman's hair out. She'd always had a jealous streak when it came to Jace. Even if she didn't like to admit it. She confessed to hiding in the stacks while she worked up the courage to face him and then found him making out with a blonde Barbie look-alike.

He sat, stunned. "I don't remember that."

"I never let you know I was there."

He scooted closer. "If you went to Boston to hunt me down, that must've meant something."

He wanted her to elaborate. Dare she?

"It meant that I've always had a wild crush on you too."

"Wild? Ooh, I like the sound of that." He reached for her hands. "Why didn't you ever say anything?"

"And risk humiliation when the guy who's openly mean to me rejects me? Why didn't you ever say anything?"

"You were mean right back. And I thought we already established that pubescent boys are insane? There's medical evidence."

She giggled and tangled her fingers in his. "Oh, I was so jealous of that blonde."

"Seeing as I don't remember her, she obviously meant nothing. As horrible as that sounds." He grabbed the legs of her stool and yanked it closer, his knees cradling the outside of hers. "I was never serious about any of the women I dated. I was too busy living my dream and none of those women challenged me like you."

"Keep going."

"The pursuit, the conversations, everything was too easy."

She could get lost in those blue eyes all day. "Go on."

He moved closer still. One hand came to rest on her leg while the other grazed her neck before his fingers dove into her hair. Her heart pounded harder with every inch of space that closed between them. "Do you think we're ready for this?" she whispered.

His gaze toggled between her eyes and her lips. "I am, but only if you think you can handle it."

Challenge thrown.

Their breaths mingled. His lips hovered over hers until she thought she'd scream. He was still torturing her, even now. And it was pure bliss.

He kissed her top lip, more nip than anything, tugging gently. Then he leaned farther and allowed his lips to dance over hers, controlled and reckless. She gave into him. To the experience. The taste of him was greater than anything she'd imagined.

Her fingers trailed up and down his neck, into the folds of his shirt, and back again. He opened his mouth to kiss her more fully, sending heat through her core and goosebumps up her arms.

She loved this man. His drive, his integrity, his heart. For years she'd loved him. She wanted the privilege of kissing him every day. If their relationship didn't follow through, she wasn't sure she'd ever recover.

He broke away and pressed his forehead to hers, his breath fast and heavy. He cleared his throat. "I think we both won this time."

She closed her eyes to revel in the moment, knowing she'd come back to it later.

And several times after that.

Jace cleared his throat again and pushed her stool away with his foot. Wiped his palms along the thighs of his jeans. "Want to step on the deck and get some air?"

"Good idea."

He took her hand and together they stepped out into the biting air. The clouds had grown darker in the time that had passed. The waves rowdier. How long had they been kissing? It had only seemed like minutes, but—

"Look." Jace pointed.

Colin's boat had moved away from the island. Jace handed her the binoculars, and she homed in on the unmarked boat vessel. They followed him from a distance for ten minutes before coming to an idle when Colin did. Dressed in scuba gear with a faded yellow tank on his back, he stepped onto the side rail. Was that a shovel in his hand? A second later, he disappeared into the water.

He was crazy! It was too cold to be diving. He'd become hypothermic within twenty minutes. And seeing as he'd taken a shovel with him, he planned to be down there awhile.

She handed Jace the binoculars. "Fire it up. Get me as close as you can to that boat."

# TWENTY-FIVE

Josephine braced against the cabin wall at the oncoming swell. The clouds had picked up pace across the sky, the shades growing in intensity. The weather system was still claiming it to be a light thunderstorm, but a warning in her gut blared.

She should never have agreed to take Jace's boat. Hers had speed, sonar, and a direct radio line to the Coast Guard. This oversight was rookie and unprofessional, and she wouldn't allow her heart to interfere with her job again.

Rain pelted the windshield as the boat crested a wave. Jace turned the wipers on high speed and raced toward Colin's boat.

"Get me as close as you can." She opened the cabin door and went out to the starboard deck. Rain, cold and unyielding, plastered her hair to the sides of her face and soaked into every thread she was wearing. Misery at every level.

Jace yelled her name, but she ignored him. His kiss had been more blissful than she'd imagined, but she had a job to do, and he was going to let her do it.

As soon as Jace's boat was close enough, she leapt onto Colin's.

"Dang it, Joey," Jace yelled and banged his palm against the wheel.

On the other side, Colin broke the surface and pulled the regulator from his mouth. He tossed the shovel onto the deck, nearly ramming it into her foot. He must've heard them coming. The man hoisted himself halfway onto the deck and froze. Shoving his mask upward, his gaze traveled up her legs to her face.

He stared at her as if she were a ghost. He blinked rain from his eyes. Eyes that held a glassy sheen. She bent and stretched out her hand. He gripped it, and she tugged him aboard. The boat dipped and swayed, first with his weight and then Jace's as he jumped aboard from the opposite side. Colin collapsed onto a built-in seat. His skin was pale, movements sluggish as he removed the air cylinder and tugged off his hood.

"What's the shovel for?" Josephine shivered.

"I lost something."

"What?"

"That's my business." His breaths were labored.

"Digging the ocean floor is not permitted."

"I'm not digging."

"Are you responsible for the cutting of ropes on lobster traps?"

Colin scowled. "No. But trespassing on someone else's boat without permission or a warrant is not permitted, even if you are the harbormaster." He turned his head in the other direction and released a violent cough. Dark circles marred the skin beneath his eyes.

She was no doctor, but she'd bet her next paycheck this man was sick. Best they all get out of the rain. "Whatever you're looking for can't be so important you have to search for it in the middle of a storm."

Unless it was valuable.

Agony clouded his gaze. "It is."

A cough came again and this time he gagged over the side of the boat. He stood and gasped for air. A gust of wind knocked the boats together.

"Since you own Duro Island, I gather that's your cabin on the other side?"

Colin nodded. She turned toward Jace, her foot slipping on the slick deck. The temperature wasn't much over freezing point and could cause the rain to turn to ice. "I'm driving his boat back. Follow us."

She turned and Jace caught her arm. "I'll drive his boat back. *You* follow *us*."

It wasn't worth arguing over as every minute in this mess would take them all closer to sickness. She jumped aboard Jace's boat, darted into the warm cabin, and wiped the rain from her eyes as best she could with wet hands. After Colin's boat moved ahead, she navigated the *Hiley Mae II* toward the pathetic dock on Duro Island.

The boat lifted and dipped with the momentum of a carnival ride. Leaping out to moor the boat, the temperamental wind lashed at the rope, making it difficult to secure. Colin trudged overboard, coughing and shivering.

Rain pelted Josephine in painful bursts. Jace grabbed her arm. "His boat is secure enough. Let's go home."

"He needs help. He's very sick."

Jace shook the water from his face and shielded his eyes to access the man stumbling up the small rise to his cabin. Concern lined Jace's mouth. The battle was clear: give into his instincts and get more information or let Colin take care of himself and get them back to Granite Harbor.

Jace grunted. "If he doesn't agree to go back with us in my boat, there's nothing we can do. We leave in five minutes."

"Look at this place. We can't just leave him here, sick." She waved a hand at the dilapidated cabin, unable to comprehend someone lived in it. "Something isn't right about this situation, and I need to know what it is."

"You can't save everyone, Joey. Especially if they don't want to be saved." Jace dropped his head. Rivulets of rain created trenches in his hair. He grunted. "Help me moor my boat."

Together, they secured the vessel and raced toward Colin's front door. She knocked and barged through without an invitation. The cabin was nearly dark, light barely filtering through the windows. Colin sat in a chair at his table, dripping puddles onto the wavy floor. "May we come in?"

"You already did." The man motioned with a quick wave of his hand, attempting to hold back another cough.

The cabin had three rooms from what she could see. An open area with a tiny kitchen on one end and a fireplace on the other, one bedroom, one bathroom, and a loft that had disintegrated long ago. At one time it would've been a great cabin, but now it was one disrepair away from needing condemned.

Colin's shivering accelerated to near convulses. Jace pushed back his wet hair and looked around. "Start a fire." He pointed to a stack of wood by the fireplace. "We all need to get warm and dry, as fast as possible."

Josephine started toward the woodpile. She trusted Jace to know what needed to be done for all their sakes.

"The m-m-m matches are in the c-c cabinet." Colin indicated the one above the kitchen sink.

She retrieved the small box then mounded some kindling she found in a metal box by the stacked wood before arranging the logs. The ashes were still putting off heat, and she hoped that would work in her favor. She, too, was shivering, and the breaths she heaved at the tiny flame she'd kindled came out unsteady.

Behind her, Colin protested at needing help, telling Jace he was fine.

Jace knelt in front of the man. "I can tell by looking at you, you're not fine. You owe this lady some answers, but first I need to see what's going on with you. May I?"

"What are you, a d-d-doctor?"

Jace looked down at the floor.

"Yes, he is. And a great one, too." Josephine went back to tending the fire, unwilling to witness Jace's reaction. He'd likely be livid with her for putting him in another situation to help someone when he wasn't supposed to, but what else could they do?

Depending on how angry Colin was after all this, he may go after her job too.

"F-f-fine." Colin allowed Jace to help him peel off the upper half of his wet suit.

She hoped it wouldn't take long to warm the room but judging by the draft she felt squeezing through the walls, her wish was likely wasted. She hadn't been this cold since the day five years ago when Ciara had talked her into joining the local Polar Bear Club. In a moment of temporary insanity, she'd followed the herd into the icy Atlantic and had nearly gone into shock. It had taken her weeks to feel warm again.

The spark finally blazed, and the kindling crackled, sending tendrils of smoke up the chimney. Jace lifted Colin's eyelids and studied his pupils, then ran his fingertips along Colin's neck. "We need to get the rest of this suit off you."

"T-t-the s-suitcase." Colin's arm shook as he pointed toward the bedroom. Josephine headed that way.

"He has a fever," Jace said. "See if you can find him dry clothes and socks. And maybe a blanket," he called after her.

It was weird going through a stranger's things in a cabin that had no electricity in the middle of a monsoon. The window leaked, creating a small puddle near the foot of his tidy cot. She found what items she could and took them to Jace. "I'll just be over here. Let me know when you're done."

She went back to the fire, adding another log. After a few minutes, footsteps shuffled closer as Jace helped Colin to the fire. She was shocked at how much Colin had aged since their conversation in the diner. His movements were akin to someone twenty-five years older than himself, and the pallor of his skin was concerning.

Seated in a folding camp chair, Colin leaned over and coughed until he gagged. She winced. The lines marring Jace's face spoke of the gravity of Colin's condition. "What is it?" she whispered.

Jace took her by the elbow and led her into the kitchen area. "Without a chest x-ray, a stethoscope, and without knowing his medical history, I can't say one-hundred percent assuredly, but it's likely pneumonia."

Another round of coughing ensued.

"He was coughing when I talked to him the other day too." She shivered. "Coughing is good, right? Doesn't it help keep the lungs clear?"

Jace sighed. "Let's hope."

Lightning flashed, followed by a boom of thunder and the howling wind. Rain hit the glass blowing horizontally. "We can't stay here but we can't go back out in this either. So much for a light storm."

Jace shrugged off his coat. "We don't have a choice. We have to stay. At least until the storm calms."

The skin on his forehead bunched. Jace unzipped her jacket and slipped it off her shoulders as if it was the most natural thing in the world. "Take off what you can and stay by the fire until you're dry. No sense in you getting sick too."

Her heart gave a little hiccup that went unnoticed as he searched the wonky cabinets for any tea or coffee. Anything to warm their insides.

Watching him, her mind tracked back to their earlier kiss, which heated her up quite nicely. The sensation was short-lived as her wet clothes sent a chill through her with every movement. She helped rummage through the cabinets and collected three cans of vegetable soup, bread, peanut butter, and a box of instant coffee. Gak, were they that desperate?

"Here we go." Jace found a plastic tote full of enameled bowls, spoons, and mugs. Some kind of camping set it seemed. At the bottom rested a small cast iron Dutch oven. How long had Colin been living like this? At least she assumed he lived here alone. There weren't enough belongings in the place to indicate there was another person.

"Hey." Jace hooked a finger beneath her chin. "I'm going back to get the First-Aid kit and thermal blanket from my boat. Heat up the soup over the fire and stay there. I want you warm."

"Hurry. Then you can help keep me warm." She gave him a playful shove.

"Gladly." Jace shoved his arms into his wet coat, walked to the door, and grimaced before dashing out.

She gathered the items and went to the fire. Colin stared at the flames, shivering beneath the thin blanket. If only they could take him back to Granite Harbor. He could get the medical attention he needed, and she could finish working. She had a grant to finish writing for the Widows of Drowned Captains Fund. She had neighbors who would notice she didn't come home. Parents who'd be calling to check on her. As old-fashioned as it may seem, people would notice their overnight stay together.

Rain pelted the parts of the roof that had been replaced with metal. The sounds of drips in less sturdy places mingled with the crackling of the fire, the only light source in the room. Nothing but a dark gray haze lie outside the dingy window. She couldn't help feeling trapped.

She didn't like it.

Jace raced in, half-drowned. His boots made a sucking sound as he walked. "There's definitely no going back until that lets up. I dropped the anchors. I also radioed in our situation, so no one worries about us. I told Jefferson to inform your parents."

"Thank you." She smiled to be polite but was far from cheerful.

Jace tossed the items onto the floor, then peeled off his wet coat and sweatshirt. His black t-shirt clung to his torso, revealing a trim yet muscular core. Next went his shoes and socks. Dirt from the floor clung to the bottoms of his wet feet as he walked.

"Gross, I know, but it's best to keep warm, dry feet." He indicated that she should do the same.

Colin held shaky hands toward the fire. She removed her shoes and socks as well. Jace removed the thermal blanket from its plastic packaging, removed the one Colin was using, and wrapped the new one tightly around the man.

"Have you been cooking over the fire since you've been here?" She pointed to the swinging hook attached to the stonework. The mortar was crumbling but otherwise the structure appeared sound.

"Y-y-yes," Colin said in a near whisper.

The lone word took such effort. Using the can opener, she cut away the lids and dumped the soup into the Dutch oven. The pot was heavier than expected and she hoped the hook was as solid as it looked.

Before long, the scent of vegetable soup filled the room and steam rolled from the spout on the kettle. Instant coffee was the equivalent of imitation chocolate, but she kept the thought to herself. This was Colin's domain, and she would be respectful. However, the safety of these waters was her domain, and she hoped he'd give her the same respect in return.

"Will you please share what you've been doing out there if it isn't dredging or cutting ropes?" She sat on the blanket Jace had placed on the floor in front of the fire, bowl of soup in hand. The area was finally starting to warm.

"S-something." Colin cleared his throat. "My wife placed years ago." His voice was raspy and the gurgle in his chest made her want to cough too, but his shivers weren't as violent as before.

"She buried it on the ocean floor?"

"No. In a sealed b-bottle. Heavy enough to stay anchored but with a buoy to help me remember where it's at. I come at times to make sure it's s-still here."

"Why can't you find it now?" Jace asked.

Another boom of thunder. She jumped.

"The buoy's gone." Colin looked away and stared into the flames as if he'd traveled back in time.

"How are you trying to locate the bottle. Sonar?"

"Yes." Another cough wracked Colin's body.

"Is your wife here with you?" Jace asked.

Colin shook his head. "She p-passed away a long time a-ago." He blinked rapidly at his bowl of soup. "What's in that bottle is all I have left of her."

His words cracked at the last.

So that's why he'd risked his health to find it. But then why not take the contents of the bottle with him years ago and not chance it in the elements? "Do you have any children?"

Someone they could call if his health became dire.

He wheezed before speaking. "A daughter."

"Does she live in Ohio as well?"

Colin's head lolled back, and he stared at the ceiling. A fat tear rolled down his cheek. "She's in a better place."

He'd lost his wife and daughter. Her heart ached for the stranger, understanding the loss. At least she'd had her adopted parents to help fill the void. Even if knowing her birth father hadn't wanted her still haunted her security at times.

"I know who's c-cutting your ropes." Colin held the bowl to his lips to drink the last of the soup.

Her senses went on alert, and she leaned toward him. "Who?"

Colin burrowed deeper into the thermal blanket. It was doing its job because his tremors were less intense. An eternity passed before he said, "Donald Sinkankas."

Jace frowned. "The governor?"

Colin nodded.

"Maine's governor is the one cutting ropes?" The man's fever had made him delusional.

Colin coughed and handed Jace his empty bowl. "He's running on climate legislation next term. His goal is to devastate the fishing industry to prove his offshore wind development program won't affect an already dying trade and his policies will be approved. He's hired a man named Abner Gannon to cut ropes and make it look as if the fishermen are warring against one another."

This time, Colin's cough produced substance that dribbled on his blanket. He took a deep breath and swallowed. "I have v-video evidence. It's on my boat, as well as a notebook with detailed information. You can h-have it."

The poor man's voice had faded to a near whisper. She opened her mouth to ask how he'd obtained the evidence and how he'd tied this Abner fella to the governor, but Jace put a hand on her arm. "Let him rest. We can get answers later."

Jace was right of course. Though patience had never been her strongest quality.

Colin closed his eyes. Her phone read four-thirty, but darkness was quickly swallowing the cabin. A thousand questions ran through her mind but she filed them away for later. The flickering flames danced shadows across Jace's face. He stared into the fire, rubbing his thumb across the back of her hand. The warmth of the fire and the rhythm of the rain tugged at her subconscience.

Warm lips pressed against her forehead. "You sleep. I've got you."

With a last look at Colin dozing, she snuggled into the hollow of Jace's neck and closed her eyes. If she was going to nap, at least it would be in Jace's arms.

# Twenty-Six

The storm was losing momentum. Jace worked the kinks from his neck and arched his back, stirring Joey who'd fallen asleep using his thigh for a pillow. They'd been sitting by the fire for hours waiting for the weather to break. Midnight was too late to get Colin into the town clinic and the man refused a hospital, as his VA insurance wouldn't cover out of state.

Jace was all too familiar with insurance red tape. Especially when it wrapped around his neck like a noose. His court date was fast approaching. He'd held two Zoom meetings with Findley since his scolding to go over strategy and paperwork. All the collected evidence leaned in Jace's favor, but that didn't mean a jury would see it that way.

Joey sat up and blinked. "Is he okay?"

She glanced at Colin lying on the cot they'd set in front of the fireplace, where he'd slept in between coughs for hours.

Jace teased his fingertips over the ends of her hair. "He's holding up. Sorry to wake you, but I'm getting stiff."

He didn't mention that Colin's fever was raging near a dangerous level. The steam from a simmering pot by the cot sprinkled with crushed cough drops from his First-Aid kit helped to loosen some of the man's congestion. Keeping the lungs active was a huge part of recovery, and if the man could stay strong until he received antibiotics, he might be all right.

"Sounds like the storm is moving out." Joey rubbed sleepy eyes. "Should we take him into town?"

"Our best option is to stay the night and go in the morning. We'll take him to Doc Greenwell. He's good at working with patients who struggle to afford care. I'm sure he'll come up with some arrangement for Colin as well."

Joey yawned. Her hair had air-dried and was matted against her face. At least their clothes were finally dry. Dripping sounds added to the cadence of the fire. They'd used every spare bowl or cup they could find to catch the drops falling around them. Where it was obvious Colin had done some repairs, it hadn't been enough to sustain the cabin long term.

She scooted beneath his arm and snuggled in the hollow of his neck. "Do you think he'll be all right?" she whispered.

"He's pretty bad, but I've seen worse. We've done everything we can do with what we have. We'll get him to port as soon as possible." Jace kissed her head and ran his fingertips up and down her arm.

He loved the privilege of touching her like this. She was silent so long he thought she'd fallen back asleep. Then she ran her palm up his chest and used it as leverage to push away and see into his face. "He has no one."

Jace studied Colin to make sure he was asleep before answering. "I can't imagine."

"I feel horrible for accusing him of cutting ropes when all he wanted was to find the last connection he has to his wife."

"You were only doing your job."

"I should have handled the whole thing more professionally. But also a good thing I didn't." She looked again at Colin. "Otherwise, he might have killed himself looking for that bottle."

"What do you think is in it?"

"I don't know, but I hope he finds it. Not having a tether to the past when you need one is devastating. Empty. Even when there are good things to fill the void, it doesn't fill it completely."

How he knew it. His looming court date surfaced again.

"Tell me." He stroked her cheek.

She sighed. "When I was six, I overheard my parents arguing about something. I was bored and nosy, so I crept to their closed bedroom door and listened. I heard my mom saying that my birth father had no right to come back into my life when he didn't want me and willingly signed over his rights when I was a baby. I didn't understand what signing rights meant but I knew what she meant about him not wanting me. I put the other pieces together when I got older."

Jace froze. "I thought both of your parents passed away in the accident."

"Until that point, I'd thought so too. But it was just my mother. My father—if I can call the man that—gave me up when she died. Couldn't handle me on his own." Tears sprang to her eyes. "My own father didn't want me. That does something to a girl."

Jace pulled her against him and held, leaving no doubt he wanted her. "Did they ever know you overheard?"

"No. They were always good about keeping my birth mom part of my life by showing me pictures and even celebrating her birthday every year. They never once said anything about my dad.

I didn't ask. I didn't want to hear details about how the man who'd given me life decided I wasn't worth keeping around."

Jace took her face in his hands, everything that he'd always loved and once despised about her becoming clear. With intensity, he stared deep into her eyes, willing his next words to build a solid foundation beneath her. "The man's an idiot. Having you could only gain the most profitable of returns."

She closed her eyes as if trying to absorb every word. Shrugged. "If he'd have only given me a chance, maybe I wouldn't have been as bad as he'd thought."

Realization hit him between the eyes. "Is that why you work so hard to prove your worth to others? Look at me." He waited until she opened her eyes. "You. Are. Worthy. Just for being you."

Her eyes turned to liquid pools, and she gave a breathy laugh. "No one's ever put it quite like that before."

"Get used to hearing it." With a quick glance to make sure they didn't have an audience, he pressed his lips to hers. Joey was everything that was right and good. She kept him focused and pushed him to achieve things he thought beyond himself. Now here she was, the one woman he thought he'd never have, needing him.

Joey may not have the past she longed for, but he wanted a part in giving her the future she deserved. He just had to get this lawsuit behind him, so he'd be worth her investment.

Josephine poured water over the embers in the fireplace. They hissed and steamed. She hated to leave the cabin cold and uninviting for Colin's return but with his condition they had no idea how long he'd be gone. There was a good chance he'd go to the hospital whether Colin wanted to or not.

Jace was outside readying his boat for the thirty minute ride back to town. Colin was sitting in the camp chair, eyes closed and slumped forward. She grabbed the dry coat she'd found in his suitcase in the bedroom and helped him into it. The fabric was lightweight, and it wouldn't keep him nearly warm enough, but it was better than nothing.

She knelt to get a better grip on the zipper. The fussy metal finally cooperated on the third tug. She zipped until it reached his sternum where she wrapped a T-shirt around his neck like a scarf. As she went to zip the coat the rest of the way, he clasped her hand with a strength that surprised her and pressed it against his chest. She started to pull away, but his eyes didn't communicate harm. They radiated sadness.

"I'm s-s-sorry."

"Don't apologize for getting sick. We'll make sure you're cared for. After that, I'll get your statement and evidence regarding the governor, and we'll come up with a plan to find your bottle."

Or at least try to.

He shook his head, and a single tear slipped from the corner of his eye. "I'm so sorry."

Her skin pebbled. If he wasn't apologizing for his sickness, then what was he referring to?

He released her hand and looked away.

A knot in the pit of her stomach told her there was more to Colin than she realized. Then again, the man was likely hallucinating from fever.

Jace walked in, blasting cold air into the room. "Ready."

She stood. "Any damage?"

"Dings and dents but nothing that'll prevent us from getting back. I got the video equipment and notebook of evidence for you to report to the Coast Guard. Be careful on the dock. The temperature dropped, glazing the dock and boat deck in a thin layer of frost."

"Thank you, Jace."

One on each side of Colin, they helped him to stand, bracing most of his weight. Jace blew out the lantern and they inched to the dock. Colin was convulsing with shivers by the time they got him settled into the boat. He mumbled that he wanted off the boat and kept trying to stand but Jace held him down with a steady hand while he eased them into deeper water before pushing the throttle. Colin finally settled but the rattle in his chest grew worse with every mile they put behind them.

After what felt like hours, they reached Granite Harbor's dock, bringing relief to Joey's chest. Jace tied off. Curious faces watched as they helped Colin to Jace's truck. At least now there'd be witnesses to their story and hopefully quell any rumors that they'd sneaked away to spend the night together.

Jace practically had to lift Colin into his truck. Colin managed to scoot to the middle, and Josephine settled beside him. The engine protested but finally roared to life. Jace let it warm for a few minutes before driving away.

Doc Greenwell didn't start seeing patients until eight, but his Cadillac was in the parking lot. One look at Colin and surely Doc would make an exception.

Jace pulled up to the curb, and she jumped out and ran to the glass-paned door. Locked. A receptionist sat behind her desk typing on her computer. Joey knocked. The receptionist looked up, glanced at the clock behind her, then went back to typing.

Great. Joey knocked again, this time more urgently. The receptionist frowned, stood, then answered the door.

Alice Underwood. Well, Alice Preston, now. "We don't open until eight o'clock."

"This is urgent."

"Then go to the nearest hospital or dial 9-1-1."

The woman's voice sounded like a recording, and after a restless night in a dilapidated cabin, it grated on Josephine's nerves. "I found a fisherman while patrolling who needs help. We believe he has pneumonia, and he's in bad condition. We came to ask Doc Greenwell to work him in."

"We?" She looked behind Josephine to Jace, who was helping Colin out of the truck.

"Oh, stop it, Alice. His condition is serious and all you can do is ask stupid questions like you hold some kind of authority? Stop being petty and get the doctor."

Alice scowled the way she did the night Josephine had won the title of Clam Bake Queen, only this time her frown produced fine wrinkles. Would the woman ever stop acting like a teenager?

Jace's face turned to stone. "And if you're not going to do it out of the kindness of your heart, tell Doc that Doctor McClintock is referring this patient to him under code 5194. And be quick. You don't want to be in violation of that."

Alice's face turned red. "Please wait inside. I'll get the doctor."

Her monotone voice spoke of indifference, but at least she was moving. For years, Joey had wanted to knock Alice off her high horse. Today seemed like a good day to do it.

Colin was shaking. A few minutes later Doc Greenwell entered the waiting room, a puzzled expression on his face. "How can I help you?"

Joey opened her mouth to speak, but Jace started an explanation that included medical terms she'd never heard before. It was best to let him handle it anyway. It was all she could do to keep rooted in this spot and not jump to Jace's defense with the high-and-mighty Alice.

Doc Greenwell took over and helped Jace get Colin to an examination room. Muffled voices sounded from behind the door. Alice glared at Josephine from behind her desk. Josephine half expected the woman to stick her tongue out any moment. Some people never changed.

Time to grow up.

Tucking her hands into her pockets, she imagined how she must look after air-drying from yesterday's baptism and getting little sleep. "His name is Colin Warner. He's a veteran from Ohio and doesn't have insurance that'll cover him here. Do what you can, please."

A door opened and Jace stepped out. He nodded to Alice and then held the exit door open for Josephine. "Doc's got it from here."

With one last look toward the closed exam room, she followed Jace to the still running truck. Colin was in good hands, but something inside of her hated to leave the man without a familiar face.

"What's code 5194?" she asked as they pulled out of the parking lot.

"I don't know. I made it up."

She snickered, remembering how Alice had snapped into action at the mention of it. Served her right.

"I told Doc about the evidence but didn't go into detail. I though it wise to have a witness that Colin gave us permission to take his belongings. Colin confirmed it with Doc."

"Good idea. Thanks for having my back."

He kissed her temple. "Thanks for having mine."

Jace drove to her house and parked in front. It was Saturday, so she'd start the weekend with a hot shower, a few hours of sleep, and a hearty meal. She'd call to check on Colin later when she walked back to her office to pick up her vehicle.

She unlocked her seatbelt. "I'm not sure what the women in Boston like, but I don't want any more dates like that again."

Jace smiled as he handed her the notebook and video equipment. Exhaustion added to the lines around his eyes. "It wasn't all horrible, was it?"

The memory of their kisses sent heat flooding into her cheeks. "There's one part I'd be willing to do again."

"Good." He leaned in her direction to kiss her but stopped. "We'll pick up where we left off after you've done something with that hair."

He winked, and she slugged him on the arm. Laughing, he pulled her to him and kissed her in a way that left her practically floating to her front door.

# TWENTY-SEVEN

THE NEXT WEEK PASSED in a blur as Josephine reported the rope cutting crime to the Coast Guard Investigative Service, provided the evidence, and issued statements to the Department of Homeland Security and the DOJ. Everyone in town was curious as to why the Feds had presence in Granite Harbor but it was perfect timing with word of Jace's malpractice suit now out in the open. While people were talking plenty about their golden boy's secret, the wild—and untrue—rumors regarding the Feds detracted a lot of attention off Jace.

Josephine stretched before flopping onto her couch. The overcast morning had allowed Josephine to sleep in, but she was still tired. She planned to pass the rest of her Saturday on the couch by the fireplace with a blanket over her lap and Jack Sparrow curled in the corner of the hearth. The feral cat still wouldn't let her near him. Though he still jumped and fled at every noise, he'd at least decided she was trustworthy enough to occupy the same room. Progress.

Jace teased her about the cat's name, but it fit him perfectly. The tom's fur was the same shade as the Disney pirate's hair and hung in mats around his ears like dreadlocks. Natural eyeliner surrounded mischievous eyes. His gait was uneven too, whether from birth or the injury she wasn't sure.

The only thing that would make this day of binge-watching Father Dowling Mysteries better would be Jace. They'd been inseparable the past week, other than work hours, of course. She physically ached with anticipation of seeing him when they were apart.

*"You. Are. Worthy. Just for being you."*

Since that night, his words had echoed across her heart and circled, trying to find a place to land. She believed he meant them, but she wasn't sure she believed the words herself. Proving her worth made her presence necessary. It made it impossible for anyone to throw her away.

The weight of validation was also a very heavy thing to carry. Maybe she could learn to dismantle the load one piece at a time. Starting with letting go of past hurt from Jace.

She was finally the subject of his laser focused drive, and it caused every cell in her being to hum with delight. She wanted to completely give into it, but the invisible force of insecurity held her back. How were people viewing their relationship now that they knew Jace's secret? What would happen if Jace was indicted? Could they build a future around that?

Would this affect her standing in the community? Her job?

Jace wasn't guilty of malpractice. She knew it to her core. But what if a jury wasn't convinced? She couldn't date a man from a prison cell.

Her phone rang, yanking her from the encumberment of borrowing tomorrow's trouble. Jack Sparrow jumped to his feet. His fur spiked into a kitty mohawk at his shoulders. He growled her direction, then tore out of the room. She didn't recognize the number on the screen. Please not another interview.

"Hello?"

"Hi, is this Josephine?"

"Yes."

"This is Linda Mulroney from the historical society. I believe we may have found the documents you've been looking for."

Josephine paused Father Dowling mid-sentence and threw her legs over the couch. She tugged at the blanket when it tangled around her feet, relieved this didn't have anything to do with the government. "Great."

"It's a logbook from 1940-1948. It lists the area's fishermen, the names of their boats, and their buoy patterns. It doesn't say anything about the Christmas memorial ceremony Ms. Fletcher spoke of, but I think it can provide you with some answers."

Josephine's heart thumped with adrenaline. "Wonderful. May I pick it up?"

"Unlike the library, our materials cannot leave this building. They're of rich historical significance and are insured as such."

"Of course." How silly of her to ask.

"However, you are more than welcome to stop by and look. We are pleased to assist you in any way we can."

"I appreciate that. Are you open today?"

"Only for another hour."

"I'll be right there."

Deciding her joggers and oversized hoodie would suffice, she set up the fireplace screen, grabbed her purse and keys, slipped her feet into sneakers, and drove to the historical society outside of town with speed that would rival the Flash.

The building was nothing more than a modular-type home, housing a large area with various items displayed behind glass, an Employees Only restroom, and what appeared to be a couple of offices. The modernity of it seemed sacrilegious to its purpose.

A petite woman around her mother's age stepped out from one of the offices and slipped her red glasses atop her head. "Welcome. How may I help you?"

"I'm Josephine Rockwell. Are you Linda?"

The woman smiled. "I am. Wow, that was fast."

"I'm a woman on a mission."

Linda chuckled. "This way."

Josephine followed Linda into the next room.

"Here it is. I've set out gloves to prevent your skin oils from transferring onto the page. I've also laid out pencil and paper should you need to copy information."

"Thank you. I know you're set to close soon. Would it be okay to take pictures with my phone? I promise to keep the flash off."

Linda's lips twisted in thought. "That should be fine."

For the next forty minutes, Joey carefully turned pages and took pictures of each one with her phone. By the time she was finished, she'd be lucky to have any photo storage left.

Linda poked her head into the room. "I apologize Josephine, but we close in five minutes."

Josephine took one more photo. "I think I have what I need."

She'd gotten all the records from 1942 to 1946.

"Well, should you need further assistance don't hesitate to call. We'll only be open by appointment from now until April first, but we're always happy to help enrich the harbor's history."

Joey peeled off the gloves and tossed them in the trashcan, thanked Linda again, and drove home.

Her living room was still warm despite the dying embers. She kicked off her sneakers and called for Jack Sparrow but wasn't surprised when he didn't greet her. Maybe with time, he'd learn to trust.

After adding more logs, she un-paused Father Dowling, releasing him from his frozen state. While he finished explaining the murderer's motive to Sister Stephanie, she dialed Jace and hoped he was back from the water.

"Hiya, beautiful." His husky voice set her insides to buzzing.

She smiled. "How was your day?"

"Freezing. Want to warm me up?"

The buoy bell clanged in the background. "Fire's crackling and I've a large stash of leftover Halloween candy."

"Woman, I've been busting my rump all day in the cold. I need something of sustenance. And a hot shower. Why don't you come to my place? I'll grill steaks and baked potatoes."

"You're cooking? I'm in."

"Bring your stash of Halloween candy."

An hour later she pulled into Jace's driveway. She kept telling herself not to fall too hard, but that was like telling a hippo to dive without making a splash. Not that she was comparing herself to a hippo. Every minute spent with Jace solidified what a wonderful man he was, not the man the media was making him out to be. She couldn't let her fear of what others thought of her to deny her this man.

She slung the handle of her laptop bag over her shoulder and got out of the car. The small grove of trees surrounding his home at the end of the lane was picturesque and secluding. She understood why he chose this property. A knot formed in her stomach when the thought entered her mind that she was grateful he'd changed dinner venues. She had nosy neighbors. He did not.

Jace didn't answer the door when she knocked twice. Or the third time. She tested the knob, and it twisted fully in her hand. "I'm here," she called, stepping into the entryway.

Nothing.

She closed the door. "Jace?"

The squeak of a door opening sounded down the hall. A muffled "coming" sounded, followed by running water and a toothbrush tapping against the sink. A few seconds later, Jace stepped into the room wrestling a sweatshirt over his head. The hem of his T-shirt lifted in the process, revealing fine dark hair on the lower quadrant of his well-defined abs.

Yikes, any more of that and she'd need a defibrillator. Or mouth-to-mouth resuscitation. Maybe both.

"Thanks for coming here. I had some calls to make, and frankly, I'm exhausted. Plus, I was in the mood for steak."

What red-blooded man wasn't ever in the mood for steak?

Weariness tugged at the skin around his eyes. Despite his yawn, she sensed an energy about him that made her curious. "Is everything okay?"

He let out a loud, slow breath and gathered her into his arms. "I'm hoping. My lawyer called this morning. He recently discovered that David took his family on an African safari a month before Arabella passed. They withheld that information from medical staff. Not understanding the significance, I'm sure, but had I known that it would've alerted me to take a different approach to her care."

"Oh, Jace." The words left her on a whisper. She leaned back just enough to see his face. "That's wonderful news. I mean—well, you know what I mean. Does your lawyer think this information will help you win the case?"

"He's confident it will. David's wife, Kimber, initialed admittance papers stating she'd reveal all information regarding the patient, including information regarding leaving the country."

"Then why didn't she tell?"

"Oversight, I'm sure. The admittance packet is thirteen pages. Add that to the worry and stress of having an unresponsive child and. . ."

"She just signed and didn't really read." Josephine, along with thousands of other Americans were guilty of that same practice. "The poor woman must hate herself right now."

Jace fixed on something behind her, toying with the ends of her hair. "Kimber's a good woman. She never would've withheld anything she thought would help her child. I would give anything to go back and change this."

"I know you would." Josephine rested her head on his chest and squeezed his waist. She hoped her embrace spoke things her words never could. "If they were truly your friends, they'd know you'd never do anything to intentionally hurt them or their child."

"They need someone to blame. It's easier that way." He gently rocked her, as if she were the one in need of comfort.

She wanted to do this forever. With him. Good, bad, and ugly, she wanted to do it all with him. Her hand reached to cup his cheek. "How are you holding up with all this?"

He swallowed. "During the day when I can stay busy, I'm fine. When night closes in and my hands are idle, all the what-ifs whisper in my ears. I'm trying to keep faith but sometimes it's hard."

Tears blurred her vision. Her heart broke for him. She slacked her hold enough to stand on her tiptoes and pressed her lips to his. He tasted like mint and grief and hope. Better than anything that had ever graced her taste buds before. He kissed her back, teasing and taking, running his palms up and down her sides.

His hair was still wet at the nape. She crushed the ends in a gentle fist, arching to kiss him more fully. He responded exactly how she'd hoped he would, letting her know his brain had moved away from thoughts of death to thoughts of living. There was a danger in allowing herself to be his escape, but oh, how she wanted to be his lifeline.

The exchange went on until she lost track of time. He pulled away, their foreheads connected, breaths ragged. Jace closed his eyes but not before she saw the sheen coating his irises. "You are the best kind of distraction."

She smiled.

He pushed her hips away from him and shook his head, putting two feet of space between them. "Steak."

"Good idea." Her lips tingled.

He went toward the kitchen, pointing to her bag on the floor as he passed. "What's that?"

She snatched it up and followed. "My laptop."

"Any word about the governor?" He opened the refrigerator, one eyebrow cocked.

"Not yet. I imagine we'll hear something soon. I went to the historical society today. I think I may have found the answers behind our traps in the boathouse." Jace pulled out the steaks. "I transferred the photos from my phone to my laptop. Some of the writing is hard to read and this way we can zoom in better."

"Smart woman." He retrieved an indoor grill from the cabinet and set it on the counter.

A swishing noise started, and a pungent odor hit her nose. "Do I smell fish?"

"Work clothes. Sorry about that. I have to run them through a cycle with baking soda before a cycle of laundry soap. Otherwise, they leave a hint of fish in all my drawers."

"Add white vinegar. I know it sounds weird since vinegar stinks, but it disinfects and neutralizes odors. I used it daily when I fished."

"I'll try that." He pulled seasonings from a cabinet. "Speaking of fishing, we have twenty-three days until the Christmas ceremony. You really think we can pull this off?"

"If we work fast."

Jace gave the metal plates of the countertop grill a light coating of cooking spray. "I'll help with this puzzle as much as I can but with the winter season, the lobster trap tree build, and the trial, it may not be much."

She leaned her back on the counter next to him and watched as he sprinkled spices on the cold meat. "I understand. It's my fault you're tangled up in this anyway. I'm not normally so needy."

Jace paused mid-season. "I've been waiting almost twenty years for you to need me. I'm not complaining."

And just like that they were back to kissing.

# TWENTY-EIGHT

*Fifteen years earlier*

Jace knocked on Joey's front door. High-pitched barking blasted through the wood, followed by a muffled voice scolding the dog and then shuffling. The door opened, and Joey's pretty face appeared through a crack in the space. "It's you. If I'd have known, I'd have commanded Moby to attack."

He chuckled.

She sighed and opened the door wider. "Come in, but don't let Moby out."

He did as bidden, closing the door behind him. The living room smelled like apples and cinnamon. A terrier puppy sniffed at his shoes, then moved to his ankles. "Good to meet you, Moby."

The dog looked up the length of him, tongue lolling, tail wagging.

Joey rolled her eyes at the cute rat. "Don't fall under his spell, too."

Jace laid his backpack on the floor and then unzipped and took off his jacket. "Does that mean *you've* fallen under my spell?"

She raised one eyebrow. "I'm protected by an entire force field. You'll never catch me."

Oh, but he'd like to.

Joey pointed to a closet. "You can hang your coat in there if you want. The table's in the kitchen."

She was a block of ice on this warm spring day. This partner project ought to be fun. What had Mrs. Hale been thinking, putting the two of them together? How were they supposed to pretend they were bestselling authors writing flattering biographies of each other when they couldn't even get along?

Jace grabbed his backpack. He'd hoped the assignment would bring an opportunity to learn why she'd been extra frosty toward him this year and maybe bring an opportunity for peace between them. Neither looked promising.

The kitchen was cozy, though clearly outdated, and it smelled like the living room with the added hint of cake. Something buttery and vanilla if his nose was correct.

"Is there a problem?" Joey pulled a chair out and sat.

"Smells like you baked something special for my visit." He draped his jacket on the back of a chair and set his backpack on the floor.

"You sure think a lot of yourself, don't you?" She retrieved the notebook and pencil from the place setting beside her. "My mom made a cake for after dinner. However, she instructed me to offer you some. She's at her quilting bee."

While he never wanted to turn down cake, penetrating Joey's force field was more important. He sat in the chair next to her, moving it so close their knees almost touched. She stiffened.

"Why do you hate me?" he asked.

Sniffling and grunts filled the silence as the puppy inspected every inch of his backpack. Through the windows, Jace spied her dad on a riding mower, cutting precise lines into the already short grass. Joey blinked in shock at his bold question.

He leaned his back against the chair and stretched one leg out to hook his ankle on the bottom rung of hers. "You've always been cold, but ever since you came home from your internship, you've loathed me. Was it horrible there, or something? Was the food bad? Did the dorm have bed bugs?"

"It was wonderful. And I. . .don't hate you." She swallowed, concentrating on her blank sheet of paper.

"Then what is it?"

Because that night at the pageant, she'd flirted with him in a husky voice that made him crazy with wanting her. Then the next day her heart was repacked in snow.

Her lips pursed. "Look, this is our last English assignment before we graduate. Let's just get it over with, please."

Her tone was a soft, pleading.

Fine. He was leaving for Portland Community College at the end of summer anyway, then for Northwestern University the next semester. What did it matter if she stayed mad at him for the rest of their lives?

Except it did matter. Very much.

They spent the next hour asking and writing about each other's interests, accomplishments, and future plans. Then came the "personality" portion of the assignment, where they had to describe each other as others perceived them.

Jace tapped his eraser on the table. "Let's see. For you, I'd say motivated, driven, hardworking, loyal, and can be trusted to work alone successfully."

He jotted notes as he spoke.

She stopped doodling little designs in the corner of her notebook. "In terms of a job interview, it looks like I'm a stellar candidate."

"Well, I would list more personable attributes, but I'm not familiar with those, as you've never let me get close enough to discover them."

Oops. That could be taken two different ways.

Her jaw hardened. "You've never tried to get close enough."

"What do you think I was doing that day on the beach? In my gesture to give you that internship?"

She crossed her arms. "Are you going to lord that over me forever? A gift should be a gift. No strings attached. Besides, I thought you gave it up because you wanted to work for Doc Greenwell instead. Not because you felt sorry for me."

He leaned closer. "I didn't feel sorry for you, Jo. I wanted to make you happy. To make you feel something for me besides hatred."

"I said I don't hate you."

"Then what is it? How can you be soft toward me sometimes and like granite others?"

She shook her head. "The assignment. Let's get it done." She lifted her paper like a bellman reading a royal decree in the town square. "I'd also describe you as motivated, driven, and hardworking, as well as the town's golden child and loose with girls' feelings."

His neck flushed hot. "How am I loose with girls' feelings?"

She leaned closer, throwing her palms out. "Sitting with me that day on the beach, handing me that opportunity, acting like you care for me. The way you looked at me with those flirty eyes. I thought it meant something. Then the first thing I see when I come home is you making out with Alice Underwood in the diner parking lot."

Her face turned as red as the kitchen curtains. She covered her mouth, clearly regretting the outburst she'd meant to keep secret. Her eyes slipped closed, and she groaned.

They'd struck gold.

"So, this force field, as you call it, is more jealousy that loathing then?"

She blinked rapidly, not meeting his gaze. "You're just loving this, aren't you?"

Jace scooted to the end of his chair to get even closer. "Am I loving that this has been bothering you for months? No, I'm not. I wish you'd have said something sooner, so I could've told you that Alice was just a summer fling. It meant nothing. We both agreed to hang out over the summer, no expectation for anything more. We had some fun, we kissed a few times, and that was it."

Her mouth hung open.

"Okay, saying it aloud does make it sound like I'm loose with feelings, but Alice went into it knowing it was a casual relation-ship."

"You are clearly not as smart as your report card claims."

"What's that supposed to mean?"

"Alice might've agreed to those terms, but it wasn't 'it' for her." Joey rubbed her forehead and mumbled, "I never thought I'd feel sorry for Alice."

Jace flung his pencil on the table. "Alice is fine. She's been dating Layton since school started."

"Have you not seen the way she still looks at you? How *other* girls look at you?"

Through the window, her dad was driving the lawnmower into the shed. Was she telling him that she was one of those girls using some kind of code language? Why didn't girls just say what they meant?

"What are you saying, Jo?"

Her cheeks filled with air, and she blew out a loud breath. "I'm saying you're clueless."

"Do you have feelings for me?"

For a second, he thought her eyes were going to bug out of her head.

"Be honest." Now her dad was closing the shed door. Jace was running out of time before her force field shut him out again.

Blood gorged her cheeks, telling him all he needed to know. "It doesn't matter," she whispered.

"It does."

"Childhood is almost over. You're leaving in the fall, and I'm staying here. It doesn't matter how I feel or how you do or don't feel. Now, let's finish this homework so I can sleep tonight."

To his detriment, she made a good point.

Her dad was walking toward the house now.

Jace moved so close to her, his knee brushed the outside of her thigh. "Let's try being friends this summer. Hang out some. If childhood is over, then let's stop acting childish."

He put his hand on her wrist and rubbed the velvety spot where her pulse throbbed. "Please, Jo."

She stared at their hands. He wasn't certain, but he thought he felt her quake. The back door opened and the sound of feet stomping off loose grass sounded in the hallway. Moby's tiny paws tore through the kitchen, his bark ripping through Jace's ears.

"Okay. Friends." She pulled her hands into her lap, but her eyes communicated the desire she'd kept secret for so long.

Why hadn't they agreed to this long ago, so they'd have time to explore the possibilities between them?

Jace returned to his space at the table. Mr. Rockwell entered the kitchen and smiled a greeting. "Hiya, Jace. Are you staying for dinner?"

"No, sir, but thank you for the offer." He tossed his belongings into his backpack. "Now that we've finished what we need for the assignment, I need to get home."

Mr. Rockwell nodded. "How's the project going?"

Joey's dad looked at her for an answer. When she didn't respond, he flicked his gaze to Jace.

Jace smiled. "It's going well, sir. In fact, I'm confident the results will be our best yet."

# TWENTY-NINE

The phone pealed so loud Josephine slammed her elbow into the outstretched drawer of the filing cabinet. She grunted and rubbed the spot through her heavy knit cardigan as she walked to the phone. Frost edged the windows. Through the glass, flurries of snow fell around the harbor.

She cradled the telephone between her shoulder and cheek. "Harbormaster."

"Josephine, this is Georgina Thorogood."

Ignoring her elbow, Josephine gripped the phone in her hand and straightened, as if the woman and her disapproving tone were in the room. "What can I do for you?"

A slight pause. "I'm reaching out on behalf of the Granite Harbor Board of Selection. Word of Jace McClinktock and his malpractice suit have tongues blazing like a wildfire."

Josephine slammed her eyes shut and made a face.

"Were you aware of his situation during the vote?"

"No, ma'am." Josephine released a long, silent breath.

"I didn't think so." Georgina's tone softened. "Otherwise, you would have made us aware."

Would she have used it against Jace to win the harbormaster position?

Yes. Undoubtedly, she would have. Shame walloped her upside the head.

"Like I said, I'm reaching out on behalf of us all. We made the right choice in voting you in, Josephine. Imagine what a mess we'd be in right now had Jace made harbormaster. You're doing a fine job, young lady. Keep it up, and don't let us down."

"Yes, Georgina. Thank you."

The woman hung up and so did Josephine. She collapsed into her chair and dropped her head into her hands. The board's praise did nothing to bolster her confidence. The reason for their approval and, thus, the phone call, was because Jace's scandal made her look shinier. Not because they felt she earned the praise.

She cringed at the repercussions for Jace. If it was this bad behind his back, she couldn't imagine how people were going to treat him to his face. Some folks were unforgiving.

They hadn't defined their relationship to one another yet and certainly hadn't declared anything in public, though it was obvious to anyone who worked on or near the dock, they were dating. What would everyone think now? Say? If they took their relationship deeper—and she wanted to—how would everyone treat her for associating with him?

Jace wasn't guilty. He wasn't. Neither of them was doing anything wrong in pursuing the other. She knew this. And yet overcoming her insecurity by standing firm on truth was easier done in her mind than in reality.

"Meeting adjourned." Pete Miller unfolded his large girth from the little booth in the back of Johnson's Grocery. Only half of the fishermen attended, as the others were retiring for the winter. Like Nick, who was heading inland next week to spend time with his children under the custody of his ex-wife.

The only one in attendance who looked Jace directly in the face now that news of his malpractice suit was the talk of the town. The others avoided eye contact and either mumbled niceties or didn't say anything at all. Pete's wife, Debbie, sniffed as she passed him on her way out.

Jace had known for months the fallout was coming. It was here.

He waited for the group to filter out before he stood, folded his metal chair, and leaned it against the wall. As he turned, Nick slapped his shoulder. The pity in the other man's eyes made Jace stiffen. "Good luck, buddy."

Before Jace could issue a disingenuous response, Nick was walking down the frozen pizza aisle. Jace ran a hand down his face and blew out a breath. He would survive this. The reaction from the townspeople were the least of his troubles. Come December twenty-first, he'd either be condemned or redeemed.

The weight grew so heavy his legs felt like lead.

Joey. He needed to see his Joey.

The bell above the entrance of Johnson's Grocery dinged as he stepped outside and hurried to the harbormaster's office. Cold, briny air gave way to heat as Jace opened the office door. Her presence hadn't been required at tonight's meeting, and he sure wished it had. She was solid for him. For his life. If he made it out of this trial unscathed, he planned to pursue this thing with Joey like he never had before.

The night they'd sat by the fire in her backyard, she said he was enough. Still, there were times she grew distant when her image was at stake. She thought she was hiding it well, but she didn't give him credit for his perceptiveness. People were his profession. He knew well how to read between lines, assess body language, and smell fear. He just hoped in time she'd come to fully trust him no matter the circumstances.

To love him.

The word slammed into him like an unexpected wave. Yet, it fit. That's exactly where his heart was headed, ready or not.

She stood beside her filing cabinet, phone pressed to her ear, the long spiral cord of the vintage telephone wrapped around her back and shoulders like an anaconda. She turned at the noise, and their eyes met. The smile she sent his way sparked a fire inside him that chased away all the gossip and whispers and judgment.

He closed the door and removed his coat. Hanging it on a peg, he moved to check the stove and added more pellets. The heat was comforting after a cold day on the water. And the icy demeanor of those he considered friends.

Joey droned on about water depth and testing to whomever was on the other end of the line. He was all about thoroughness in the workplace, but all he wanted was her full attention. Instead, he waited patiently, taking in every detail of her face and form as the sun sank lower on the horizon. He checked the clock. Only half past five. Night arrived earlier each day.

Finally, the phone's handset clicked in its cradle.

"Hiya." Behind her desk, Joey reached for her mug and raised it to her lips, not quite hiding that seductive smile that warmed him through.

He stalked toward her and braced his arms on her desk. "You're a workaholic." He sniffed the air and leaned over to see into her mug. "And a chocoholic."

He took the cup from her hands and set it aside. "Your physician is prescribing an evening of rest with a healthy dinner of clam chowder shared with someone you find irresistible."

"Jack Sparrow will be so excited."

"Very funny."

She giggled and leaned closer. "Someone I find irresistible." She tapped her chin with a finger. "I wonder who that would be?"

He moved in to claim her lips, but she swiveled away, laughing.

She opened the filing cabinet and rooted around inside. He rounded to her side of the desk and lowered onto a corner, careful not to damage any important papers. "Shame that you can't think of anyone because I know a guy who happens to have a copy of *Panning For Answers*."

She whirled, bumping the filing cabinet door with her hip, slamming it shut. "The new documentary on unsolved mysteries of the Gold Rush?"

"The one and only."

She slipped the seductive smile back on and stood in front of him, forearms braced on his shoulders, fingers playing with his hair. "Have I mentioned how irresistible you are?"

Jace threw his head back and laughed.

Her lips twisted in a suppressed smile.

Legs bracketing hers, he hooked his fingers in her belt loops and tugged her closer. "I'm on the clock," she whispered.

His gaze flicked to the wall clock behind her. "Technically, your shift ended four minutes ago."

"Displays of affection in the office are unprofessional." Her fingertips grazed his scalp, making him crazy. "Besides, you stink."

"It's part of my charm. All the boats are moored, the dock is empty, and you said yourself I'm irresistible."

She sighed. "You are."

"Panning For Answers," he chanted in a whisper.

She groaned and then her lips covered his. She tasted like chocolate and the promise of a future.

The door squealed open.

Joey pushed away from him and held a fist to her mouth, her face the color of steamed lobster.

Jace turned to find Cooper, his sternman, standing in the open doorway, looking ten kinds of awkward. "Sorry." The man fidgeted. "Uh, I'll just call you later."

"No worries, man. Come on in." Jace stood and walked around to the other side of the desk, not bothered in the least.

Joey's hand slipped over her face, and she rubbed her forehead a few times before lowering her hand. "How can I help you?"

She scowled at Jace. "I told you it was unprofessional," she whispered loud enough for all to hear.

"You kissed me." Jace shrugged, then slapped Cooper's arm. "I'm irresistible."

Cooper shook his head, palms out. "I get it. I was young once too." Cooper nodded at Joey. "Don't fret, ma'am." Cooper's fisherman gear belied his Midwestern background. "I was on my way home when my wife called. Family issue. I need the day off tomorrow, Jace, if it isn't too much trouble."

"Of course not. I hope everything's okay."

"I hope so, too. See you Friday." Cooper moved to the door.

"Take care."

Joey half-waved, her face still radiating embarrassment. The door closed, and she groaned.

"It's okay, Jo. People kiss. He understands."

He took a step toward her.

She jabbed a finger at him. "You stay over there."

"But I'm irresistible."

"Yes, you are, but we have work to do before there's any more of. . .that."

"We both worked full shifts today and you want to do more work? I thought my college professors were bad."

"We're running out of time to solve this before the lighting ceremony." She went back to the filing cabinet and retrieved a stack of papers. "I printed off the pictures from the logbook to make it easier. The pictures of the traps and buoys are on my computer."

She collapsed onto her rolling chair.

"How am I supposed to help if I have to stay over here?"

"Fine, you can join me. But no touching. Or kissing."

"None?"

"Nada."

"What about after my willingness to sit through a two-hour documentary?"

She stared at him tenderly, the gears in her brain visibly turning.

He raised a brow. "What are you thinking?"

"That when you first kissed me, I was afraid it was a fluke, and I'd wake up to find you'd changed your mind." She shuffled her feet. "But this is the real deal, isn't it?"

Jace grabbed a folding chair and carried it next to her. He took her hand and entwined their fingers. "It is for me. I have no idea what's ahead but if the trial works in my favor, I want a shot at a future with you."

They stared at one another, neither asking what would happen to them if the trial didn't work in his favor.

She pressed her other hand to the side of his face. "Are you trying to prove your irresistibility? Because if so, it's totally working."

He kissed the tip of her nose. "Back to work, Rockwell."

They spent the next hour combing through information, matching buoy patterns with boat and captain names. Some patterns dated back to the 20s, while others belonged to fishermen who'd been established mere months before the war. So far, they'd matched twelve but had dozens to go.

Jace stretched his back. "Yellow buoy with three vertical black stripes."

Joey's finger traced the pages, looking for such a description. A minute later, she snapped. "Ah-hah. Johannes Geingrich, captain of the *Sea Storm*."

He wrote down the info, while she drew a star next to the man's name. His stomach howled.

She glanced at him from the corner of her eye. "One more?"

"One more." He clicked on the next picture. "White buoy with two thick black vertical stripes."

She skimmed the pages on her desk. The sun had set completely now, and the pellet stove was dying down. Jace tried to hold it in, but the yawn came anyway. How was he going to sit through a two-hour documentary when he could hardly keep his eyes open?

"Got it. The end is smudged though." She brought the paper to her face. "Martin Warner? I think that says Warner. Captain of the—"

She paused.

"Of?" His stomach roared again.

"Captain of the *Hiley Mae*." She turned the paper and pointed to the passage. "The mother boat to yours."

The *Hiley Mae* pre-dated World War II. The knowledge still had Josephine's curiosity tingling well into the next day. No one, not even Jace's dad, Seavey, had known the name went back that far. Jace's boat was the second generation, but she intended to ferret out the historical details along with the rest of the search.

She braked at the four-way stop and motioned for the driver opposite her to proceed while she adjusted the defrost. With no traffic behind her, she waited to go until her windshield cleared.

Doc Greenwell's clinic sat on a little knoll ahead on her right. A man emerged from the entrance, hovered against the cold, and walked toward the only vehicle in the patient parking lot. Colin. Josephine eased through the intersection and continued at a snail's pace as she watched him.

She'd called the Bangor Hospital twice after Doc Greenwell had informed her of his admittance but since she wasn't family, and Colin hadn't signed a release paper giving the staff permission to share information with her, she'd gotten no answers regarding his health.

Flicking on her turn signal, she turned into the parking lot as the other car pulled away. An Uber. She was hoping to speak with him, but she wasn't going to chase the driver down. A chat with Doc Greenwell would work just as well.

Josephine parked and walked into the clinic. A shiver stole through her as she transitioned from the cold into the warm lobby. Alice looked up from her computer and frowned. Her personality was as cozy as a mattress of nails.

"Do you have an appointment?" Alice's curt voice echoed through the waiting area. A mother and child waited on a small couch in the back corner.

"No." Josephine was tempted to walk out and leave the door wide open to thaw Alice's demeanor.

"Do you wish to make an appointment?"

"No. I'd like to speak to Doctor Greenwell."

Alice offered a counterfeit smile. "I'm sorry, but for that you'll need to make an appointment."

Normally, Josephine didn't like to throw her title around, but today, she'd do it gladly. "Official harbormaster business that involves one of his patients. No appointment needed."

Josephine produced her credentials for Alice's view to prove her point.

Alice made a face, lifted the phone from its cradle, tapped a button, and informed a nurse that Josephine wanted to speak to him in a professional capacity.

The woman took her job as seriously as her snobbery.

A few minutes later, Doc Greenwell opened a door, greeted Josephine, and motioned for her to follow him to his office.

He eased into his worn leather chair and clasped his hands atop his desk. "What brings you in on this fine warm day."

November in Maine was never warm and, Alice's demeanor dropped the temperature at least another twenty degrees. "I'm inquiring about Colin Warner."

He grinned. "Figured you might be."

"I know you can't say much due to privacy laws and all that, but it's my job to keep the water and harbor safe, so I was hoping you'd give me some idea of what's going on. His involvement in the rope cutting case puts him at a great risk."

"Any updates?"

"Not since I handed the evidence over to the Coast Guard and gave my statement."

Doc Greenwell leaned back in his chair. The leather and hinges groaned with the action. "Normally I wouldn't get involved, but I'm always willing to cooperate with local authorities." He winked. "The timely diagnosis of pneumonia saved his life. He was bad. Maybe the worst I've seen. The specialists were able to get the illness under control with strong antibiotics and fluids. We were able to get him financial assistance through a special program within the VA."

"I'm glad to hear it. So, he'll recover well?"

"If he cares for himself properly. Physically and mentally." He stretched the last word out as if wanting her to take the bait.

"Is there anything else I need to be aware of that would possibly affect the safety of Granite Harbor's citizens?"

Doc Greenwell crossed his arms over his wide chest. "Since I cooperate with local authorities, I can tell you that Colin suffers from PTSD."

"Oh." Josephine sank onto the chair in front of his desk.

"The confined space of the ambulance that transferred him to Bangor set him off. They had to sedate him. They later learned why through his medical records from a VA hospital in Ohio. He's suffered from PTSD ever since returning from the Middle East in '91. He worked in intelligence."

That's how he'd gotten video footage of the rope cutter and discovered the connection to the governor—it was his specialty. And now his reluctance to board Jace's boat and ride in the cabin too small for three adults made sense. "Is he a threat to anyone or himself?"

"I don't believe so. He was very open about it with hospital staff and with me today. He's simply a man who sacrificed to protect our country, returned with trauma, and is doing his best to live life one precious day at a time."

She looked down at her lap and nodded, ashamed to have asked the question. Colin's skills and his willingness to continue helping the citizens of this country despite what he'd been through spoke of his integrity.

Her gaze flicked back to Doc's. His mouth parted and he leaned forward but remained silent.

"Anything else?"

Doc Greenwell glanced away, concern in his eyes. "The rest isn't my story to tell."

"Fair enough." Colin's personal business was his own. If it didn't interfere with the safety of Granite Harbor's visitors or residents, he was as entitled to his privacy as anyone.

"Thanks, Doc." She started to rise but Doc held up his hand. "I'd like to speak to you about another matter I should keep quiet on too, but. . ."

"You like to cooperate with local authorities."

"Exactly." A small grin lifted one side of his mouth. "It's about Jace. He's too vital to the medical community to waste his talents on lobstering. I offered him a position here not long after he arrived, but he refused. He thinks it wouldn't be good for the clinic's reputation or mine. That's sea spit. What this town needs is a good, reliable doctor, and I'm ready to retire."

She blinked.

"Talk some sense into the man. This ridiculous lawsuit will pass, and when it does, he needs a job worthy of all the time and money he spent on education."

"I don't know what help I'll be."

"Nonsense. You're capable of persuading him back to common sense more than anyone."

Where she wasn't sure about that, she did agree Jace shouldn't waste his talent. "I'll do what I can."

"That's all I ask. If anyone can help him find his way again, it's you."

# THIRTY

A LIGHT SNOW SPRINKLED the gray water and the tops of Jace's gloves as he hooked the gaff and guided the line into the winch. He might get another month before the weather became too harsh to make venturing so far offshore worth the risk.

The first trap broke surface, spewing icy water out the sides and on the deck as Jace placed it on the counter. Dad acted as sternman today, measuring keepers and shorts and banding claws. He tossed one into the drink as Jace earthed another trap.

"I don't miss hauling in this weather, for certain." Even with his age and arthritis, Dad was faster than Cooper. Though Cooper made an excellent sternman.

"Can't claim to love it all that much myself," Jace called over the noise of the winch.

"You look exhausted."

"I am."

"It's hard balancing romance with this profession, isn't it?" Dad tossed a bug back into the water.

The reason Jace's mother had left. The unspoken words hung in the air like sea smoke.

"My hours at the hospital weren't all that conducive either." At least Joey understood the way life was here. Jace's mom had been from away and couldn't hack it—motherhood or being a fisherman's wife.

"Things getting serious?" Dad stacked the empty trap to the side while Jace sent the last one down the counter.

"She's amazing."

"Kind of a waste spending all those years hating each other, huh?"

"Eh, we never hated each other. Not really. In truth, the thought of loving her scared me, and her rebuff was a defense mechanism."

Dad nodded. "I know you've a lot going on right now, but it's clear she makes you happy. It's good to see my boy happy."

"She does." Jace stared at the white caps rolling and churning in the distance.

"But?" Dad grew still. Waited.

"She's holding back." Icy wind hit Jace and made him shiver. "I don't blame her. Not until we know the future is open for possibilities."

"My knees are wearing spots in the carpet I've spent so much time in prayer."

"Thanks, Dad." Jace blinked the moisture from his eyes so it didn't freeze.

Jace changed the subject by telling Dad about their conversation regarding her birth father when they were at Colin's cabin and the traps they'd found in the boathouse. "The deeper we investigate, the more I get the feeling we may not like what we find. And she seems to think that because her dad didn't want her, she needs to prove how valuable she is to me and this community, so we'll think she's indispensable. She battles the fear that she'll never be enough. It's a void I don't know how to fill."

Dad tossed the last two lobsters in the drink and eased against the counter. "You're not meant to."

"What do you mean?"

"Love isn't about filling voids. We're human. We can't possibly undo the damage someone else has done and fill it with our own selves. That's why many relationships fail, and we set ourselves up for it. Love is about being the bridge when the other needs a way across. We hold their hand and help them over the void. Each and every time."

For a man of few words, it was the most philosophical thing Jace had ever heard.

"What?" Dad made a face.

"That was very wise."

"With age comes wisdom, son. Unfortunately, a lot of my wisdom was gained the hard way." He sighed. "Enough of this emotional stuff. Tell me more about these old traps."

Jace grabbed the bucket of herring, and they began stuffing nets with bait. "One of them belonged to a Martin Warren, owner of the *Hiley Mae.*"

"No kidding."

"That name sound familiar at all?"

"Can't say as it does." Dad threaded the rope through the trap. "You might ask Holden, though."

"Joey's dad?"

"He's the one I purchased the *Hiley Mae II* from when you and Josephine were the size of sardines. It was already named. Maybe he knows the history."

"Huh. Boat's been with you so long, I never thought about who owned it before."

Dad looked around the vessel and patted its side. "She's been a good one. Classic and reliable."

"That she has."

"Now"—Dad shoved the last net with bait into a trap—"you don't really plan to do this for the next thirty years, do yah? This town could use another good physician. And I know you miss it."

Jace nodded. He did. There was no point in denying it. Should he be acquitted and he and Joey fall deep enough to get married, set hours and a steady income would be nice.

"Think about it." Dad patted his shoulder and lined up the traps.

"I will."

Jace waited for Dad to be free of the line before he drove ahead, letting gravity yank each trap back into the water.

Joey's hands worked magic.

Jace leaned forward allowing her thumbs to dig deeper into the tissue around his shoulder blade. His cheeks burned from the wind, despite using a protectant cream. He was tired to the marrow of his bones, and he couldn't get Dad's words to stop running circles in his brain.

"Ah." He winced. "Yeah, right there."

She adjusted on the couch behind him and dug harder into the muscle, using her elbow. "Sorry but my fingers can't take anymore."

The pungent odor of the balm she'd applied beneath his shirt beforehand filled the space. Jack Sparrow glared at him from his puffy bed on the hearth, his yellow eyes assessing every move. The cat still wouldn't let anyone pet him, but he seemed to be settling well into the spoiled life of a house cat.

"That's good. Thanks." Closing his eyes, he pushed through the pain onto his knees and turned to face her.

She frowned and put her hands on the sides of his face. "Poor thing."

Jace curled his lip. "I'm not a wimp." He stood. "But if you feel sorry enough for me to add some kisses to my regimen, I could swallow my pride."

"I thought you'd never ask." She spread a throw blanket over her lap and patted the cushion beside her. He eased onto it, picked up her legs, and stretched them across his lap.

She tangled their fingers together. "I'm sorry you had a rough day."

"It wasn't so bad. It was nice to spend the day with Dad."

"How is Father McClintock?"

"Wanting to see you." He rubbed circles on the back of her hand with his finger. "He wants to know if you have plans for Thanksgiving or if you'd like to join us for turkey TV dinners and football?"

"As appealing as that sounds, I've already committed to Thanksgiving with my parents. I'm sure they'd be happy to set two more places at the table, though."

"Sold."

Her lips met his.

Upbeat piano music played from the television.

Joey broke away. "Ooh, it's on."

He groaned. She settled her head against the couch and wiggled against his side.

"What is this again?" he asked.

"Murder, She Wrote. You'll love it. I promise."

Jace watched as three women with big hair strode across the screen wearing neon windbreaker jackets and pants. "Doubtful."

"First of all, you're sorely lacking in your vintage TV mystery show experience. Second, getting into the mindset of Jessica Fletcher may help us solve our own boathouse mystery."

"My lack of TV knowledge stems from studying for hours on end when I wasn't working the boat with Dad."

"Point taken. It's a good thing you have me to enlighten you now."

Since Jace could see he likely wouldn't get anymore kisses until the old lady had solved the mystery of who murdered the aerobics instructor, he changed the subject. "Speaking of our mystery, Dad told me that he purchased the *Hiley Mae II* from your dad when we were babies."

Joey paused the TV. "What?"

"He said if anyone knows the history of the boat, it's probably your dad."

"But Dad's never fished. He's always worked as a manager at the co-op."

Jace shrugged. "That you know of."

Her forehead knotted. "Well, if he did fish, the boat couldn't have been passed down in our family. My grandfather was a fisherman, but he survived the war and fished until retirement. I met him a few times before he passed away. And his last name was Rockwell."

Jace ran his fingers lightly up and down her arm. "Jo, the owner of that buoy's last name was Warner. I know he lives in Ohio, but have you considered it might be a relation to Colin?"

"I have."

"I feel like we've interfered in the man's life enough already. Maybe we should let this go."

"But why? Wouldn't you like to know if your boat has a story, has ties to someone who fought in WWII? What if you and Colin turn out to be related?"

"We're not related. And with all due respect to every serviceman, does it matter if my boat does? It won't change anything. We have things to take care of in the here and now."

"Like what?" She quivered at his touch.

"Like us going on an official date. In public."

A declaration he was staking his claim.

She leaned away to look at him. "That'll make us officially official."

"Aren't we anyway?"

"We are to me, but then we'll be official to everyone."

"Everyone knows we're together anyway."

She balled the blanket in her fist. "It's just a bold statement."

Amid the town gossip and the trial—she may as well have finished her thought.

Disappointment seeped in. "Other than you, Cooper, and my dad, I've been avoiding people as much as possible for months now to escape judgement. I can't run forever. It's out now and I've got to face it. If we're serious about each other, it's something we'll have to face together. I know how I feel about you. If you feel the same, let me take you out Friday night."

Her grip on the blanket tightened before it began to ease. "Okay." A slow, unsteady smile crept up her face. "I'll be sure to eat an early lunch, so I'll be hungry."

"Until then, let's enjoy each other without the rest of the town watching."

Jace chased after her lips, and she giggled. "What about Jessica?"

She pointed the remote at the TV.

"The eighties are gone. Now come here."

She tossed the remote behind her, creating a dull thud as it hit the carpet.

# Thirty-One

Josephine's stomach tied a sailor's knot as Jace held the door for her. The Occidental Octopus, known by the locals as Double O's, was a family-friendly joint open from October fifteenth to April first and housed an open mic stage for local talent. Serving a small variety of soups and chowders and hot sandwiches, two sardine fishermen and their wives had run the place for locals during winter for the last twenty years. With a full house nearly every Friday night, they'd be lucky to find a seat.

A waitress walked by with a tray full to bursting.

"That double-decker grilled cheese looks amazing," Jace said, nestling his hand in the small of her back. It nearly had her salivating too but declaring their relationship boldly and publicly had her nerves on edge. Stupid. Everyone knew anyway.

A group of four wedged through the crowd to the exit. Sissy Chambers raced toward the kitchen, carrying two empty pitchers. "There's a table in the back corner. Grab it before it's gone. I'll be back to clean it in a minute."

Before either of them could thank her, she was gone. Jace grabbed Josephine's hand and led the way, nodding at friends as they went. Someone released a catcall, but Josephine ignored it, hoping it was meant for someone else.

Jeffrey Talbott played a mellow tune on his acoustic guitar from the stage. Josephine stood awkwardly, unsure what to do with her hands while they waited for their table to be bussed. People were staring. Was it because of their declaration or the scandal surrounding Jace?

She took off her gloves and shoved them into her coat pockets.

Jace leaned toward her ear. "You're starting to make me think you're embarrassed to be seen with me."

She knew by the tone of his voice he was teasing, but she felt like a jerk all the same. "It's not that. I just don't like being the center of attention."

Jace pointed at the tables surrounding them. "You're not."

At closer glance, people were eating and chatting with one another, most not paying her and Jace any mind at all. The few who did either smiled or waved.

"You put a lot of unnecessary pressure on yourself." He slid his arm behind her back. "It's okay if you're not perfect. If *we're* not perfect. It's also okay to not care what others think."

Guilt pricked. He was right. Even if she hated to admit it. She'd been so concerned about everyone's reaction, she'd made herself believe everyone was gawking at them when they weren't. That was concerning. How often did she do that to herself?

"Sorry for the delay." Sissy swooped in and tossed the table's contents into a large bin, perched it on her hip, and then wiped the table with a bleachy rag. "Drinks?"

"Coke, please." Josephine removed her coat.

"Make that two." Jace pulled out her chair as Sissy raced away.

A few minutes later, Sissy returned with their drinks and took their orders.

Jace settled against the back of his chair and stretched his arm across the table, palm up. His confidence reassured her, and she began to relax. Music played while they talked about the lobster trap Christmas tree lighting ceremony, Jace's recent truck repair, and the overdue library book she still hadn't read.

A loud cackle sounded from a table behind them, causing most of the customers to turn around. Hemingway slapped the table, face to the ceiling, revealing his few remaining teeth. His granddaughter and her boyfriend sat one on each side of him, a basket of fried pickles in the middle.

"Telling stories again." Jace squeezed Josephine's hand and winked. "At least he's in a good mood tonight. And not spitting."

"I heard Grantley's boyfriend can charm the skin off a snake. Guess he has a way with grandpa's too."

"We should ask him about the history of the *Hiley Mae*."

"Grantley's boyfriend?"

"Hemingway." Jace craned his neck to better see the table behind her. "Dementia's an odd thing. Sometimes people can remember things from fifty years ago, even though they can't remember the last five minutes. You're confident that's him in the old photo? The kid with the fish? We should ask him what he remembers."

"I don't know. I'd hate to ruin his good mood."

"The guy loves telling stories about the town. I think it's worth a shot."

Sissy brought their food and refilled their drinks. Two tables beside them emptied and the waitress began cleaning the mess. Hemingway flagged her over but before she could reach their table, he yelled, "I'll take an order of fried donuts."

The waitress put a hand on her hip. "You just finished an order of fried donuts."

The skin on Hemingway's face swirled and dipped with his frown. He eyed the waitress, seemingly assessing her for truth. "I'll take an order of fried donuts."

"It's your belly, not mine. Coming right up."

Grantley shouted *to go*, and Sissy nodded.

Jace popped the last bite of grilled cheese into his mouth and chewed as he stood. He ambled over to Hemingway's table and introduced himself to Grantley's boyfriend, Aiden. As if he'd known them forever, Jace pulled a vacant chair up to the table, and straddled it.

More tables thinned, and from what Josephine could hear, Jace made small talk with the trio while she finished her tomato soup. She was wiping her mouth with a napkin when the name Martin Warner hit her ears. She scooted back her chair and joined Jace, waving a hello to the group.

"Martin Warner. . ." Hemingway scrunched his face toward the ceiling. "Now, why does that sound familiar?"

"'Cause you know everyone, Hem." Nate Kay turned from his seat behind Hemingway and grinned. The bristled-jaw man was a good twenty years younger than Hemingway, but old enough he might be able to add some information to the mystery.

Josephine put a hand on Jace's shoulder. "Martin would've been a fisherman before he left to fight in WWII. I know he had a son, but I'm not sure what his name was. It's possible that the two of you were boyhood friends."

Hemingway stammered and stuttered as he thought. Josephine got the feeling that his inability to answer the question was agitating him. The rest of the group must have sensed it too because Nate turned sideways in his chair and faced them. "Let's see. I went to school with a Carl Warner back when the schoolhouse was on League Road. I remember him having a sibling or two, and I think they were much older than us. Hmm. . .Pete or Peter. I think the sister's name was Rosemary."

"Peter!" Hemingway slapped the tabletop, jarring a fork to the floor. "Peter was a good man. Had my back many a time." His deep belly laugh echoed through the place. "Like the time I forgot my arithmetic homework and Peter made himself sick, so I'd have to walk him home. Bought me another day."

Such a tactic wouldn't work nowadays but Granite Harbor students were taught in a one-room schoolhouse then.

Jace folded his arms on the edge of the table. "Do you remember what happened to Peter?"

Hemingway scratched his cheek. "Let's see. I know he inherited his dad's boat when he died 'cause I was wicked jealous. Thing sat for years, as we were just kids. He got married sometime after me and June Bug and moved inland somewhere—I don't know."

Josephine had sat through many stories about his June Bug over the years. Her death had devastated him, and he hadn't been the same since.

"What about Carl?" Josephine asked Nate.

"If it's the same family—sounds like it is—Carl's mom remarried after being widowed for a time. Carl passed away in our mid-twenties. Some heart condition no one knew he had. Left a wife and child behind."

"How sad," Jace said.

"I wonder what happened to Rosemary?" Grantley moved her glass in a circle, swirling the liquid.

Sissy approached the table carrying a white sack. "Fried donuts to-go. Take it easy, Hem."

"You too, Sassy."

They all looked at each other and tried not to laugh, as the mistaken name fit her when riled.

Nate's wife, Gertie, finally joined in the conversation. "The Rosemary you're wondering about wouldn't be Rosemary Wells, would it?"

"The old singer?" Nate shook his head. "Nah, surely not."

Once in a great while, Josephine would hear someone mention the famous Rosemary Wells from Granite Harbor, but that's as far as her knowledge on the matter went. "Did Carl and his wife have any children?"

"A son." Hemingway's eyes glittered with unshed tears. "I got to hold him once when he was a babe. Don't know what happened to the kid or his mother."

"That's all right," Jace said, standing. The pointed look he gave Josephine said they'd pushed Hem's memory far enough. "We appreciate all the information you offered. Enjoy those donuts. Make sure to put them in an air-tight container when you get home, or they won't be any good tomorrow. I learned that the hard way a few weeks ago."

Josephine waved and followed Jace back to their table where he looked at the bill, then threw down two twenties. He helped her into her coat, and they left, fingers entwined.

"Well, it may not be all we'd hoped but we have more information to go off of than we did." Jace let go of her hand long enough to zip his jacket higher. A light snow began to fall, the streetlights making it sparkle like glitter.

"We're running out of time before the ceremony." She'd never been able to connect the dots on her own family tree, so helping others in the community connect theirs meant a lot to her.

Jace stared ahead as they walked to his truck. "We have what we need for the ceremony. If we don't solve the mystery of the *Hiley Mae* before then, that's okay."

Was it? Leaving things undone wasn't in either of their natures. And there was something in the missing pieces of the puzzle that she felt she was meant to find.

# THIRTY-TWO

JACE WASN'T SURE IF he'd ever thaw out. Stiff from the cold and dreaming of a hot shower, he rowed the last few strokes to the dock. Cooper looked like something left in the freezer too long, pale with little ice crystals clinging to his ski mask. Thankfully the temp was supposed to warm up ten degrees the next few days. Jace tied the skiff to the dock with frozen fingers while Cooper climbed out.

The dock was slick with sea spray but the line running from piling to piling allowed them to stay upright in between the new strips of grip tape. The pipe on Joey's office roof belched gray smoke. He could picture her wrapped in a thick sweater, the room filled with the scent of coffee, her mug half full, desk messy.

A man he didn't recognize walked out and slammed the door. Jace went alert. Storming to his vehicle, the guy got inside and peeled out of the lot faster than Jace could blink. "I wonder what that was about," Cooper said over his shoulder.

"I'm going to find out. See you Wednesday." They were going out every two to three days now as they'd set the traps even further offshore, and the lobsters' movement naturally slowed along with their appetite in colder waters. Jace understood. Except for the slowing appetite part.

Jace gave the door a quick knock before going in. Face in her hands, Joey spread two fingers apart to peek through. Seeing it was him, she inhaled a deep breath and crossed her arms over the paperwork spread across the desk. "Hiya."

"Who was that guy?" Jace tugged off his gloves and moved to the pellet stove.

"Henry Scott, if that's his real name. Some minion of the governor's. Seems they've made an arrest, and they want the name of the person who captured the evidence. I wouldn't tell him, so he cussed me and left."

Jace's fingers had thawed enough he could make fists. "Did he threaten you?"

Joey pursed her lips to the side and glanced away.

Jace swirled and stomped to the door, threw it open, and stepped outside, ready to tear the man's head off. He searched the parking lot. "He's gone."

"He's not worth the effort. Close the door. It's freezing."

He did and returned to the place in front of her desk. She rolled her neck from side to side, hair bobbing around the glasses she'd pushed on top of her head.

"You're in a dangerous position," he said. "I don't like it."

Joey rubbed her forehead. "I don't either, but I'll be fine."

"You can't guarantee that."

"None of us can." She yawned as she stood. Her eyes glinted with mischief as she rounded her desk. "But I have you to protect me."

Her arms wrapped around his neck.

He threw her past words at her. "This is completely unprofessional."

She chuckled and ran her fingertips through the hair at his nape.

"Your wily ways don't distract me from my concern." He settled his hands on her hips.

"Oh, yeah?" She moved her lips over his.

Maybe it would, a little.

He slid his hands up to her waist and under her shirt just enough to press his icy palms on her warm back. She ripped away, gasping.

"That was mean."

He laughed. "Now, back to the topic at hand."

"I'll inform Sheriff Jones, Homeland Security, and the DOJ. Can we ditch this place and eat?"

"Promise?"

Her features softened. "I promise."

"Then, let's eat. Afterward, you can watch some who-did-it show while I nap."

"As appealing as that sounds, I was going to scour the old records I dug out of the storage closet for info on the *Hiley Mae*."

Her obsession with finding answers concerned him. "You sure you want to dig into all this? We've identified all the traps and buoys and sent ceremony invitations to all the out-of-town families we could connect. We accomplished what we set out to do, Jo."

"I know." She rubbed her forehead again. "I figured you'd understand, seeing as when you're treating a patient you keep going until you find the answers."

That hit him below the belt.

"I do." He rolled his shoulders. "Tell you what. I heard Maggie's has chili on their menu this week. I'll get some and then help you sift through the records."

She tipped her head to the side. "You're the best, you know that?"

"I do." He gently knocked her forehead with his. "I'll be back."

Jace walked to his truck and let the engine warm while he checked his phone messages. His lawyer had left a voicemail regarding the upcoming trial. Jace's stomach clenched. Torn between wanting answers after months of waiting and wanting to put it off for as long as possible, he decided on the latter, tossed his phone onto the seat, and drove to Maggie's.

Twenty minutes later, he was back at Joey's office with a take-out bag and two Moxies. "Food's here."

No answer.

The storage closet was open, and a yellowish bulb blazed.

"Jo?" Careful not to mess anything up, he sat the take-out bag and drinks on her desk. then stepped into the small closet.

"Food?"

"I. . .I can't believe this."

"What is it?"

She frowned. "A mooring record from 1989. Colin Warner owned the *Hiley Mae II*. That means he'd have sold the boat to my dad before my dad sold it to yours."

An icy blast hit Josephine in the face as she left the grocery store, arms wrapped around a large paper bag. Flyers and tape in hand, Jace sidled over and spied its contents. "Got enough hot chocolate?"

"Actually, no. One can never have enough."

He reached inside and pulled out a pink glittery packet. "What's this?"

"An avocado sheet mask. For my face. Sparrow and I are going to have a spa day."

"Count me out. Wanna swap?"

"Nah, I've got it." They headed toward his truck. "I put several flyers inside. Are you done out here?"

"Covered."

Jace opened the truck door. "That cat isn't gonna let you get near him with that thing."

He pointed to the mask.

"It's not for him. The catnip is."

"You realize that's weed for cats, right?"

She shrugged. "We all have our vices."

He took the bag and set it on the floorboard, chuckling. "We sure do. And you're mine."

His lips took her by surprise. They teased for only a moment then left her in the cold. Movement caught her attention in the row behind him. She shoved Jace away, pulse racing. "It's him."

She raced toward Colin, stopping for the oncoming car. He hadn't been home the two times she'd gone to his cabin to check on him. He was almost to the store's entrance when she shouted his name. Colin stopped and cocked his head. The second time she called, he turned around.

Legs burning, Josephine was panting by the time she reached him. "I've been looking for you but haven't seen you around."

"Why?" His forehead crinkled. Suspicion darkened his features.

"I wanted to make sure you'd made a full recovery. And to let you know they've made arrests in the rope cutting case. A man with ties to Governor Sinkankas tried to get me to reveal your name but I refused. Wanted to warn you."

Colin stood at attention and assessed the parking lot like a sniper would his surroundings. "Did he hurt you?"

Josephine frowned. "No, I'm fine. I've informed the authorities."

Jace's footsteps approached, and his hand settled between her shoulder blades. "Glad to see you've recovered."

Colin's eyes shifted to Jace and then back to her. "I appreciate all your help."

Jace nodded.

"I'm sorry you never found your bottle." Josephine tucked her hands into her coat pockets.

Colin looked her over once again. "Me too, but I ended up finding something even better."

She frowned.

"See you later." He moved to leave.

"Wait." She put a hand on his arm. "I also wanted to talk to you about something."

Colin took a step back. "What about?"

She told him about finding the traps and buoys in the boathouse, how they'd been able to trace them to members of the community who'd lived in Granite Harbor at the time, and the upcoming lobster trap Christmas tree lighting ceremony. "While researching, I discovered that you were the one who sold my dad the *Hiley Mae II*. How ironic that the connection would lead to another one between us—between our families—so many years later."

Colin didn't respond.

An awkward silence hung thick in the air, causing Josephine's stomach to knot.

Cold seeped into her jeans and made her shiver. "We'd be honored if you'd come to the ceremony and represent your grandfather and the Warner family. It's on December first at seven. If your father is still living, we'd be honored to have him too."

Colin's lips thinned. "He's not."

"Sorry to hear that. Will you come?"

"No." Colin took another step away. "I'm on my way out of town right now. Just stopped in to get some snacks."

Josephine's insides wilted. "Oh. Well, under the current circumstances, I understand. Take a flyer anyway in case you change your mind. And, please, be safe."

She wanted to thank him for his service to their country but then remembered she wasn't supposed to know about that. Instead, she reached inside her coat pocket and pulled out a folded paper that she'd tucked away when she'd ripped off one corner trying to tape it to a window. She thrust it at Colin and he took it, lifting his coat sleeve just enough to reveal a bluish tattoo. *H.M.*

Hiley Mae? If that's what the mark stood for, and the boat meant enough to him to permanently attach it to his body, why wouldn't he come to the ceremony? She opened her mouth to ask but Jace put a hand on her arm, stopping her. He shook his head.

Colin looked down at his boots. "I'm sorry."

"But—"

He disappeared inside the store.

Jace kissed her temple. "That's all you can do, sweetheart."

She turned, heart aching. "He wants to come. I can feel it."

"Maybe. I don't know." His arm engulfed her shoulders, and he pulled her close.

"Between me and you, Doc Greenwell said he suffers from PTSD. Has ever since the first Gulf War."

Jace grimaced. "That explains a lot, then. Probably why he keeps to himself and wants to avoid large crowds."

"Yeah. I just hate that every trap is going to have a representative except his."

"It'll be a great ceremony all the same." Jace started the truck and turned on the heat.

"I saw a tattoo on his wrist. It says H.M."

"Really?" Jace backed from the parking space then threw it into drive. "Hiley Mae?"

"I'd bet on it."

"Huh. Strange."

Josephine stared out her window and watched the scenery flash past. Strange and getting stranger.

# THIRTY-THREE

Jace scrubbed a towel over his head, then used it to clear the fog on the bathroom mirror. He leaned against the counter, noting signs of the old man taking shape across his features. The last nine months had aged him from the inside out, the graying hairs at each temple telling the story.

He rummaged through the drawer for a comb, knocking a loose Q-Tip to the floor. The comb sliced through his hair as his phone pealed from the other room. He had plans with Joey after church to make labels for the traps with the deceased soldiers' names, but she'd mentioned not feeling well last night. If she wasn't up to it, he'd take care of lunch, build a fire, and they could veg the rest of the day.

Jogging to his bedroom, he snatched his phone up on the last ring and answered, too late to let it go to voicemail when his brain registered the call was from his lawyer. Like always with these conversations, Jace's stomach clenched in anticipation of bad news. "Hey, Findley."

"Are you sitting down?"

"No."

"Find a seat."

Bile burned a path up Jace's throat. He flopped onto the edge of his bed in nothing but his boxers and pinched the bridge of his nose. "I'm sitting."

"Pollack Insurance has dropped all malpractice charges. You're free to go back to work as soon as you sign these papers in my office."

Air whooshed from Jace's lungs. It was over? Just like that?

"How? When?" He'd heard Findley, but his brain wasn't quite sure to believe him.

"After it came out that the Garretts withheld information about their African vacation and the Bos Med team finished the investigation on their end, Pollack decided continuing with a trial wouldn't be in their favor. They dropped the charges."

"Is. . .you're sure? It's over? Like *over* over?"

"You're a free man."

This seemed too easy after the hell he'd been through the past several months. Moisture sprang to his eyes. He let out a shaky breath.

"Jace?"

"I'm here. That's. . .wow, that's—great news."

He rubbed a palm down his thigh, fighting back a dam of tears.

"That it is, buddy. I know you've got your lobster thing going but I need you to come in as soon as you can to sign these papers. I'm sure your superior at the hospital will have some things for you too. They're working on a public statement right now to clear your name."

"Thanks, man. For everything."

"Of course. Since you weren't at fault, Bos Med is covering my fees."

More great news.

"Expect a call from your superior. I'm sure they want you back to work as soon as possible with the staffing shortage."

With another round of thanks, Jace hung up and stared in stunned silence at the carpet between his feet. *Thank you, God.*

A free man. Free to go back to Boston. Free to return to doctoring. Free from the bobbing of a boat, the lashing of an icy wind on his face, the uncertainty of a haul and market prices.

But going back to his old life meant leaving Joey.

As much as he looked forward to a brighter future, truth was, he wasn't willing to give her up.

Snow twirled outside the window of Josephine's living room. Thin curtains usually masked the full view, but she'd pushed them back as the wintery scene made the room all the cozier. She needed cozy as her safety net today. Between reporters stalking the dock wanting interviews about her takedown of Governor Sinkakas and the spam calls blowing up her phone—likely more reporters or death threats—she needed an escape.

The logs in the fireplace crackled. Jack Sparrow dozed on the arm of the couch, swallowing the entire thing. While he still didn't trust her enough to sleep deeply when sharing a room, he inched a little closer to her every day.

Jace sat on the floor beside the coffee table, long legs outstretched. He was everything she needed today. The leftovers from their smores sat on the edge of the table next to her laptop, small wooden signs, and the metallic paint markers spread between them. Each sign would hold a deceased soldier's or nurse's name. They'd completed four and still had several to go.

She scrolled down the screen on her laptop. "Christopher Morris."

Jace had surprisingly neat penmanship for a doctor, so he penciled in the name then handed the sign to her to trace with the metallic marker. Every time they completed a sign, he'd steal a kiss. Something about him was different today, though she couldn't decide what. There was a light in his eyes that was definitely different.

"At this rate, we'll be working until dawn." She giggled as he nuzzled her neck with his nose. The cat woke, wide-eyed, poised to run if either of them made a wrong move.

"I'm not in any hurry. Are you?" Warm lips pressed against her skin where his nose had tickled.

Goosebumps raced across her arms. "I'm not." There wasn't any place she'd rather be than right here with him. "You're in a particularly good mood today. Care to share with the class?"

He glanced at Jack Sparrow. Perceiving no threat, the cat yawned and rested his chin against his front paws, ears perked. "I don't know. Think he can handle the excitement?"

"If he doesn't, I'll make him walk the plank."

Jace smiled. "My lawyer called this morning. The insurance company has dropped all charges."

"Ah!" She vaulted from her knees into his arms. "That's amazing!"

At her shout, Jack Sparrow leaped off the couch and sprinted across the room into the kitchen, paws slipping beneath him in his haste.

She laughed and put her hands on Jace's cheeks. "This means you can go back to doctoring and saving lives and—" her enthusiasm dropped along with her shoulders. "Does this mean you're going back to Boston?"

He turned his face and kissed her left palm and then tangled his fingers with hers. "Only long enough to resign from the hospital and sign over my loft to the current tenant. That is if you'd like to see me stick around."

"You know I do, but are you sure?" The last thing she wanted was for him to one day resent her for staying.

His thumb rubbed the sleeve of her sweater. "Someone has to be here to keep you safe from the reporters and protestors. And all the psychos angry that a criminal is getting what he deserves."

"Don't stay just for that. I'll be fine."

"I'm staying because I don't want to spend a day without you."

She kissed him, long and sweet, grateful he felt the same as her. "Will you be content lobstering or are you going to consider Doc Greenwell's offer?"

He leaned back. "What do you know of Doc's offer?"

"Oops." She chewed her bottom lip. "I guess I'm not as good at keeping secrets as I'd thought."

"Apparently not." He shifted positions so she could settle better against him. "How'd you find out?"

"Doc told me when I stopped by to inquire about Colin's pneumonia. Somehow, he seems to think I have the power to make you see reason."

Jace played with the ends of her hair. "You can. Kissing you all day seems perfectly reasonable."

He leaned forward but she scooted back.

"Nope. Not until we get these signs finished. We have a week and three days until the ceremony. Work, then play."

He tried to swat the marker she pointed at him. "I like the sound of that."

She playfully rolled her eyes.

An hour later, the finished wooden signs filled the coffee table. A new murder mystery streaming series based off an author's books and set in Montana played quietly in the background. "Last but not least, Martin Warner."

She sighed, not meaning for it to come out so forcefully.

"It'll be okay. Colin will be okay." Jace patted her hand.

"I know. I just. . .I can't get over that he has H.M. tattooed on his wrist. I'm certain it stands for Hiley Mae. And since the boat obviously meant that much to him, why did he sell it?"

Jace popped his neck. "The boat's probably named after a family member. Maybe his wife? Only he knows the answer to that. I think you're part bloodhound. You get a scent, and it drives you crazy until you find it."

"To a fault." She crisscrossed her legs. If her parents would hurry and get back from their antiquing excursion in Portland, she'd ask them what they knew. It wasn't a conversation to have over the phone on their anniversary trip.

She scratched her head. "The genealogy website I subscribed to when we started this investigation was helpful in tracking out-of-town family members to invite to the ceremony. I could use it to see if I can find anything else out about Colin."

"Honey, let it go."

"Honey? I think I like that. Has a bit of southern charm to it."

"You're exhausting." He kissed her cheek. "Cute but exhausting. I'm going for another bowl of chili."

"Save some for me," she called after him.

"No promises."

Pulling up the genealogy website, she typed in Colin's full name and the state of Ohio. She narrowed the results by adding an approximate age and that he'd served in the Gulf War. Five results filled the screen. She glanced through them, starting with the first, but none of them showed record of a previous Maine address until the last one. She clicked on it.

A tree sprouted from the bottom right-hand corner of the page and branches grew upward from there. Where a connection had been found or input by a website member, leaves blossomed. She clicked around until she found the name Martin Warner, wife Hiley Mae Hendricks. Beneath that branch were their children Peter, Carl, and Rosemary. The names mentioned that night at Double O's with Hemingway and his granddaughter.

Josephine clicked on Peter but found no familiar names connected. Next, she clicked on Carl's name. His wife had been Matilda Bruhn. Children listed—Colin Warner, wife Anne Hannity.

She held her breath. Blinked. That couldn't be right. Anne Hannity was—

A tiny leaf waved on the branch between Colin and Anne, revealing there was record of a child. Heart pounding in her ears, she swallowed and clicked on the leaf with a shaky finger. Hiley Mae Warner, born on June 1, 1993, daughter of Colin Warner and Anne (Hannity) Warner, Duro Island, Maine.

The room started closing in on her. June first was Josephine's birthday. Anne Hannity was the name of her birth mother.

Sweat broke out on her forehead. Chili threatened to rise from her stomach.

"I turned the burner on low. The chili was getting cold. Want me to grab you another bowl? Hey, what's wrong?"

The sound of ceramic hitting a table sounded amid the blood rushing in her ears. "Jo?"

Jace took her face in his hands. "What is it?

His gaze roamed her face, checking for signs of health distress.

She sucked in deep breaths. "He's. . .he's. . ."

All she could do was point to the computer.

Jace frowned at it. "He's what? Who?"

"He's my father. Colin. I. . ."

She swallowed bile. "*I'm* Hiley Mae II."

# THIRTY-FOUR



The scent of evergreen and cinnamon hung heavy in the air. Josephine reached into the branches and unearthed a Christmas ornament she'd gotten years ago at the town's lobster trap Christmas tree lighting ceremony. The shiny, fired clay pine tree filled her palm. Muti-colored lights were painted on, and tiny red hearts peeked from between the branches as ornaments. *All Hearts Come Home for Christmas* was etched on a border at the bottom.

She looked out the window at the falling snow, her chest growing a little heavier. Not all hearts came home for Christmas. Her birth father's hadn't after asking Santa for it every year until she was thirteen. Now that she was much older and her Christmas wishes had changed, Jace's heart hadn't either.

They'd had a great summer together after graduation. For the first time in their existence, they were cordial to one another in public and even hung out a few times with a group of friends. Once, they'd sat together in the park, without the group, when the antique club sponsored a movie night in the park and had played *The Outsiders*. He'd shared his popcorn. She'd shared her M & M's.

Again, at Maggie's Diner when he'd come in to pick up a to-go order, he'd spotted her and Ciara eating lunch and had joined them instead. They'd laughed until her sides hurt.

Then again, at the end of summer, when Justin Metcalf's parents had hosted a community party at the beach to send off all the collegiates. Jace had stayed by her side at the campfire most of the evening, finding little ways to flirt with and touch her. When it had grown dark enough for the stars to shine, he'd scooted close and stared at her lips as if trying to decide if it was wise to kiss her. To her disappointment, he'd hugged her instead and promised to see her at Christmas.

Except he hadn't come home.

He'd finished his classes at Porland Community College and had gone to Boston to move into his dorm at Northwestern University early so he could spend the holiday in the city with friends.

Father McClintock's disappointment had been palpable when she'd seen him at the Christmas Eve service at church last week. She supposed he'd noticed that hers was too by the way he patted her shoulder and told her to "hang in there."

Moby woke from his nap by the fireplace and sniffed the box of decorations she was taking down until next year. The dog had grown so much since they'd gotten him. How quickly time passed, and life changed. Just a few short months ago, she was still a teenager. Now she was working full time and taking a few classes at the community college via her scholarship. And Jace had finally gone out into the world, seized it, and was thriving. She was happy for him, but sad for the friendship they'd finally found that would fizzle out like seafoam retreating on a wave.

Mariah Carey's *All I Want for Christmas is You* came onto the radio for the hundredth time. Christmas was over and, frankly, the song was just depressing this year. For some reason, it reminded her of the kelly green dress she'd worn in the pageant. The one that had sucked the words from Jace's tongue.

She chuckled at his audacity to enter her in the pageant without permission. Jamar had flagged her down on the way home from her shift at the grocery store one night. He'd left a party and was too tipsy to drive. He'd crawled inside and after a good scolding, she drove him home. Somehow conversation had drifted to Jace, and Jamar had let it slip that Jace was the one to forge her entry paperwork. Whether or not he did it to be mean or because he had faith she'd win the scholarship, she'd never know.

The diva singer hit a high note, while the background continued repeating the famous lyrics. If Josephine had communicated her interest in Jace, would he have come home? She'd never know.

She stared out the window again, thinking. A clump of snow fell from the top branches of the spruce tree and slid to the ground in a heap. What if she could talk Ciara into going to Boston with her and finding Jace? His reaction to her visit would tell her once and for all if there was any hope of a relationship together. As pathetic as it was, if there was even a smidgen of hope, she'd wait for him.

Yeah. That's what she'd do. When spring came and the weather made traveling less treacherous, she would go to him. Find her courage and tell him how much she cared for him.

# Thirty-Five

Sleet pelted Jace's body and bounced off, making pools of tiny snowballs on the dock. He helped Lauren carry the crate to the scale. Cooper followed behind with the other. They needed to get this done, loaded, and get home before the roads were too dangerous for travel. He looked to Joey's office. The lights were out. No smoke belched from the pellet stove.

Lauren tapped his arm. "She came in long enough to grab a few things and then left. Said she was working from home for a few days."

Concern raced up his spine and left a path as cold as the sleet. Ever since she'd found out that Colin was her birth father, she'd curled in on herself. Had barely answered his texts. Sent all of his calls to voicemail. Hadn't shown up for work. He realized that three days wasn't long enough to process the shock of her life, but he was concerned that she was processing it in unhealthy ways.

Horrible timing with news of the governor being the highlight of every news outlet in print and online.

"Thanks." He nodded to Lauren, and they worked to get the last of the crates weighed and loaded on the box truck for the co-op.

A part of him wanted to hunt Colin down and throttle the man for abandoning his infant daughter and not revealing his identity to her in person when he had the chance. Had she been able to hear Colin's reasons and ask questions, the pain might be a little less now. She might let Jace offer comfort. After all, he was familiar with the emotions that came from knowing a parent chose to leave.

But this was Joey's cross to bear, and if she wouldn't let him help her carry the load there was nothing he could do. And not being able to bring relief to a situation was something Jace didn't tolerate well. He'd arranged to spend the last part of the week in Boston tying up his loose ends, and he didn't want to leave without knowing Joey was in a good place.

Was *he* in a good place?

The question whispered across his heart and had been for days if he were honest with himself. The idea of easing back into the medical field made him anxious, especially in a small town like Granite Harbor where everyone knew the details of the malpractice accusation. Some folks would find him unsuitable even when his name was publicly cleared.

For the most part, everyone accepted him now as a lobster-man, but would they accept him as their doctor?

He slapped Cooper on the shoulder as they walked to the parking lot. "Drive safe."

"You too, man."

Jace yanked on the door twice before it opened. His wind-shield wipers were covered in tiny white balls. The engine groaned but started, and he revved it to give it a boost. He waited several minutes for his defroster to warm the windshield enough he could see through it.

Whitecaps rolled in the gray water and the wind picked up. He thought back to all the evenings he'd spent at Joey's house, curled up together on the couch by the fireplace, watching television, and sharing kisses. That's where he wanted to be tonight. Warm with her in his arms.

That's where he wanted to be every night. Forever.

If he planned to make a future with Joey, he had some hard decisions to make. A small-town practice with a wife who worked in the same town sounded like a great plan. If Joey'd even have him when the time came. He just didn't know if he could risk losing another patient again. But he also didn't want all his hard work, years of education, and remaining amount of student debt to haunt him from a cold, uninviting lobster boat.

Josephine's phone rang for the third time that morning, followed by the ding of a text. She tossed it on her unmade bed and collapsed onto the mattress, pulling the covers up to her chin. Between Jace and the spam calls and texts, her phone battery was getting a work-out. She wasn't angry with Jace—none of this was his fault—but she needed space. Time to process that she'd faced the man who'd given her away and didn't even know it. Had helped to save his life even. That she'd touched him and assisted him and spoken to him.

Without knowing he was her father.

Why hadn't he said anything? Why didn't Colin want her to know?

Everything she thought she knew about her life was different. Her adoption story, even her name! She was Hiley Mae Warner. Named after her great-grandmother. Josephine was essentially Hiley Mae II, the name Colin—her birth father—had given his boat as a tribute to his grandfather's boat. The boat he'd sold to her adopted dad around the same time Colin had given up custody. She'd never known Dad had tried making a living as a lobsterman before taking the job as manager at the co-op. He'd never mentioned it and neither had anyone else, except the night Jace said Father McClintock suggested she ask Dad about it. The very boat Hemingway said was hers the day he was yelling and spitting on the dock. The boat her boyfriend now owned.

She dropped her head in her hands and moaned. This was messed up. More tangled than the sheet at the foot of the bed from her restless sleep. So insane she decided to stay under the blankets with a carton of Chunky Monkey and a true crime show and ignore her existence.

Another text.

A tear slipped down her cheek as Jace's name lit up her screen then disappeared seconds later. Just days ago, he'd declared he was making a life here despite his ability to return to Boston Medical and her heart had soared. Now, here she was, ignoring his calls and texts while dodging reporters and trying to make sense of her life.

Was this thing with Jace too good to be true?

All of the other proverbial rugs had been yanked from beneath her. Would a future with Jace be too?

She needed distance to get her head on straight. She needed answers to fill in the gaps.

Muting the TV, she stared at her black phone screen. A minute later, another ding sounded, reminding her she'd yet to read the previous texts. She sighed so deeply it made her lips flap together. A stray tear rolled down her cheek as she decided to open the messages.

> *Tried to see you before I left but you wouldn't answer.*

> *I'm looking at the Boston skyline from the hospital for the last time and thinking of nothing but you.*

> *I'm sorry for your loss but happy for your gain: Holden and Marian, your incredible intelligence, determination, and strong will. Your new standing in the community. Us.*

> *Hang in there, Jo. I'll be home soon. (Heart emoji)*

Home.

The very place she'd been chasing to fit into now felt like a foreign land. Maybe when Jace returned he could offer some perspective. Help her navigate all the unknowns. With no guarantees of the future, she'd have to trust him when he said he wanted to build a life with her.

She did trust him.

Squeezing her eyes tight, she knew what she had to do. She had to find answers, heal, and move on. Something jiggled at the foot of her bed and her eyes flew open. Jack Sparrow glared at her, kneading the bed with his giant paws. This was the closest he'd gotten to her so far. Each day since Jace rescued him, Jack had gained confidence one inch at a time. Looked like he'd decided to trust too.

The next afternoon, Josephine walked inside her childhood home and slammed the door behind her. She hadn't intended to be forceful, it'd just sort of happened. Moby was tucked into his typical corner of the couch, a fleece blanket wrapped around him like a cocoon, his little nose and eyes and the tips of his ears peeking out. He rolled his eyes to see who'd disturbed his peace but wasn't concerned enough to greet her.

"Hey, boy." She bent and kissed his wet nose.

"Josephine, is that you?" Mom's muffled voice grew louder as she peeked out from the kitchen. "Hey, sweetheart, lunch is about ready."

Josephine's stomach clenched. Now that Mom had mentioned food, her nose registered the scents, but her stomach soured.

She inched into the kitchen, feeling sicker with each step. Dad sat at the table, tablet in hand. "There's my Joey-girl. We missed you. Come here and see if you can help me unscramble this word."

"I didn't come over to play games." She swallowed. Both parents turned and studied her, apparently catching the tension in her voice. "I came to ask why you never told me my real name is Hiley Mae."

The linen towel in her mother's hand dropped to the floor. Dad set down his tablet. Her parents looked at each other before Dad nodded.

"I guess we owe you some answers," Mom said, her face aging ten years in five seconds.

"I guess so," Josephine said.

Dad shifted in his chair. "Sit down, honey."

"I don't want to sit down." Josephine—Hiley—whoever she was, gripped the back of a chair. "I want the truth. All of it."

Mom took out the casserole and turned the oven off. "Your mom was my best friend growing up. Her parents used to summer here every year. They were from Virginia. We were pen pals all winter. The day you were born, I promised to take care of you and love you like my own should something ever happen to her. A godmother, per se, without either of us calling it that."

It was information Josephine already knew, the story she'd been told dozens of times over the years. She waited for more.

Mom wiped a tear. She pulled out the chair next to Dad and sat. "Two summers before you were born, the summer we graduated high school, your mother met a man named Colin Warner, on leave from the Army. At the end of the summer, Anne didn't go home with her parents like usual. She and I got an apartment together and carpooled to Bangor three days a week, while she attended classes at the community college, and I worked in the perfume department at J.C. Penney's.

"Anne and Colin were crazy about each other. They wrote letters all the time and spent every minute together whenever he had leave."

Doc Greenwell's mention of PTSD from Colin's military experiences fit into place. Josephine pulled out a chair and plopped onto it.

"In the summer of 1990, they eloped while he was on a short leave. Anne's parents were angry with her for not pursuing her education at a refined university and marrying a man 'more suited for her station.' Shortly after, he was sent to Kuwait on a special mission. We were fighting what they call the Gulf War. Though he couldn't tell your mother what the mision was, we all knew it was dangerous. Anne was devastated."

Tears were flowing in tandem now, and Dad patted his wife's hand.

Dad cleared his throat. "He was injured but not badly enough he couldn't finish his tour. He came home on leave a couple of times after the war ended but he wasn't the same. He re-enlisted without speaking to your mother about it first—before she had a chance to tell him she was pregnant. Anne spent her entire pregnancy and delivery without him, though we helped as much as she'd allow us.

"When you were five months old, we were babysitting you. Anne was on her way home from work. She hit a patch of black ice and slammed into the guardrail. She wasn't wearing her seatbelt and was thrown from the car."

Josephine looked down at her shaking hands, imagining the scene unfold.

"We worked it out with Child Protective Services to act as foster parents until Colin's tour ended. He consented by signing the papers overseas and when he returned stateside six months later, you already belonged to us in our hearts."

Josephine's nose began to drip. She reached for a napkin. "And he just let you keep me? What about my grandparents?"

"Colin's parents had already passed away. Anne's didn't want to raise another child. They thought a nanny and, later, boarding school was best. None of us wanted that for you. Colin wouldn't consent to let them raise you and the judge decided since your grandparents hadn't tried to be a part of your life thus far, placing you with them wasn't in your best interest."

Josephine blew into the napkin. "Why didn't Colin want me?"

"Oh, honey." Mom reached for a napkin as well and blew into it. "He wasn't right between grieving your mother and the things he'd experienced overseas. No one understood it at the time, but he had PTSD. He hadn't bonded with you during Anne's pregnancy or your birth. Without the connection to Anne, he didn't know how to be a father. He was a mess."

Dad leaned his elbows on the table. "He gave me his boat and signed permission for us to file for adoption. The judge awarded it."

"How—" Josephine swallowed the lump in her throat. "How did the McClintock's end up with the boat?"

Dad took off his glasses and rubbed the bridge of his nose before putting them back on. "The adoption fees were way more than we could afford on a fisherman's salary, so I sold the boat to help pay the fees. Having you meant more than a fishing vessel. I landed a good job with the co-op."

A sob escaped and Josephine clamped a hand over her mouth. Mom reached for her, but Josephine waved her away. She had to get all her questions out before she crumbled. "Why haven't you ever told me all this?"

Mom wiped her eyes with the heels of her hands. "Because we were happy. You were happy. Colin insisted we have your name legally changed, keep the details of your adoption quiet, and have no contact with him. People didn't really talk about mental health at that time. Even though he wasn't raised in Granite Harbor, he knew that Duro Island was close enough that the stigma of his mental condition would transfer to you. Living in a small town can have its disadvantages too."

Sensing the black aura of the room, Moby padded into the kitchen, his claws clicking on the linoleum. He scratched Josephine's leg, whining to be held. She picked him up, and he licked the tears from her cheeks. His aged teeth gave him foul breath and she turned her head.

Josephine tucked his little furry head beneath her chin. "Colin's been mooring boats here off and on for years."

Dad knotted his hand together. "He returns now and then over the summers, works odd jobs, and keeps an eye on you from a distance. I think after enough passed that he could function, he regretted giving you up. But it was too late."

She sobbed into Moby's fur. The poor dog was shaking, probably concerned over her blubbering. Whatever was in the bottle Colin had been trying to find all summer, it was his last connection to his wife and child. His last connection to Anne. To Josephine. *I found something better.*

The echo of his words sliced her heart. Didn't he know it didn't have to be his last connection? She was alive. They could try to get to know each other.

Did she want that?

Her lungs squeezed as if she was suffocating.

"I have to go." She kissed Moby's head and handed him to Mom.

"Honey, wait," Dad called after her.

"I have to go." She ran from the house and drove to the harbor. The water was flat calm, as were the clouds. The air was arctic.

Unsure what she was doing, she drove to the harbor and paced the dock. When a white van with the letters QRV-TV Channel 6 parked beside her, she hopped aboard her boat, started the engine, and sped away without a solid plan.

It took forever for the cabin to heat. She sliced toward the horizon, numb in both body and spirit.

Thirty-minutes later, she found herself at Duro Island. Had she done that on purpose? She must have. She should go inside. See if Colin were still there.

He wasn't. He'd told her that day at the grocery store he was on his way out of town.

But, what if?

*Josephine, you're being irrational.*

She wasn't going to find some magical answer in that dilapidated cabin. She knew this, yet it didn't stop her. Colin might not need a connection to her, but she desperately needed a connection to the pieces of her that had been missing for years.

She slowed the throttle and eased toward the island. The dock had deteriorated even more since her last visit. She tied off and carefully walked up the hill to the cabin, unsure what she expected to find.

Her knuckles hit the wood. Stupid, really, but it wasn't her home, so she knocked. When no one answered like she knew they wouldn't, she forced the swollen door open with her hip. Daylight filtered through the grimy glass windows. The structure was cold and uninviting, just like her birth father.

Her gaze took in the cobwebs and dust. "We might have been good together, the pair of us," she whispered to nothing.

At the table, she pulled out a rickety chair and recalled the night she and Jace had stayed there. The night she asked Colin where his daughter was. *"She's in a better place."* Josephine thought that meant she'd died but now realized he was referring to Josephine's place with her adopted parents. Then, she remembered the anguish in his voice the next day when he told her he was sorry. It hadn't been the fever talking after all.

Grief swelled within her. She doubled over and let the pain spill out.

# Thirty-Six

Jace's muscles relaxed when the Welcome to Granite Harbor sign appeared in his windshield.

Home.

His life in Boston had been good until Arabella's tragic passing. He'd learned and grown as a person as well as a physician and made great memories. Jace was grateful. But it was time for a change. It was time to come home for good. Indulge in all the nuances of small-town life, the tight-knit community, the atmosphere.

Joey.

The last of an orange and purple sunset streaked across the sky. He needed to see her. He also needed to sleep in his own bed after the stiff mattress in the budget hotel last night. Maybe over the weekend, he'd start the living room remodel he'd been envisioning for months.

He turned left toward Joey's house and slammed on his brakes when several vehicles sped past him and ran the stop sign in the direction of the dock.

What on earth?

An uneasy ball bounced around in his gut. He turned the car around and followed.

The dock parking lot was full which was strange for a winter evening. A large group of people stood by the dock, far enough away not to be in the path of others running to the boats but close enough to see any action. A woman in the crowd buried her face in her gloved hands, shoulders shaking. Another woman wrapped her in a hug and rocked back and forth. Jace's stomach sank. Something bad happened.

Throwing the truck into park, he turned off the engine and shoved his keys into his pocket. He slammed the door and raced toward the group. That's when he recognized the crying woman as Grantley, Hemingway's granddaughter.

"What's happened?" Jace shouted as he approached.

Maggie, the diner's owner, grabbed his elbow. "Hemingway. He came down to the dock in a rage, spitting and pushing and threatening. He hopped on the *Codfather* while Neisser was gassing up and took off. Ripped the hose right off the pump. Gas is leaking out all over the dock and into the water."

"Is everyone okay?"

Maggie shrugged. "He's still out there. Some of the guys went after him but Hem had a head start. They're not sure where to even begin looking."

"Could Joey locate it through the GPS?"

"Don't know. No one can find her. She's not at home or anywhere in town it seems."

Couldn't find her? Joey may be reeling from everything going on in her life but she wouldn't ignore the needs of this town. Fear gripped Jace. Where was she?

The governor's minion sprang to mind.

Jace jogged toward the boats, scanning where each one moored. Her harbormaster issued boat was gone. Had she already gone after Hem?

His fists clenched. She couldn't be out there alone with the raging old man. He'd seen plenty of patients gain superhuman strength when angry or scared. Out in the ocean alone with a crazed man wasn't safe, and Joey was stubborn enough to try it.

Jace started for his boat when Grantley gripped his arms. "He was napping and the next thing I knew, he was poised for a fight. Nothing I said calmed him down. I don't think he even knew who I was. He shoved me down and took off. This new medicine—it's supposed to help. What's going on?"

"What's he taking?"

Voices shouted and men scrambled around them.

"Excalibur. You know, the commercial that claims it slays the symptoms of dementia?"

"All medications have side effects. Those kind in particular can have the opposite affect if they're not a good fit for the patient." A siren sounded down the road. "Call his doctor and tell the authorities everything you can. Leave nothing out. Make sure they know Joey's boat is gone and she hasn't been located as well. I'll do what I can to find your grandpa."

He didn't wait for her response, only sprinted to where the *Sea Wolfe* was pulling away. The odor of gasoline hung heavily in the air. Jace leapt aboard, the momentum rolling him forward and onto his side. Ken looked behind him and cursed. "Ya crazy igit! Give me a wicked scare, as if we don't have enough going on already."

Jace stood and found his sea legs. "Sorry, but I came to help. No sign of Joey?"

"Not that I seen." Ken pushed open the throttle.

"Has anyone alerted the Coast Guard?" Jace gripped the doorway of the cabin to steady himself as Ken turned out of the harbor.

"Pete Miller was working on it. The rest of the men were trying to stop the leaking pump. Crazy, Hem. He needs put in a facility before he hurts himself or someone else."

True. The man's care had obviously become too much for Grantley. Jace just hoped that whatever happened tonight, everyone went home alive.

The temperature had dropped below freezing. The last sliver of daylight streaked the sky. Josephine rubbed the chill from her arms and opened the throttle. She shouldn't have stayed at the cabin so long, but she'd lost track of time. She looked forward to a hot bubble bath and another carton of Chunky Monkey, if she could get past any reporters still stalking her office.

A flash of light burst in the distance, like a flare, only orange not red.

Strange.

Another flicker. A fire?

As she grew closer her breath caught. Something was on fire. She pushed the boat harder. Her mouth dropped open. A boat!

Adrenaline surged her into action. She idled the engine, and her boat eased toward the other one. Flames danced along the deck. Where was its captain?

She fumbled for the radio as the outline of another boat approached from the opposite direction. "Coast Guard this is harbormaster, Granite Harbor. We've got a boat on fire in the open water. Over."

Static filled the line a moment before a female voice asked, "Do you have coordinates?"

Josephine read the device on the instrument panel. "Latitude forty-three degrees north, longitude minus sixty-eight degrees west."

"Help is on the way."

Josephine grabbed her fire extinguisher. She walked onto her boat's deck, trying to assess where to begin. White foam burst through the flames, tamping them down. Someone had beaten her to it. A deep voice yelled her name.

Cal White, on the aft end of the *Codfather*. "Toss me your extinguisher!"

Judging the distance, she rocked her arms a few times before pitching it into the air. Cal cradled it like a football, then pulled the pin and fought the flames. She turned on her spotlight and aimed it at Cal. Hemingway sat propped against the outside of the cabin wall, coughing. His cheeks were splotchy red and spittle ran down his chin. What was he doing on the *Codfather*?

When the flames were under control, she guided her boat closer, dropped anchor, and leaped aboard. A fog of breath filled her vision upon impact. Hemingway tried to stand but couldn't. His grumbled curses filled the air. Cal and Nathaniel inspected the boat for damage and any lingering signs of fire. Josephine talked to Hemingway in a calm, soothing voice.

"Hey, Hem. What's going on?" she asked.

The old man's glare turned murderous as he finally stumbled to his feet. She stayed several feet away.

Cal and Nathaniel gave her the short version of the story as lights from another boat approached. Hopefully the Coast Guard.

Hemingway charged at her, but Cal stepped in his path. They grappled for a moment. Josephine was shocked at how much strength the old man had. Why was he attacking them? The other boat sidled next to hers.

"Joey!"

She turned and saw Jace as a splash hit the water behind her. She spun at the sound. Hem and Cal had gone overboard. The water was freezing. They'd be hypothermic within minutes.

Nathaniel growled and donned a lifejacket, then jumped in after them. He pumped his arms and legs toward a sputtering Hemingway. Joey fumbled for the life ring and tossed it toward Cal, wondering if the specialized blankets the coalition had raised money for were aboard.

Blood seeped from Cal's forehead and trickled down his face. He held the life ring in a limp grip. She opened the bench seat and found another lifejacket. She almost had it secured around her when a hand clamped around her arm. "Oh, no you don't."

Jace unzipped his coat and shrugged it off. "I'll guide him in. You take care of his wound."

Before he could protest, she jumped overboard and screamed in shock at the blast of icy water.

"Dang it, Joey," Jace yelled.

Tremors wracked her body but she managed to slip the lifesaver around Cal's head and down to his torso. She pushed it from behind as Jace pulled the rope. Her breath clouded her vision. So cold.

Two sets of arms reached down from the boat and helped pull Cal aboard. She bobbed in the water, her brain freezing over and clouding her thinking. She closed her eyes for a second and thought of those poor people the night of the Titanic's demise.

Splashing had her opening her eyes. Nathaniel was struggling with Hemingway, who fought him all the way. Nathaniel needed help if they were all going to get home before hypothermia took them all.

Nathaniel pulled back his fist and punched Hemingway in the face. The old man's eyes rolled in his head, and he slumped over.

Shock had her swimming to the men. She helped keep Hemingway afloat as Nathaniel guided them toward the *Codfather*. Something creaked. Popped. A mini explosion went off somewhere, forcing her backward.

Debris shot into the air and fell around her head. She blinked. Why was everything in slow motion? No matter which way she tried to swim, she couldn't move.

"Joey, give me your hand. We've got to get off this boat!"

Jace.

Why couldn't she move?

An acrid scent filled her nose a second before pain split her skull and everything went black.

# Thirty-Seven

Jace released Joey's hand as the ambulance doors opened. He'd already gone over protocol with the EMTs, tracking every move they made. They were a well-trained and knowledgeable staff. The knot on her head concerned him as the abrasion felt to be swelling beneath the skull. It was unclear what had hit her when the starboard side split apart.

The *Codfather* was irreparable between the damage the fire had caused and the explosion. Apparently, Hemingway had run into some things on his joyride and damaged components. Jace had jumped in after Joey as the front of the boat rocked beneath him. He'd gripped her by the back of her lifejacket and swam her to Ken's boat until the Coast Guard transported the injured to theirs minutes later.

Keeping the blanket wrapped around him, Jace bent to jump out of the ambulance. Other than being wet and still trying to warm his bones from his swim in the Atlantic, he was fine. But he wasn't letting Joey go through this alone. He couldn't lose another person he loved if he could prevent it in any way.

And love her, he did.

Had since elementary school when they'd competed for the highest grade on the math test and every competition since. He'd loved her drive, her determination, her passion. Now, he loved her heart.

Red and white emergency lights reflected on the front of the hospital. He followed the team inside. His chest cracked open when they rushed Joey behind the swinging doors, leaving him alone in the emergency room. He assured the nurses he was fine but allowed them to retrieve a set of scrubs he could wear. At least then he'd be dry.

Minutes turned to hours in the waiting room while they ran tests and made Joey comfortable. Her parents arrived around one in the morning. It had taken them much longer to drive to Bangor from Granite Harbor than it had taken Jace and Joey with the Coast Guard transport to the hospital's nearest dock and an ambulance escort from there. Jace had updated them as best he could, explained medical lingo, and did his best to comfort and assure them. His brain was weary, his body tired, and his heart broke as they'd relayed the details of their last conversation with Joey regarding her identity.

Colin really was her birth father. Jace struggled to wrap his mind around that. Was Duro Island where Joey had disappeared before Hemingway stole the boat?

Questions and visions of his sweet Joey flashed through his mind as he dozed in the hard plastic chair.

"The doctor is ready to see you now."

Jace's bleary eyes popped open, and he sprang from the seat. The threesome followed the nurse down the hall and around two corners to a room in the back. Joey lay asleep, her hair matted with dried salt water and a little dried blood. IV fluids dripped from a bag into a tube that snaked into her arm. A monitor blinked beside the bed, tracking her vitals.

The doctor walked in a moment later and introduced himself. "The MRI revealed a nasty concussion, but with rest and medication she should recover without long-term damage."

Marian Rockwell's breath stuttered. "Long-term damage?"

"Memory loss, cognitive disfunction, headaches, insomnia, depression. She may experience these symptoms for up to six weeks, but I'm confident they'll be temporary."

Holden put an arm around his wife's shoulders. Jace cleared the gravel from his throat. "Any breaks, frostbite, or hypothermia? She was in the water longer than she should've been."

The doctor wrote some notes on a clipboard. "No breaks or frostbite. Her body temperature was low when she arrived, but the heated blankets and hot packs used during transport kept her out of danger."

Relief washed over Jace.

They asked a few more questions. Jace listened intently while studying the doctor's bedside manner and the patient and gentle way he dealt with the family. This was who Jace was. Doctoring was a vital part of the human experience. Not only for answers and healing but as the mediator for concerned loved ones. No matter what he'd gone through in Boston or what lay ahead, this was a part of him he couldn't tuck away and ignore and live happily.

As soon as Joey was out of danger, he would meet with Doc Greenwell about joining his practice.

Marian walked to Joey's bedside and kiss her daughter's forehead. Joey's eyelids twitched but she didn't wake. Good. She needed all the rest she could get.

Jace yawned despite his attempt to hold it in.

"You must be exhausted." Holden offered his hand to Jace. "Thanks for watching over her tonight. We're blessed she has you in her life."

Jace's throat clogged with emotion. "I'm the blessed one. How about I get you a hotel room for the next couple of days, so you'll have a close place to rest until she's released."

"That'd be great. Thank you, son."

The man patted Jace's arm as he turned away.

Son. Jace could get used to that.

A week later, Joey woke on her couch, disoriented from a long nap. Once her vision adjusted, she remembered that Jace had come over that morning. Was he still here?

Something weighed heavy against the top of her head. Something that purred. She flicked her gaze upward.

Jack Sparrow lay on the arm of the couch, snuggled against her hair. He'd never touched her before, had never come close enough. But there he was, as if he'd missed her while she'd been in the hospital. As if he understood she needed support and the extra TLC. As much as she hated to move and spook the feline, her back was stiff and cramping, and she needed to stretch.

"Hey, pretty girl." Jace walked in with two mugs and placed them on the coffee table. He slid an arm behind her back to help her sit which sent Jack into a running panic.

Upright, the room spun, but the dizziness was getting better with each passing day.

"Better?" He kissed her.

"Much," she mumbled around a yawn. "I'm tired of sleeping, but I'm so tired."

He handed her a mug of hot chocolate filled with whipped cream and chocolate jimmies.

"You're a great boyfriend."

"You make it easy."

Was he blushing?

How adorable.

He joined her on the couch. The scent of warm chocolate and wood smoke filled the room. The fire was dying which was okay. Jace was all the warmth she needed. Having a doctor around—and a handsome one at that—was a nice perk.

"It's good to see you smile." He took her hand in his and settled them on his thigh.

"You make it easy."

He kissed her head this time. "How're you feeling?"

"Better."

"Good. I have to leave for a few hours. Dad, Cooper, and his wife are helping me load, set up, and secure the traps for the ceremony tomorrow. I'll bring dinner back with me. Your mom should be here in a few minutes to keep you company until then."

She groaned. "I don't need a babysitter."

"Until your symptoms are gone, you do." He kissed the back of her hand.

"I wish you'd let me come and help."

"Uh-uh. You need your rest, so you'll feel like attending the ceremony. Besides, I can't have you stealing my thunder. I was chosen as the honorary citizen, and I plan to wear my crown proudly."

A ripple of anxiety ran through her. "I don't think I'm going to attend the ceremony."

"Oh. Well, if you don't feel up to it, I understand."

His disappointment was palpable, and guilt stabbed her. She blew out a breath. "I'm not ready for the barrage of reporters who are stalking me for two kinds of interviews now or anyone in town, really. I can't face them. Not yet."

She stared at the bubbles her whipped cream made as it melted.

He moved and sat on the coffee table facing her so she couldn't hide. "What do you mean?"

Josephine swallowed the tears that had plagued her non-stop nowadays. "I'm a failure, Jace. My statement to the DOJ failed to keep the governor behind bars. In the short time I've been harbormaster, I've divided the fishermen with my progressive ideas, revealed a scandal that put our town on the map, discovered I'm not who I really am, and put several lives at risk. Had I been at my post the night Hemingway took the boat instead of chasing ghosts and running away from hard things, I could've stopped things long before they got out of control."

Jace frowned. "Don't do that to yourself. Hem took the *Codfather* so fast no one, not even the people that were on the dock, had time to act. You still would've been chasing after him. As for the governor, he has money to pay people in high places for his freedom. That's not on you."

She opened her mouth to speak but he held up a finger.

"Your real name may be different, but you are still the same fierce, wonderful, loveable Joey I adore. The one we *all* adore. Even if your progressive ways aren't popular."

She shook her head, shoving down another cry. "I let my emotions get in the way. I wasn't where I should've been. I've let everyone down and I'm not ready to face them yet."

He took her mug, set it to the side, and took her hands in his. "No one blames you for this. Hem's going to be okay rehabilitating in a facility where he'll be well cared for. It's what he's needed for a while now. If anything, this town is proud of you for doing your job and finding him, for risking your life by jumping in to help Cal. And those thermal blankets used to keep us all from hypothermia? We'd have never had those aboard had it not been for your effort with the coalition to purchase them."

She turned away, closing her eyes—and her heart—to the truth. How she wanted to believe him, but she'd battled the demon of inadequacy so long, she didn't know how to view herself as anything other than lacking.

"Look at me." Jace's tender words made her comply.

"Your worth does not lie in your job or your name, your standing in the community, or how other's see you. Your actions, your grit, your service to others, your beautiful heart—that's what makes you who you are. That's what makes me want to be around no other woman but you. For the long haul."

Jace winked at the pun and knelt on one knee if front of her. His calloused thumbs brushed away her tears that came even though she tried to stop them. He leaned forward and pressed his lips to hers. "If you don't feel like going tomorrow, I won't pressure you. But don't skip out because you're afraid. Promise me you'll think about what I said. I meant every word. Besides, the celebration won't be the same without our beloved harbormaster."

A knock sounded on the door a moment before it opened to a feminine voice. "Honey, I'm here."

Jace gave her another quick kiss then stood and greeted Marian before walking out the door, leaving Josephine to battle between the woman she thought she was and the woman he'd just claimed her to be.

# Thirty-Eight



Josephine was not in a Christmassy mood despite her handsome date clad in a festive button-down under a suit coat. His jeans fit him to perfection as did his new boots from Beans. Since she was still healing from her ordeal, she'd dressed for warmth and comfort over style.

Jace stood from lacing up her boots. "Ready?"

As she'd ever be. "You look handsome."

He grinned. "You said that already."

"Truth is always worth saying twice."

"In that case, I love you."

She blinked. Had he just—?

His lips grazed hers before she could even process his statement. Her thoughts went fuzzy, and it had nothing to do with the concussion. He pulled away and a satisfied smirk lifted the corners of his mouth. "Come on. The town's honorary citizen can't be late for his own speech."

She locked the door, and he escorted her to his truck. The cab was toasty and comforting. She settled her head against the seat. She'd only felt dizzy twice that day and they'd lasted mere seconds. Not including the dizziness he'd caused by confessing his love for her. Jace promised not to keep her out too long and to take good care of her after she got back home.

That was the part of the evening she was looking forward to most.

The harbor was already full of cars, many parked along the sides of the road. The town was aglitter with lights and bows and pine garlands. She'd only been gone from her office for a week and in that short amount of time, the town had turned into a Christmas wonderland. Her moody spirit lifted and some of the anxiety eased the huge knot in her stomach.

Jace parked and helped her out, keeping hold of her waist as they walked to the dock. She spied the lobster trap Christmas tree from a distance and the display looked every bit as beautiful and vintage as the pictures she'd seen from the days when lobstermen used wooden traps for this very purpose.

A campfire blazed on the grassy knoll where a vendor was selling hot chocolate, coffee, and roasted nuts. The air smelled of Christmas and hope.

Debbie Miller waved at Josephine from the ramp then yanked off her gloves and started clapping. Spectators looked around to see what the commotion was about, and then they started clapping too. Josephine tightened her hold on Jace. "Congratulations, honorary citizen. You have a standing ovation."

He steered them down the ramp. "They're not clapping for me, Jo. They're clapping for you."

Her smile fell, shocked why anyone would be clapping for her. Someone whistled to her left, followed by a whoop to her right. When they reached the lobster trap tree, Jace let go of her and clapped along. "Our beloved harbormaster," he shouted.

The crowd grew even more boisterous, making Josephine want to both laugh and hide. She fiddled with her hands, unsure what to do with them. Her smile had to look awkward.

Jace brought his lips to her ear. "I told you no one faults you."

The band of expected rejection she'd strapped around her heart broke free. Seeing herself as anything other than not-good-enough was going to take some time to undo after years of training. "Thank you," she mouthed to Jace.

She stepped aside as he quieted the crowd and told them how angry he was initially about his nomination. He explained that he'd been in a bad place but that the discovery of the lobster traps and the journey to finding the story behind them had reminded him how much he loved this town and its people and the history that preceded them.

"I'd like to thank everyone who helped set up and make this possible. It is my absolute pleasure to present you with this year's Christmas tree and to honor those soldiers, nurses, and their families who sacrificed during World War II for all for the freedoms we enjoy today. Please join me in a moment of silence."

Hands joined together. Heads bowed. Jace's palm found the small of her back. She wished Colin were here to join in the celebration of his grandfather—her great-grandfather—so she could thank him for his service to their country and maybe have a chance to bridge the gap between them.

Jace continued by announcing the name of all forty-nine soldiers in alphabetical order. Debbie concluded the ceremony by starting a light-hearted rendition of "We Wish You a Merry Christmas." The evening and the community had come together beautifully. Josephine was proud to be a citizen of Granite Harbor.

The last note ended and Jace kissed her cheek. "You've been standing for a while. Let's find a seat by the fire."

She started to complain then noticed how weak her legs felt. As they headed that way, many stopped to shake Jace's hand, hug her, and wish her a fast recovery. They ran into her parents who were holding hands and laughing like two teenagers. Jace settled her on a straw bale with a blanket across her legs while he fetched hot chocolate and roasted nuts.

Doc Greenwell and his grandson strode by, stopping when they noticed her. "Best celebration we've had in years."

"It is, isn't it? Jace did a fantastic job."

"Indeed." He resisted the pull of the toddler coaxing him away. "I'm glad you finally talked him into joining my practice. He'll be a wonderful addition to our community."

Josephine was stunned for the second time this evening. Why hadn't he told her he'd officially taken the job? "Um. . .yeah, me too."

"Come on, Pappy." The boy with a blue knit cap yanked on his grandpa's arm.

"Duty calls." Doc Greenwell patted her shoulder before moving on.

Jace returned a few minutes later with their goodies and pressed the side of his body against hers. "Are pecans okay?"

"Perfect." She removed her glove, dug into the bag, and popped a few in her mouth.

She tried to be patient and let Jace tell her about his job when he was ready but she'd never been good at waiting. "Congratulations on your new position, Doctor McClintock."

Jace turned to her. "I wanted to be the one to tell you, but I was waiting for the right time."

"The right time?" she teased.

"Tonight was about you and the fallen soldiers and nurses. Not my new career."

She loved his selflessness. "There's nothing wrong with throwing your good news in the mix." She threaded her arm through his and rested her head on his shoulder. "I'm glad you're sticking around."

"Did you doubt it?"

"A little. With your talents I knew you'd never be content on a boat. Now you'll have a reason to stay."

"You're my reason to stay. I love you, Joey."

Her heart slammed against her ribs and her spirit lifted like a helium balloon. "You said that once already."

"The truth is always worth repeating."

"Then I love you, too." She touched her lips to his. "I love you, too."

Father McClintock was right. Confession was good for the soul.

# Thirty-Nine

Jace reached beneath the Christmas tree they'd put up in Joey's living room and handed her a small box. "Last one."

She smiled, silhouetted by the snow falling outside the window. The weatherman had predicted upwards of eight inches by nightfall, and he should be heading home.

But he wasn't about to miss his first Christmas with his fiancée.

He still grinned like an idiot every time he thought about it.

The stubborn box lid gave her trouble, but she finally got it open. She pulled out a white notecard. "An address?" Her forehead wrinkled, and then her eyes grew big. "Ours?"

"Not yet." They'd decided on a Valentine's Day wedding, something small and intimate with immediate family and friends, so house-hunting would begin after the holidays. "Colin's."

She blinked.

"Turns out I have Matlock skills too. I contacted Colin and told him you'd discovered that he's your birth father. I asked him if it would be okay for you to write to him sometime, when you feel like you're ready. He gave permission."

"Oh." The word left her mouth in a quiet breath. "I'd like that."

"I figured you would. I know both of our pasts have things in it we wish we could change, but we've got the rest of our lives to make our futures what we want."

"Thank you." She placed her hand on his cheek and kissed him in a way that made him anxious for their wedding.

Before they got carried away, he ended it and pressed his forehead to hers. "Merry Christmas."

"Merry Christmas."

A guttural meow sounded beside them, and they both laughed as Jack Sparrow stretched and then flopped onto his new kitty couch in the corner.

A gust of wind and icy droplets hit the windows. Joey rubbed at her arms.

"You cold?"

"Not really. The sound of it makes me think I'm cold."

Jace added another log to the fire and walked to the window. "It's really coming down."

She nuzzled against his side and wrapped her arms around him. "I don't want you to go, but I want you safe."

"We haven't even eaten lunch yet."

"If you don't leave soon you might end up trapped here."

"I can think of worse things than getting trapped in a warm house with the woman I love."

"Like what?"

He thought for a moment. "Mr. Edwards' physics tests."

"Ugh, definitely worse. I'm glad those days are over."

Jace bent and kissed her the way he'd always imagined doing when daydreaming about her in Mr. Edwards' class.

"Mmm." She snuggled even closer, as if it were possible. "All hearts come home for Christmas after all."

He ran his fingertips through her hair. "What do you mean?"

"It's a phrase I learned long ago. Having you here is my favorite gift of the day."

"Mine too." He palmed the back of her head and kissed to many more Christmases together.

# Author's Note

I hope you enjoyed Josephine and Jace's story, as well as visiting the fictional town of Granite Harbor. Community is important (and I'm blessed to live in a great one), so I wanted to portray a tight-knit and picturesque small town where people love and serve one another. I enjoyed studying the lobster industry and adding in some of the Maine lingo and dialect to the story.

This book is five years in the making. The idea came to me so clearly and I wrote the first draft quickly but put the story away when other publishing opportunities came. In the end, I wrote two different versions each at two very different word count lengths to maximize my chances of getting a contract. That was insane. LOL When I decided to quit my day job last year and write independently full-time, I knew it was time to finally bring this story to the market. I went through it yet again, and this time added five thousand words. Here it is and I'm glad to say there will be no more versions of this book. This is it. (Smiling widely.) This is also book fifteen for me!

However, there will be three more books in addition to Christmas in Granite Harbor, all set in the same small town and all featuring characters you've come to know and love. What's next you ask? Remember Lauren the wharfrat and Ross the lighthouse groundskeeper and the tension between them in chapter eight? They're getting their own story and it's a doozy! I already have a cover designed and it fits the story and series theme perfectly. I hope you'll join me for book two, Summer in Granite Harbor. Be sure to check out my other books in the meantime. You can find a complete listing at https://candicesuepatterson.com. Signed paperbacks are always available on my website or through my personal store at https://candice-patterson-shop.fourthwall.com. Each title comes with fun book swag and comes at a discounted price over other retailers.

If you'd like to learn more about the lobstering industry, here is a list of books I used for research that I highly recommend:

The Lobster Chronicles by Linda Greenlaw
The Lobster Coast by Colin Woodard
Stern Men by Elizabeth Gilbert
The Last Lobster by Christopher White
Lobsters: Gangsters of the Sea by Cerullo

# Acknowledgments

Words are important. They can inspire, build up, encourage, entertain, and inform. They can change a life. I don't take the honor of writing novels lightly.

None of my books would be complete without thanking the "sisters of my heart"—the Quid Pro Quills—for being my support group, prayer partners, reality checkers, brainstormers, and all-around best friends. Robin Patchen, Pegg Thomas, Kara Hunt, Jericha Kingston, and Susan Crawford—you push me to be a better writer. I couldn't survive my fictional worlds without you.

To my agent Linda S. Glaz of the Linda S. Glaz Literary Agency. Thanks for all you do!

To Marti Chabot, my favorite Mainer. Thanks for reading this story to make sure I made all things Maine authentic.

Big thanks to Rockport, Maine's harbormaster, Abbie Leonard, for kindly answering my questions. Any mistakes found in regards to the occupation of harbormaster are entirely mine.

To my husband, Adam, for always being willing to help me flesh out my plots and characters when I get stuck, for listening to me drone on for hours about books and writing, being patient when I'm on a deadline, and for always loving me no matter what. I'm so thankful God gave me you.

To Levi (Olivia and Cecilia), Silas, and Hudson—no matter how many books I write or what else I do in life, you are my greatest accomplishments. It's a joy seeing God working in your lives. Thanks for supporting my dream all these years. Now go chase yours!

Above all, I thank my Lord and Savior, Jesus Christ. All honor and glory are His.

Thank you, dear readers, for taking time out of your busy lives to spend it with my characters. Until next time. . .

Candice lives in Indiana with her husband, three sons, and her first grandchild. She studied at the Institute of Children's Literature at age sixteen. Her novels have been recognized by Midwest Book Review and Publishers Weekly. When she's not tending to her chickens, snuggling with her Great Pyrenees, drinking coffee, or dreaming of Maine, she's working on a new story. Candice writes Modern-Vintage Romance--where the past and present collide with faith. Visit https://candicesuepatterson.com.